To Wager with L(

Girls Who Dare, Book 5

By Emma V. Leech

Published by Emma V. Leech.

Copyright (c) Emma V. Leech 2019

Cover Art: Victoria Cooper

ASIN No.: B07WTMKMND

ISBN No.: 9781708436384

All rights reserved. Without limiting the rights under copyright reserved above, no part of this publication may be reproduced, stored in or introduced into a retrieval system, or transmitted, in any form, or by any means (electronic, mechanical, photocopying, recording, or otherwise) without the prior written permission of both the copyright owner and the above publisher of this book. This is a work of fiction. Names, characters, places, brands, media, and incidents are either the product of the author's imagination or are used fictitiously. The author acknowledges the trademarked status and trademark owners of various products referenced in this work of fiction, which have been used without permission. The publication/use of these trademarks is not authorized, associated with, or sponsored by the trademark owners. The ebook version and print version are licensed for your personal enjoyment only.

The ebook version may not be re-sold or given away to other people. If you would like to share the ebook with another person, please purchase an additional copy for each person you share it with. No identification with actual persons (living or deceased), places, buildings, and products is inferred.

Table of Contents

Members of the Peculiar Ladies' Book Club	1
Prologue	2
Chapter 1	5
Chapter 2	21
Chapter 3	29
Chapter 4	43
Chapter 5	58
Chapter 6	66
Chapter 7	78
Chapter 8	86
Chapter 9	96
Chapter 10	110
Chapter 11	122
Chapter 12	131
Chapter 13	143
Chapter 14	152
Chapter 15	160
Chapter 16	172
Chapter 17	181
Chapter 18	193
Chapter 19	202
Chapter 20	214
To Dance with a Devil	232
Chapter 1	234

Chapter 2	246
Want more Emma?	258
About Me!	259
Other Works by Emma V. Leech	261
Audio Books!	265
The Rogue	267
Dying for a Duke	269
The Key to Erebus	271
The Dark Prince	273
Acknowledgements	275

Members of the Peculiar Ladies' Book Club

Prunella Adolphus, Duchess of Bedwin – first peculiar lady and secretly Miss Terry, author of The Dark History of a Damned Duke.

Mrs Alice Hunt (née Dowding)–Not as shy as she once was. Blissfully married to Matilda's brother, the notorious Nathanial Hunt, owner of Hunter's, the exclusive gambling club.

Lady Aashini Cavendish (Lucia de Feria) – a beauty. A foreigner. Happily and scandalously married to Silas Anson, Viscount Cavendish.

Mrs Kitty Baxter (née Connolly) – quiet and watchful, until she isn't. Recently eloped to marry childhood sweetheart, Mr Luke Baxter.

Harriet Stanhope – serious, studious, intelligent. Prim. Wearer of spectacles.

Bonnie Campbell – too outspoken and forever in a scrape.

Ruth Stone – heiress and daughter of a wealthy merchant.

Minerva Butler - Prue's cousin. Not so vain or vacuous as she appears. Dreams of love.

Lady Helena Adolphus – vivacious, managing, unexpected.

Jemima Fernside – pretty and penniless.

Matilda Hunt – blonde and lovely and ruined in a scandal that was none of her making.

Prologue

Dear Jemima,

I do hope that you are well. It's been so long since any of us heard from you. I had hoped you would attend St Clair's ball, but Kitty tells me you won't be there. It's an age since we saw you last. Is everything all right? I warn you I intend to call on you the moment I'm back in town and I shall expect an excellent excuse for your lack of correspondence. If anything is troubling you, you may confide in me. You know that, don't you? I would help if you'd let me. Please do reply, Jem, dear. We worry for you.

—Excerpt of a letter from Miss Matilda Hunt to Miss Jemima Fernside.

The morning of the 31st August 1814. Holbrooke House. Sussex.

Harriet's eyelids fluttered as the early morning light pierced her tender brain. Good Lord, but her head was pounding. She raised a hand, pressing tentative fingers against her aching temples. She must be unwell, she decided, realising that her stomach felt uncertain too; an unpleasant acidic swirl in her guts certainly boded ill. With a soft sigh, she shielded her eyes from the sun, intent on sleeping some more. The bed was deliciously warm, and she wriggled back, luxuriating in the comfort of its embrace. It even smelled good: a touch of bay rum, soap, and something musky and… masculine.

Wait.

What?

Harriet froze as she registered a contented murmur from behind her—from extremely close behind her.

She started awake, and looked down in horror to discover she was all but naked—wearing only her shift—and that a man's muscular bare arm encircled her waist, just below her breasts. As she stared, the arm tightened, pulling her closer and, with growing alarm, her beleaguered brain registered the heat of a broad chest pressed close against her back, not to mention… not to mention….

Harriet squealed as the hot, hard length of a very masculine member pressed firmly against her bottom. Flailing with panic, she turned in the confines of the embrace that held her captive and came face to face with a pair of startlingly beautiful aquamarine eyes.

A very familiar pair of aquamarine eyes.

Oh, good God.

Harriet gasped, too stunned to say a word as Jasper St Clair gave her a crooked grin that was famed throughout the *ton* for having the ability to make sensible women lose their senses, and their virtue.

"*No*," she breathed, too horrified to find anything more to say for the moment, though she felt sure an avalanche of words would follow just as soon as she gathered her wits… and her undergarments, which appeared to be scattered about the summerhouse.

Good heavens! They were alone together, in the summerhouse, and from the looks of things, they'd been there all night. What had they done? What had *she* done? Harriet racked her aching brain, but the wretched thing refused to cooperate. All she could remember was the feel of Jasper's arms about her, the press of his lips against hers….

Oh no.

Oh, no, no, no, no….

"Good morning," he said, his smile fading a little in the light of her obvious dismay.

"W-What—?" she began, only for them both to jolt in alarm at the sound of the summerhouse door opening, the recognisable scrape of the ill-fitting wood grating over the flagged stone floor.

Laughter and chatter reached them, too late for them to move, for them to hide or gather their things, and suddenly they had an audience.

Jasper reacted first, snatching up his coat from the floor beside their makeshift bed, which seemed to be compiled of a nest of assorted blankets. He covered Harriet as best he could and then held her to him, meeting the astonished gazes of the assembled company, who were staring at them with looks ranging from delight and amusement to appalled fascination.

The blush that scalded Harriet's cheeks was so fierce she thought she might spontaneously combust, which seemed a rather happier outcome than facing Lady St Clair, Matilda and Mr Burton, Jasper's brother Jerome, and two of his cronies from his school days whose names escaped her. She did remember one of them being the biggest tattle monger she'd ever come across.

Good God. She was ruined.

"Ah," Jasper said, his voice a little less urbane than usual. He cleared this throat, and when he spoke again, the words were firm and very, very clear. "It seems you are the first to congratulate us. Harriet has agreed to marry me."

Harriet's head whipped around to stare at him again, open mouthed at the bare faced lie. Jasper just grinned at her and kissed her on the nose.

"*Got you,*" he whispered.

Chapter 1

Dear Papa,

I'm so excited for tonight's ball. Everyone who is everyone will be there. Did you hear that our good friend, Kitty has married Luke Baxter – he is the heir to the Trevick earldom? The old earl died recently and now his heir is also dying and won't last the year out. I'm afraid to say I can feel little sympathy for the man. He was not a kind or Christian soul. I'm so happy for Kitty though, and to think of her being a Countess! Such a romantic story. It makes one hope that such things are not restricted to fairy tales, and yes, Papa, before you ask, of course I shall keep my eye out for any eligible gentleman ready to sweep me off my feet.

—Excerpt of a letter from Miss Ruth Stone to her father, Mr George Stone.

The previous night. The St Clairs' summer ball. 30th August 1814, Holbrooke House, Sussex.

Harriet watched as Jasper swept Kitty around the lavishly decorated ballroom. They made a striking pair, Jasper's golden good looks set against Kitty's lush, dark beauty. Harriet sighed inwardly. It must be nice to be beautiful. Not that she cared for such frivolous things. Beauty was nothing more than pretty wrapping paper: tear it off and what lay beneath was exposed for all to see. Sometimes the paper matched the loveliness of the gift within, but more often than not it was a disappointment.

Not in Kitty's case, she had to admit. Kitty had become a dear friend to her and was just as lovely inside as out. Vivacious and good natured and full of fun she was the kind of girl who was always laughing, always looking for the best in life, and something of a handful. Harriet smiled as she saw Kitty's husband Luke watching her dance, the soft shine of adoration in his eyes. She would lead him a merry dance that was for sure, and he'd love every moment.

Though she tried to resist the urge, Harriet looked back at Jasper and felt her heart twist in her chest. Why did he have to be so handsome? She'd told herself time and again that her stupidity was at an end and she no longer cared a damn about him, but she knew it was a lie. Unfortunately, Kitty had figured it out too, and the way she was talking to Jasper—not to mention the intent look on his face— sent an unpleasant prickling chasing up and down Harriet's spine.

Surely Kitty would not talk about her, would not betray a confidence? Except it hadn't been a confidence. Harriet had not admitted or denied anything. Kitty had simply guessed that Harriet's animosity towards Jasper did not stem from mere dislike.

"I think he hurt you," Kitty had said, and Harriet hadn't been able to find an adequate reply.

It had been tempting to tell her, to blurt out that Jasper Cadogan had stolen her heart and then crushed it and tossed it aside. She hadn't, of course. Harriet never shared her feelings with anyone. She never had, until the time she'd forced herself to be brave and trust in Jasper, and she never would again. If you gave people the chance, they hurt you. Far better to trust in science and reason, and things that were quantifiable, things that could be measured and weighed, their qualities dissected and discussed, spread out before you with nowhere to hide. These things were tangible and solid, proven… unlike love, which seemed to Harriet to be a mythical beast she could not bring herself to believe in. Not anymore, at any rate. Not for her.

Yet still, after all these years, her gaze was drawn back to him and a dull ache filled her chest, longing and loneliness and sorrow making her feel brittle and hollow and damned bloody angry. He'd done this to her, she reminded herself, and then she remembered what else Kitty had said.

I think he hurt you badly, but I don't think he has the slightest idea how or what he did. You owe him an explanation, Harriet. It's not fair to keep punishing someone for years and years without giving them a chance to redeem themselves.

It was true she'd seen the hurt and confusion in Jasper's eyes often enough when she'd insulted or cut him, yet the wounded puppy expression was one at which he excelled. She'd seen him use it to his advantage. Just because that look made her heart soften and her insides quiver didn't mean it was real. He could wrap women around his finger, and he did. Everyone knew his reputation, knew he'd bedded some of the most glamourous women of the *ton*. He certainly never missed an opportunity to mock her for being a bluestocking, making her feel every bit the awkward creature they both knew she was. So what on earth could he want with plain, bookish Harriet Stanhope?

His last paramour had been a Mrs Tate. She was here tonight and had been sending Jasper covetous looks from across the dance floor. Dressed in red satin with her gleaming mahogany locks in an effortlessly simple style that had no doubt taken hours, she was a breathtaking sight. Mrs Tate was gorgeous, sophisticated, witty, and utterly at ease with herself. She radiated the confidence of a woman who knew her own worth, knew a thing or two about the world, and knew how to make a man want her without lifting a finger. In comparison, Harriet felt like exactly what she was: a wallflower, a bespectacled bluestocking who never knew the right thing to say and would rather sit in a corner with a good book than attend a ball. Why would a man like Jasper ever want Harriet when he could have the likes of Mrs Tate? It was a simple enough equation, yet one that Harriet had forgotten to calculate for a brief moment all those years ago, too full of hope that everything she'd ever dreamt of could be hers.

What a fool she was.

Past tense, however. She'd *been* a fool, and she would not be again. From now on she would use her head, not her heart, to guide her... but perhaps Kitty was right. Perhaps her bitterness had become cruelty. Jasper could not help who he was any more than she could. She knew and understood that animals were born with instincts to act in a certain way. It appeared some men had evolved less than others, their physical urges too close to the surface, their wants and desires overriding morality or decency. He'd not known his actions would hurt her so deeply. He couldn't, or his bewilderment at her treatment of him wouldn't be so marked.

It was time to let go of the hurt and the anger. Time to forgive him and move on, for her own sake as much as his. She had a new life ahead of her, one in which Jasper would have no part. She'd not even told her brother, Henry, yet—she'd been waiting for the right time—but she would.

Soon.

***

Jasper looked down at Kitty with gratitude.

"Mrs Baxter," he said, smiling at her. "Your husband is a very lucky man, and I am very grateful to you."

Though she had no way of knowing if her words had given Harriet reason to reconsider, Kitty had spoken to her on his behalf, and Harry had promised to consider her words. It wasn't much, perhaps, but it was something and Jasper would hold on to it. If Harry would only drop the wall she'd erected between them, perhaps he had a chance. A frail and slender one, but it was better than nothing.

"Perhaps you could dance with her tonight? It's such a magical evening," Kitty said, before adding in a theatrical whisper, "why, *anything* could happen!"

Jasper snorted, his hopes not daring to go to those lengths. "Yes, she might not throw her drink in my face, *if* I'm lucky."

"Oh!" Kitty said, her dark eyes brimming with mischief. "I almost forgot the dare!"

"The what?" Jasper asked, intrigued.

"The dare," Kitty repeated, squealing with excitement. The dance drew to a close, and she took Jasper's arm, gesturing for him to lean in so she could speak privately. "It's The Peculiar Ladies," she said, bouncing with impatience.

Jasper returned a blank look. "I'm sorry, I don't follow. The Peculiar what now?"

"Oh, our book group. We're The Peculiar Ladies," Kitty said in a rush, ignoring his expression of bemusement. "And we all have to take a dare from the hat. Mine was to dress your bear in evening clothes."

"Well, that explains a lot," Jasper said with a bark of laughter. "But I thought Harriet did that?"

"She helped me," Kitty admitted. "In fact, she was marvellous. I couldn't have done it without her."

Jasper smiled, pleased at this evidence of Harriet's sense of humour. He'd seen it often when they were children, but it seemed to have vanished ever since, and he had the uncomfortable feeling that it might be his fault.

"Anyway, Harriet took her own dare tonight."

"Oh?" Jasper stilled, his heart thundering in his chest. Could this be it? Could this be the chance he'd been waiting for? "What is it?"

Kitty's eyes twinkled. "To bet something she does not wish to lose." She grasped his arm, squeezing tight. "She'll kill me for having told you," she said, her voice urgent. "For heaven's sake, make the most of it. Don't mess it up."

He looked down at her, seeing his hopes reflected in her eyes. She wanted her friend to be as happy as she was, he could see that, and damn if he didn't want it too. He wanted to see Harriet look at him the way Kitty looked at Luke. He longed for it.

"I won't, you have my word," he said, praying it was true. He smiled at her, hoping she knew how grateful he was. "I'll give it my all or die trying."

***

Matilda smiled as Prue waved a greeting.

"There you are!" Prue exclaimed. "I've been looking for you."

"Yes, you owe me the next dance, Miss Hunt," said her dashing husband, the Duke of Bedwin, smiling at Matilda. "I hope you've not forgotten."

"As if I could," Matilda said, embracing Prue before greeting Prue's cousin, Miss Minerva Butler, and Bedwin's sister, Lady Helena.

"It's lovely to see you, Miss Hunt," Miss Butler said with a warm smile.

"Yes, it's been ages," Lady Helena agreed. "You must come and visit us."

Before Matilda could answer, there was a shriek of laughter, and they all turned to see Bonnie dragging a grinning Jerome Cadogan onto the dance floor. There were tuts and murmurs of disapproval from the older generation, and Matilda frowned with unease.

"Oh, dear," Prue murmured.

"I know," Matilda replied. "I've spoken to her, and I know St Clair's spoken to Jerome, but—"

"But they're having fun," Lady Helena said with a wistful sigh.

"The kind of fun that could ruin a young lady's reputation," Bedwin said, his expression dark.

"Oh, Robert, darling, couldn't you speak to him?" Prue asked, clutching at his hand.

Bedwin stared at his wife in horror. "Damned if I will. It's none of my affair. Besides which, it looks like your Miss Campbell is the instigator. You must speak to her."

Prue scowled. "Oh, very well, but you should at least speak to St Clair. He's your friend."

"Miss Hunt just told you St Clair has already had words. What do you think I can do?"

"I don't know," Prue said, sighing. "Only it's clear the poor girl is besotted with his brother, and I'd hate to see her get hurt."

"She thinks it's her last chance to have fun," Matilda said, her heart aching for Bonnie.

She turned back and discovered Minerva, Prue, and Lady Helena all looking at her.

"Gordon Anderson," they said in unison.

Matilda pulled a face and nodded. "The poor girl."

They stood in silence for a moment, considering Bonnie's fate, and the appalling Scot whom she'd described often and at length. He sounded ever more dreadful every time she spoke of him.

"I need some more punch," Lady Helena announced, breaking the silence and giving her brother an appealing glance. "Please, Robert."

She held out her empty glass to the duke, who sighed.

"You're getting through that at a rate this evening, Helena," he said, a suspicious glint in his eyes.

"Because it's delicious," Helena said, beaming at him. "Much better than the usual dull brew that's offered. I usually spend all evening wishing I could drink champagne, but not tonight."

She gave him a rather hazy smile.

Matilda watched as the duke's suspicious expression deepened. He lifted the empty glass to his nose, muttered a curse, and upended the glass to allow the dregs to trickle onto his tongue.

"Damn me!" he exclaimed, outraged. "No wonder you're enjoying it, that's the most potent fruit punch I've ever tasted."

"Robert?" his wife asked, looking at him in concern. "What's in it?"

"What isn't?" he replied, shaking his head. "But from the way all the young ladies have been consuming it, this should be a lively night."

***

Harriet sipped at her punch, absently wondering why it tasted so much better than usual, and watching the colourful whirl of colours as the dancers flew about the ballroom.

"Care to dance, Harry?"

She stiffened at once, the familiar voice sending awareness skittering through her like hens scattering before a fox. How the devil had he found her? She'd thought this dark corner the perfect hiding place. Harriet forced herself to turn and look at Jasper.

Something that might have been panic rose in her chest as she noted the hopeful gleam in his eyes. *It's not real,* she reminded herself, *he looks like that for all the women. You're nothing special.*

"No, thank you, my lord," she replied. Remembering her promise to be less awful to him, she strove to keep her tone light and pleasant. "B-But thank you for asking."

There, that was perfectly civil.

"Oh, come on, Harry," he wheedled. "You've not danced all night. Please... won't you dance with me?"

See? muttered a little voice in her head. This was the problem with Jasper Cadogan. He couldn't understand that every woman in the room wasn't willing to fall into his arms at a moment's notice.

"I don't like dancing, Lord St Clair. I believe I've reminded you of that before now," she said, before realising her voice had grown tart. She took a breath and forced a stiff smile to her lips before adding, "But thank you again for the kind offer."

"That's not true," he said, his voice far too low, far too intimate. "At least, you always used to love dancing. You used to beg me to dance with you."

To her intense frustration, a blush seared her skin. It felt as if it began at her toes and rose in a swift wave, until all the visible parts of her were a bright pink, almost the same colour as her gown.

"We were children then," she said, doing her best to keep her tone calm and even. She would not lose her temper with him. Not tonight. She turned back to concentrate on the dancers again. "Things change."

"I know that," he said, and despite herself she looked up at him, taken aback by the sorrow in his voice. "You've changed, Harry."

And whose fault is that? She wanted to rage at him, but she didn't, couldn't. She'd never let him know how badly she'd been hurt. She'd been made a fool of too thoroughly already, and she'd not live through it again.

"That's Miss Stanhope, *my lord*," she replied, lifting her glass to take a drink before discovering it empty. Without another word, she set off to fetch another.

"No, it isn't."

With irritation, she looked over her shoulder to discover Jasper following her.

"What?" she asked, threading her way through the crowd.

Jasper moved closer, taking her arm to stop her progress and leaning down to speak in her ear.

"It isn't 'my lord,' and it isn't 'Miss Stanhope.' For heaven's sake, Harry, we've known each other since we were babies."

Harriet tugged her arm free and opened her mouth to give him a set down, before remembering her resolution. Damn, but this was harder than she'd realised.

"Excuse me, my lord. I'm dreadfully thirsty."

She curtsied and then hurried off again, not terribly surprised to arrive at the refreshments room and discover he was still following her. See, *this* was why she had to be rude to him, nothing else got through his thick head. There was the usual crush of people at the refreshments table, but Harriet pushed through to the huge punch bowl. The crush of bodies and the humid evening air had given her a raging thirst and—despite it being dreadfully unladylike—she downed one full glass of punch with a sigh of relief before refilling her glass.

She drank this one a little slower but remained where she was. Jasper's attention had been taken by Matilda and he was trapped in the doorway. It was only a temporary respite, however, as Harriet couldn't leave the room without going straight past him. Whatever Matilda was saying to him, Jasper didn't look best pleased.

Good, she thought. Perhaps his brother was up to his usual tricks and Jasper would be forced to sort him out.

Heavens, but it was hot tonight. Harriet sighed and wished she'd brought a fan. Instead, she drained her glass and filled it again. Perhaps if she eased her way around the edge of the room, she could slip out behind Jasper without him noticing.

Her progress was slow and not entirely steady, and Harriet leaned against the wall for a moment to catch her breath. She felt a little giddy. No doubt the heat was making her feel faint. Fresh air, that was the thing....

Sadly, she made it to the doorway just as Matilda left Jasper alone. He turned to her at once, as though he'd been perfectly aware of her attempt to escape the whole time.

"Oh, go away, Jasper," she said with a sigh. "I'm too hot and I don't have the energy to fight with you."

"Good," he said, his expression rather fiercer than before. "It's about time. Come along...."

Jasper grasped her arm, towing her behind him as Harriet held her drink aloft, trying not to spill it. Irritation simmered under her skin.

"Jasper!" she protested, too annoyed not to use his given name. "Leave me be, you obstinate wretch."

"Not on your life," he shot back. "Not tonight. Tonight we're going to talk."

What?

Oh no.

That sounded like a dreadful idea.

"Let go of me, you... you elvish mark'd, abortive, rooting hog!"

That got his attention.

He stilled, turning back to look at her with amusement. "What did you call me?"

"A rooting hog," she replied with dignity. "Among other things."

"Yes, that's what I thought you'd said." His lips twitched. "Hmmm, *Richard the Third*, if I remember correctly. How many other Shakespearean insults can you remember?"

Harriet sighed, impressed that he was correct and wishing she'd kept her blasted mouth shut. It had been a game they'd played together as children, she and Jasper and Jerome and Henry, each of them abusing each other with the worst insults they could dig up. Harriet had astonished them all with her inventive curses until they'd discovered what she already knew, that Shakespeare was a marvellous source of material.

"All of them," she said darkly.

Jasper chuckled and carried on his way, his grip on her hand firm and unyielding.

"Let me go," she said in a harsh undertone. "People are *looking*."

"They wouldn't look if you weren't making a scene," he replied, perfectly cheerful.

Harriet gave up and followed him out into the garden. Perhaps she could escape him outside.

To her annoyance, he didn't stop at the terrace but carried on, dragging her into the gardens.

"Jasper Cadogan, if you don't let me go I'll—"

"You'll what?" he demanded, stopping at last in the seclusion of a dark corner. "Hate me forever? Never speak to me again?" He gave a huff of laughter. "I'm not sure how else you can punish me, Harry."

There was something soft and bruised in the way he spoke, and Harriet acknowledged a stab of guilt. Perhaps Kitty had been right. Perhaps this had gone on long enough.

There was a taut silence as Harriet didn't know what to say next. She was too afraid to give him an inch, to invite any kind of friendship between them. He was her weakness, her Achilles' heel, and the only way she'd ever kept him at bay was to stay angry with him, to build an impenetrable wall of ice around her that he couldn't cross. If she let that go, she'd be at risk, vulnerable, and she couldn't allow that. Still, soon enough she'd be gone, and she'd not have to see him anymore. She could put him from her mind, and from her heart, for they'd hardly mix in the same circles then. She'd be safe.

Harriet let out a breath. She'd apologise, assure him she didn't hate him, and then she'd go up to her room and write a letter. The sooner she was safely away from here the better. Her carefully made plans would have to be brought forward, that was all.

Before she could speak, however, Jasper beat her to it.

"What are you going to bet, Harry?"

A strange sensation, akin to ice water sliding down her back, snapped Harriet's attention back to Jasper. His aquamarine eyes were intent, and something in his expression made her heart beat faster.

"W-What?"

"You have a dare to complete. To bet something you do not wish to lose."

Kitty Connolly, I will wring your pretty neck!

"What of it?" Harriet demanded.

Her head was spinning again, her heart beating too fast. She was filled with the desire to do something reckless, to run away into the darkness and never be seen again.

She gasped, beyond shocked as Jasper caught her by the waist and pulled her close. Suddenly she was sixteen years old again and gazing at the boy she'd loved her entire life.

No.

No, she would not be that girl again. That stupid, stupid, girl.

"I dare you, Harriet," he said, his voice low and so intimate the hairs rose on the back of her neck. She couldn't breathe. "I dare you to stop hiding, from me, from life. I dare you to go back into that ballroom and dance and laugh and have fun. I dare you to dance with me, with an open heart and no pretence between us. I dare you to dance with me, look into my eyes, and tell me I mean nothing to you."

Harriet stared up at him. Surely her heart ought not beat at this ridiculous pace. It could not withstand such punishment, and would burst at any moment…. Only it didn't burst. It just kept on thundering, battering against her ribs like a panicked bird trying to escape a trap, and this *was* a trap.

"And what do I get if I win?" she asked, all too aware of the breathless quality of her voice.

"I'll leave you be," he said, his grip tightening on her waist. "You'll never be plagued by me ever again. I won't seek you out, won't speak to you. You'll be free of me, for good."

"You m-mean it?" she asked, grasping at his words.

It was what she'd wanted, what she'd been planning for: a way to escape him, to put him behind her, and he was handing it to her. All she need do was pretend to enjoy herself for a few hours. She could manage that, surely?

"I mean it," he said, his voice harsh. "But don't forget your forfeit, Harry."

There was a warning note there that she ought to have heeded, but the possibility of being free of this maddening connection that held her tied to her past was too tantalising.

"Which is?"

"If you fail—"

"Yes?" She watched him, trying to read his expression and wondering at the determination she saw there, or… was that *desperation*?

"You'll give yourself to me."

Harriet blinked, not understanding.

"I'll…?" she began, frowning.

Jasper laughed, but it was not a sound she associated with him. It was darker, that desperate edge audible once more.

"You'll show everyone the real Harriet, the one I grew up with, the one I knew was bold and brave and funny, and then, at midnight, you'll dance with me. You'll dance with me and you'll look into my eyes and tell me how you feel about me. If you can tell me I mean nothing to you, if you can put your hand on your heart and swear that there's nothing between us, that you don't care for me… you'll never see me again. But if you can't… if you can't, I will take you down to the summerhouse and make love to you. You'll be mine, Harry, just like you were always supposed to be."

Harriet stared at him. She wanted to tell him he was mad, she wanted to slap his face and kick him in the shins and stamp her feet and rage, but she couldn't. The idea of Jasper taking her to the summerhouse and making love to her was so overwhelming she couldn't even breathe, let alone move.

"Did I hurt you, Harry?" he asked. He cupped her face with his hand and stared down at her, his voice tender now. "I swear I never meant to."

That was probably the only thing that could have snapped her out of the trance she'd fallen into. She pushed away from him, out of his arms.

"Of course not," she said, striving to calm herself, to reach for the anger that protected her. If she could stay angry with him, she'd be safe. All she had to do was prove him wrong, and she'd be free of him, for good. "And I'm not hiding from anything, or anyone."

"Prove it," he said, with a gleam in his eyes that boded ill.

"Fine!"

She could get her dare done and rid herself of this wretched man once and for all. Then she could get on with her life in peace, knowing she was free of him.

"You'll do it?"

"Why not?" she retorted, draining what remained of her drink and throwing the empty glass at him. Jasper caught it, deft as ever, blast him. "This will be easy, and you'd better keep your promise."

"Oh, I'll keep it," he said, a maddening smile curving over his lips.

Drat the arrogant wretch, she'd make him pay for this.

"Would thou wert clean enough to spit upon," she threw back at him.

He frowned at that, considering. *"King Lear?"*

"Ha!" she said triumphantly. *"Timon of Athens."*

Jasper rolled his eyes. "Time's running out, love," he warned.

"Argh!" Harriet replied and stomped off back to the ballroom.

Chapter 2

Dear Miss Stanhope,

Thank you kindly for the book by Watts which I greatly enjoyed. "Logic, or The Right Use of Reason in the Enquiry After Truth With a Variety of Rules to Guard Against Error in the Affairs of Religion and Human Life," posed some interesting questions which I should be glad to discuss with you when we next meet. In anticipation of that meeting I enclose "Conversations on Chemistry," by Mrs Jane Marcet, with whom I am acquainted. It is an introduction to the subject in which you have shown such interest and I hope you will find it a useful starting point.

—Excerpt of a letter from Mr Inigo de Beauvoir to Miss Harriet Stanhope.

Still the night of the St Clairs' summer ball. 30th August 1814, Holbrooke House, Sussex.

Jasper stood in the dark of the garden and wondered what the hell he'd just done. He must be out of his bloody mind. Harriet was so damned stubborn she'd prove him wrong if it killed her. She'd go out there and be witty and lively and funny and everything he knew she could be, because she *was* all of those things, she'd just forgotten. The lurking suspicion that he'd caused that change made him feel sick.

How? How could he have done it?

For the thousandth time he remembered the year he'd truly noticed Harry for the first time. He'd been eighteen, and Harry sixteen. For all his life, Harry had adored him and he'd known it. She'd put up with being dragged through mud and playing the hapless heroine for him and both their brothers to alternately rescue or kidnap. Christ, they'd almost drowned her one year! She'd never complained, and had always stared at him with such admiration from behind those spectacles... until she'd turned sixteen, and then it had been Jasper's turn to stare back.

It had taken him by surprise, so much so that he'd found it difficult to speak with her at all. He'd spent the entire summer getting up the nerve to kiss her, but when he had it had been perfect—more than perfect—and it had changed everything. It had changed him. With his usual hopeless timing, it had finally happened on the morning he'd left to go abroad, desperation at leaving without her having a clue as to his feelings giving him courage enough to take his chance. He'd not seen her again for over a year, when everything had changed in his absence. He still remembered the anticipation he'd felt at seeing her again, and the bewilderment when she'd cut him dead.

Yet, once again desperation had motivated him to act rashly, and no doubt the outcome would be just as awful. She'd look him in the eyes and tell him she didn't give a damn for him, and he'd be honour bound to let her go. His heart clenched.

"Please," he said, staring up at the cloudless sky above him. "*Please,* let me win her back."

***

Harriet seethed all the way back to the ballroom. How dare he? How dare he dare her? And such a ridiculous dare it was. Well, she'd show him....

Suddenly, she was looking out over the whirling crowd of dancers again and her stomach twisted into a knot, because no one ever asked Harry to dance. She was a bespectacled wallflower who hid in dark corners and would rather die than be noticed.

How the devil was she to prove otherwise?

A wave of cold travelled over her, followed by intense heat, as she realised what forfeit she'd agreed to. Oh, good heavens.

Lurching a little, she staggered sideways to lean against the wall. Everything seemed to be spinning before her, and not just the dancers.

Harriet, you imbecile!

She would lose this bet and then... and then... Jasper would take her to the summerhouse and....

The hot and cold sensation intensified as a strange ache coiled low in her belly. Oh, no. She did *not* want that, she assured herself. Yet as she imagined being in Jasper's arms—imagined his hands on her, his lips—something inside her burned with longing. Her breath caught and panic rose in her chest. If he touched her that way she'd be lost. She'd be sixteen and madly in love all over again, and she'd hand him the power to destroy her utterly.

That would not do.

"Jerome!" Harriet almost shrieked his name as she hurried across the ballroom to him.

As ever, Bonnie was glued to his side.

Harriet wondered if Jerome was the only one who didn't realise Bonnie was in love with him. Poor Bonnie... another case of love causing misery. Oh, not yet, because Bonnie didn't appear to have grasped the truth. Jerome would never love her back, and he certainly wouldn't marry her. Harry knew Jerome as well as she knew her own brother, and Bonnie simply wasn't his type. She was too bold, too outspoken, too much trouble. The wicked devil would only make the most of her company, have fun with her while he could, and then he'd leave, and Bonnie would be devastated. Oh, not that Jerome would take advantage. He wouldn't act the cad; he simply wouldn't notice the damage he'd done. Men so often didn't.

"Harry!" Jerome exclaimed, grinning at her. It was an echo of Jasper's smile, though Jerome's broken nose gave him a slightly more rakish air than Jasper's Greek god perfection would allow for. "Are you having fun?"

"Are you foxed?" Harry asked, frowning a little.

"Me?" Jerome replied, looking affronted. "As if I would be, at a family affair. I've drunk nothing but fruit punch all evening, just as I promised Mother."

Beside him, Bonnie sniggered, and they exchanged a glance before dissolving into laughter. Harriet shook her head at them.

"Well, never mind that. You must dance with me," she said curtly.

Jerome straightened up, his expression instantly sober. "You want to dance?" he repeated, looking as if she'd just told him she wanted to perform the dance of the seven veils, not the quadrille or whatever it was everyone was gathering for now.

"Yes."

"With me?"

He looked so astonished that Harriet's temper rose.

"Yes," she repeated, striving for patience.

"You want to dance... *with me?*" Jerome parroted the entire demand again, clearly needing to be certain.

"Yes, please, Jerome, if it wouldn't kill you," Harriet pleaded, wondering if she'd have to beg him. Was it really such a terrible request?

"But you never dance, Harry."

"Well, I do tonight!"

Having had quite enough of this nonsense, she snatched up Jerome's hand and dragged him onto the dance floor.

Once in position, Harriet caught sight of Jasper watching her and remembered she was supposed to be enjoying herself. She forced her face into something resembling anticipation and smiled at Jerome.

"Are you quite well, Harry?" Jerome asked, concern in his eyes. "Have… Have you been drinking the punch?"

"Quite well, thank you," Harriet replied, smiling so broadly her face hurt. "I say, Jerry, can you get some of your friends to dance with me too?"

Jerome blinked, stunned into silence, which was just as well as the dance spun him away from her and it was several seconds before they were reunited. She wouldn't put it past him to bellow a reply over the entire ballroom. Subtlety was not his strong suit.

"S'pose I could," he replied, narrowing his eyes. "Why? What's going on?"

"Nothing," Harriet said, trying to keep her smile fixed in place. She could feel Jasper watching her; his gaze felt as if it was burning a hole in the back of her neck. "Just decided it's time to stop sitting in the corner, that's all."

"Well!" Jerome clapped his hands together, satisfaction glinting in his expression. "And about bloody time, too. Certainly I can find you some dance partners. Cholly owes me a favour, for starters."

Harriet sighed. It would have been nice to think he'd not have to blackmail his friends into dancing with her, but it was hardly surprising. Harriet knew she was not popular. She never had been, outside of Jasper and Jerome, and that was only because they'd grown up together. With people she didn't know, Harriet didn't have the slightest idea of what to say, and so she said nothing. Naturally, she appeared awkward and diffident, if not outright unfriendly, and when she did finally speak, she usually said something of the sort that stamped the word *bluestocking* on her forehead. Besides which, she was not exactly beautiful. Not ugly, either, but simply... unremarkable.

Her hair was an unremarkable shade of brown, neither dark nor light, as were her eyes. She was of average height and her figure neat enough, but neither exceptionally slender nor voluptuous. Harriet was the girl that people walked past without noticing, and that was fine, she told herself. If anyone ever noticed her it was either *oh, the girl with the spectacles,* or a combination of sniggering and bewilderment because she'd said something no one else understood.

Still, she didn't have to enjoy this, only convince Jasper that she was, and it really didn't matter why they danced with her, only that they did. So she pasted an expression of delight onto her face and beamed at Jerome, who returned a cautious smile, and around they went again.

***

Jasper watched as Jerome said something to Harriet and she tipped her head back and laughed. Jerome looked a little startled, as did those dancing on either side of them, but it seemed Harriet's laughter was infectious. Everyone grinned at her and she laughed again as Jerome chuckled and shook his head.

Damn it, you bloody fool, Jasper cursed himself. He'd played this all wrong. He was going to lose her.

As the night wore on, Harriet's dance partners came and went, all of them shaking their heads and laughing when they left her. Indeed, some didn't leave. They remained to talk to her and fetch her glasses of punch between dances. When they finally parted, they looked bemused at having been so entertained, which only made Jasper gnash his teeth harder. They were only now seeing what he'd always known. Harriet was a remarkable young woman when she was relaxed and happy. Once upon a time it had only been him who'd seen it, but he *had* seen it, he'd seen it before anyone else had and surely that meant something. It bloody well ought to. Some of her dance partners looked regretful as they walked away, and it seemed quite a few secured a second dance with her.

Jasper felt his jaw clench tighter. She'd better have saved the midnight waltz for him.

By now, he didn't know if he was longing for midnight or willing it away. For all that jealousy was burning him from the inside out to see her having such fun with every other eligible man but him, he was terrified that she would simply look him in the eyes and tell him he meant nothing to her. Perhaps she'd say that she hated him, or perhaps she merely disliked him. Somehow, he preferred hatred to anything less… at least it was a strong reaction. To be merely disliked seemed a pitiful fate. He could not even believe that she would look into his eyes and tell him she loved him, that she'd always loved him and always would. Yet surely she cared, just a little? His heart felt squeezed in his chest.

She had once. She had for years and years. He knew she had, and he'd taken it all for granted, fool that he was, but perhaps she could again? Might she give him the chance?

No matter what, he would jump on the slightest sign that she cared for him and take her down to the bloody summerhouse. Oh, not that he would force himself on her, he wasn't a blackguard, but he needed to be alone with her, needed a chance to win her back, and he didn't know how else to try when she wouldn't speak with him. He knew that women desired him, knew every other woman here believed him exceptionally handsome; it was only Harry who seemed immune to his charms. The trouble was he didn't care what anyone else thought, and he never had. Harry judged people on their minds. She had no interest in a handsome face or a strong physique, and that was where everything fell apart. She thought him a fool, and he couldn't pretend she was wrong.

He wished he was clever enough to impress her, and it wasn't as if he'd not tried. He'd tried bloody hard at school, studying until all hours until he'd realised it was hopeless, and it was less humiliating to pretend he didn't care than to keep failing.

Naturally she despised him for not caring, for acting as though he had no interest in learning, in anything beyond the superficial, yet he was too mortified to explain the truth.

If she knew she'd pity him, and that would crucify him.

Finally, midnight arrived and Jasper crossed the floor towards her. *Please*, he prayed as he walked towards her, *please, give me a chance.*

Harriet was waiting for him, and all the laughter had gone by the time he reached her. She was wide-eyed as she looked up at him; he thought perhaps she was trembling. He hoped so, because if it wasn't her it was him. Not that this wouldn't be humiliating enough when she told him she wanted him to leave her alone. He wasn't entirely a fool, he knew that was the only reason she'd accepted his dare, in order to never be bothered by him again.

Jasper swallowed and took her in his arms, drawing her closer than he ought but unable to stop himself. If this was the last time he'd hold her, he was damned well going to make the most of it.

Chapter 3

Dear Matilda,

How kind you are to worry so about me. I assure you there is nothing dastardly or Gothic in my disappearance. Far from it, I'm afraid for I should be vastly entertained by a villain at this point. Sadly, there is no riveting mystery to entertain you with. My aunt has been a little under the weather these past weeks and she frets when I'm away from her. She's been such a dear to me that the least I can do is give her my company.

So there, you see. A dull explanation, but nothing to upset your tender heart.

I hope I have put your mind at rest.

—Excerpt of a letter from Miss Jemima Fernside to Miss Matilda Hunt.

Still the night of the St Clairs' summer ball. 30th August 1814, Holbrooke House, Sussex.

Harriet shivered as Jasper drew her into his arms for the waltz. Strangely, she'd enjoyed herself this evening, as Jasper must well know. For once her nerves had deserted her, and she'd danced and laughed and had a rather wonderful time. How odd, when she'd always despised dancing. Yet, if she were being honest, that wasn't entirely true. Jasper had been quite correct; she hadn't *always* despised dancing. She'd just never learned to enjoy it with anyone but Jasper and his brother. Harriet had learned with Jasper and Jerome and her own brother, taking turns with each of them under the dance instructor's tuition as she was the only girl. She'd loved those lessons, they'd been full of laughter and fun, and she'd loved dancing with Jasper most of all, because she'd loved him most of all too.

Though she'd told herself all night that she was dreading this moment—for she must tell a bare-faced lie to walk away from him once and for all—she found now that dread was far from her thoughts. She smiled as she remembered those lessons, remembered how patient Jasper had been when she'd trodden on his toes, and the way he'd grinned at her when he spun her into a complicated turn, and she didn't trip up.

"What are you smiling at?" His voice was soft, and she was too lost in the memory's sweetness to find an easy lie.

"I was remembering our dance lessons," she admitted, knowing it was a dangerous thing to say in the circumstances. She had to tell him he meant nothing to her. She had to get free of him once and for all.

"That was my favourite time of the week," he said, surprising her.

"You rotten liar," she retorted, shaking her head in disbelief. "You hated dance lessons and always said it was a waste of a perfectly fine afternoon."

Jasper stared down at her and she made the mistake of looking into his eyes. Lord, but he was beautiful. His eyes were remarkable, neither green nor blue but a tantalising mixture of the two, a bright aquamarine that stole her breath whenever she saw them.

"That's true," he allowed, smiling a little. "But only up until the summer you turned sixteen. Then… then it was what I lived for."

Harriet's eyes stung and she looked away. Despite her best intentions, she gave a snort of laughter.

"You could have fooled me," she muttered, though so quietly he likely hadn't heard her.

"Harry," he said her name like a plea, aching with sadness.

She forced herself to look back at him, determined to end this once and for all. If he was really as unhappy as he sounded—which she could not believe for a moment—then he deserved to be rid of her every bit as much as she needed to be rid of him. This was it. She would tell him she didn't care for him and they could both move on.

The moment her gaze met his, the words died in her throat and her breath caught as she saw the look in his eyes.

"Harry," he said again. "Don't you care anymore? Don't you care just a little?"

She felt giddy all at once, overcome with heat and emotion and the way he was looking at her, as if… as if he wanted to carry her off to the summerhouse and make passionate love to her.

Oh, good Lord.

No man had ever looked at her that way. She doubted anyone ever would again. Fool. The only reason Jasper looked that way was because she'd rebuffed him for so long. He was like a boy denied a treat, wanting it beyond reason simply because he'd been told no. Yet, an uncomfortable truth rose as she stared up at him and recognised that unrestrained desire.

She felt it too.

She wanted him.

She wanted him badly, and she was indeed a fool to think she could just walk away and he'd not plague her any longer. He would always plague her, even if she was on the other side of the world. He was under her skin and he'd always be there.

Then, perhaps this would finally rid her of him. She snatched at the idea even as a faint voice told her it was preposterous. Harriet hushed it, too eager for a reason to believe in this new and alluring possibility. Perhaps if she gave in to her physical desire, her stupid heart would recognise that it had only been lust, not love. Certainly Jasper would be done with her. He'd lose interest once he'd had what he wanted, and she'd come to her senses once and for all. Why not just get it over with and put them both out of their misery?

In that moment it seemed perfectly logical. A perfectly reasoned argument. Harriet could deal with a logical argument, it was emotions she struggled to comprehend. This wasn't her heart leading her. That *would* be foolish. No, this was a cold, calculated decision that would set her free.

"Harry, answer me, for the love of God," he begged.

She didn't answer him. Answering him was far too dangerous. No. Far better to just get it over with now the decision had been made. The dance ended, and she didn't let go of his hand but tugged at it, pulling him from the dance floor.

"Harry," he said, his voice urgent. "What are you doing? You promised to answer the question."

She ignored him and forced her way through the throng, heading outside the open doors and into the darkness beyond.

"Where are we going?" he demanded, an odd note to his voice as she hurried down the steps and into the garden. "Harriet, for heaven's sake, slow down! Where are we going?"

She still didn't answer, moving so fast she was breathless.

"Harry!"

"To the summerhouse," she said over her shoulder, impatient now and not slowing her pace.

There was a stunned silence.

"The summerhouse?"

The hand she held tugged back and with such forced she stumbled into him. Jasper steadied her, his hands at her waist once more. She stared at his cravat, which gleamed a snowy white in the moonlight. Looking into his eyes was a very bad idea, as she'd already concluded, so she forced her gaze to remain riveted on the pristine linen.

"Why are we going to the summerhouse?" he asked, and she thought he sounded breathless too.

All that running had winded them both, she supposed.

"You know why," she replied, irritated by the question. It had been his dare, hadn't it?

He tilted her chin up, forcing her to look at him. Damn it, those dreadful eyes… there should be a law against them. They gave him an unfair advantage over lesser mortals.

"Harry," he said, staring down at her so intently that she wanted to turn away. "Do… do you mean to say that… that you do care for me?"

Harriet closed her eyes, the only way to avoid that searching gaze as she shook her head. If he looked into her eyes he'd see that lie for the frail thing it was.

He dropped his hand, and the silence stretched out so long she was almost tempted to look at him. Almost.

"Why, then?" he asked, his tone bleak.

"I…." she began, only to falter as a blush scalded her cheeks. Still, he couldn't possibly see that in the moonlight. "I desire you." The words were uneven, forced out as they were. "And you'll feel better when you've… you've…." Harriet licked her lips, uncertain of how to phrase it but she supposed they were past polite conversation at this point. "When you've had me, you'll stop acting like I mean something to you and leave me in peace."

There was a huff of laughter, though he didn't sound especially amused. "Is that how this works?"

"Yes," she said, relieved that perhaps he'd begun to understand.

"You'll be ruined," he said.

Harriet laughed this time. "No, I won't," she said in disgust. "My worth has nothing to do with my virginity."

"In society's eyes it does."

"Oh, stuff society. Besides, no one will ever know." She opened her eyes and dared to look at him. "I'm going to the summerhouse. Are you coming or not?"

"I'd better, I suppose," he said, an odd look glinting in his eyes. "If you're certain it will cure me of this godforsaken obsession with you."

"It will," she retorted, with a decisive nod. "I've reasoned it out, scien... scientifically," she said, stumbling a little over the word. "And I'm rarely wrong when I do that."

"Harry... have... have you been drinking?"

Jasper's voice was cautious, as well it might be. He knew that Harriet never drank. Losing her grip on reason, losing control... that was a terrifying and appalling idea and good heavens, no. *Never!*

"Of course I've not been drinking!" she exclaimed. "The very idea." She turned to glare at him and stumbled on the uneven ground. Jasper reached out and steadied her. "I've drunk nothing but the fruit punch."

"Hmmm," Jasper replied, frowning a little.

Soon enough they reached the summerhouse and Harriet leaned against the door, pushing hard to open as it scraped on the stone flags like it always did.

"I should have that fixed," Jasper said.

Harry laughed. "You say that every time we come here."

"We've not been here in years, Harry," he replied.

"Nonsense. We came here when you arranged for Kitty and Luke to meet in private."

"We didn't come in."

Harriet threw up her arms. "Fine, we've not been here for years," she agreed, deciding to let him have his own way.

"It's been eight years. Eight years since I kissed you, and I don't think a day has gone by when I've not thought of it."

She turned to look at him and smiled, shaking her head in open admiration. "Gosh, you really are very good at this, aren't you?"

He stiffened, the movement visible even in the darkness of the summerhouse. The small single room was all shadows, with a little glimmer of moonlight catching here and there.

"Good at what?"

Harriet waved her hand, gesturing roughly in his direction. "Seduction," she said, feeling another wave of giddiness and reaching out to grab hold of a chair back to steady herself. "You know just what to say to get a woman's clothes off her, don't you?"

"You appear to be fully dressed."

Harriet huffed, dismissing the sardonic tone to his voice. "We've only just set foot through the door. I imagine the most practised rake needs a few minutes to work his magic, even if he does look like a fallen angel."

She flushed then, recognising the gleam of interest in his eyes at her unintended compliment. Still, she'd already admitted she desired him, and he knew he was gorgeous. The way women threw themselves at his head wherever he went would give the humblest of men a clue. To her knowledge, Jasper had never been humble. Nonetheless she turned around, not wanting to see his smug look when he commented on her admission.

"I'm not a rake, Harry."

That surprised her. Not only that he'd not taken the opportunity to tease her for likening him to a fallen angel, but that he'd deny it. Everyone knew of his affairs, the stories were legion.

She snorted. Not the most ladylike sound and she regretted it immediately, but really... why deny the obvious.

"I'm not," he insisted. "Half of those stories that go around aren't true, and the rest are grossly exaggerated."

Harriet rolled her eyes and turned to face him. "So, you've not been having an affair with Mrs Tate?"

He had the grace to look somewhat sheepish but held her gaze. "I never said I was a virgin, either." There was a slight twitch to his lips. "But I finished with her some time ago."

"Oh?" Harriet replied, striving for nonchalance. What did she care if it was over between them? It was none of her business, yet, she couldn't deny that she was glad. "That's why I have the pleasure of your attention, is it? At a loose end?"

"Damn it, *no!*"

There was real anger in the explosion of his words, and she jumped, startled, and yet was too slow to react when he closed the distance between them and took her in his arms. His mouth was on hers, hot and fierce and urgent and in that moment Harriet's resistance—what little of it remained—held up a white flag and surrendered.

Memories assailed her of another kiss, given in this same place. It had been a tentative, sweeter kiss, full of hope and expectation, and she could not help but compare it to this. They had nothing in common. She'd be so young and naïve and idealistic, and Jasper had just been playing, practising his technique, no doubt.

This was different.

A man who knew what he was doing gave this kiss and wanted what she'd so blatantly offered him. It was ferocious and intense, and his arms locked about her, pulling her closer, so close she could hardly breathe. She felt possessed and desired and it was wonderful, dramatic, and not a little overwhelming.

Harriet melted into his embrace, sinking her hands into his hair and finding it warm and silky. Jasper deepened the kiss, plundering her mouth as if he'd die if he couldn't kiss her, as if she was air and he'd been drowning until their lips met.

Yes, was the only coherent thought in her mind, and, *don't stop,* and how strange and pleasant it was not to think. Harriet thought about everything, considering things from all angles, weighing her decisions with mathematical precision, but thought was beyond her now. There was nothing but the heat of Jasper's body burning through his clothes, the strength of his arms about her, and as he grasped her bottom and hauled her against his arousal she burned too.

Harriet gasped and pressed closer as heat thrummed beneath her skin, the ache that had settled over her flesh earlier that night descending to pulse between her thighs in a steady and insistent throb that seemed to repeat his name.

Jasper, Jasper, oh, yes, please, Jasper.

The next she knew his hands were at the fastenings of her gown and she laughed at the speed with which she was divested of both it and her petticoats.

"Still denying you are a rake?" she said, chuckling and shaking her head with bemusement as she watched her stays tumble to the floor and feeling oddly detached, as though this was happening to a different Harriet, a braver Harriet, one who'd forgotten she was afraid of Jasper, and that she needed to stay far, far away from him.

"Yes," he said, pulling her back to him and nipping at her earlobe as one hand slid beneath her chemise, smoothing up her thigh. "I was lonely, Harriet. Lonely for you, that's all. You only needed to crook your finger, and I'd have come running."

Harriet smiled, dazed but not entirely beyond sense. The things men would say to get a woman naked. Strange too, when she'd already agreed to this.

"There's no need to try so hard," she whispered, startled to hear the words slur and then gasping as his fingers grazed her sex. She shivered and clung to him. "Oh, yes," she murmured.

Jasper stilled and drew back staring down at her.

"Don't stop," she pleaded, her body alive with anticipation.

"Are you quite certain you've not been drinking?" he asked.

"Oh, Jasper, *really?*" she exclaimed, impatient now. She tugged at his hair, drawing him down for another kiss and he groaned against her mouth as his fingers trailed gently back and forth through the soft curls between her thighs.

"Harry, oh, God, Harry, I want you so much."

"Yes," she agreed, beyond saying anything more than that. "Yes, yes, yes."

"We need a bed," he said, the words desperate as he looked about the room. He let her go, so suddenly that Harriet stumbled and had to catch hold of the chair back to steady herself. Thankfully, Jasper didn't seem to notice, too intent on gathering blankets and arranging them on the floor, before tossing a mismatched assortment of cushions onto the pile. Satisfied, he pulled off his boots and cast them down with an astonishing lack of care, knowing what store he placed on the impeccable shine they bore.

His coat and cravat followed, and Harriet watched with rapt fascination as he unbuttoned his waistcoat, flung it to the floor, and tugged his shirt from over his head. Her mouth grew dry as his hands moved to the fall on his trousers and she hardly dared breathe as he pushed them and his small clothes down in one fluid movement before kicking them aside. He was breathing hard now, whereas Harriet thought she might have entirely forgotten how.

Good heavens. A fallen angel indeed.

She stared, unashamedly, studying him like a work of art, for he was that in every sense of the word; so very beautiful. Jasper Cadogan was a masterpiece of male perfection but all heat, flesh, and blood instead of cold, unyielding marble. Her gaze travelled over him, taking in every part of him, from broad shoulders and muscular arms to sculpted abdomen and taut belly, committing it to memory as her eyes moved down to the proud jut of his erection, where she could not help but linger for a long moment before returning to his face.

To her surprise, Jasper hesitated. Was he blushing?

"Still want me, Harry?" he asked, sounding strangely uncertain.

A helpless smile curved at her lips and she nodded. Jasper let out a breath.

"S'not the first time I've seen you naked," she said, and then clapped her hand over her mouth, appalled by the admission. Why on earth had she said that?

Jasper gave a delighted bark of laughter and tugged her back into his arms. Harriet gasped at the feel of his naked body, the fierce heat of him against her through the thin fabric of her shift.

"Oh?" he said, staring down at her with devilry glinting in his eyes. "Have you been spying on me, love?"

He didn't exactly sound displeased by her revelation, but Harriet still burned with mortification. What was wrong with her?

"Come now, you can't leave it at that. When was this?"

"Years ago," she mumbled, wanting to bury her face in his chest but finding his skin hot and silky beneath her touch. She could barely think at all. "You were eighteen."

Harriet had thought him the most beautiful thing she'd ever seen in her entire life when she'd come across him skinny dipping with her brother in the lake, in that long, glorious summer when she'd been happy. Yet he'd been still a youth then, poised on the brink on manhood. Now he was a man in truth, and he took her breath away, made her heart ache with longing, and the secret place between her thighs pulse with desire.

Unable to stop herself she touched a fingertip to his chest, trailing through the scattering of darker gold hair until she found the flat disc of his nipple and circled it. Harriet watched, intrigued as the skin grew taut beneath her touch, and could not deny the impulse to lean in and lick the tiny nub. Jasper groaned, and the sound thrilled down her spine, a feeling of such power that she couldn't help but revel in it. She did it again, circling with her tongue now before sucking lightly.

Jasper cursed and suddenly she was being lifted and taken to the floor, laid carefully among the nest of blankets and cushions he'd arranged for them. He kissed her again, undoing the tie that held her shift tied at the neck and tugging it open to expose her breasts.

"Harry," he breathed reverently as he cupped her soft flesh. "You're so lovely."

Harry laughed a little, amused that he was trying so hard but touched all the same. At least he was making an effort.

He stared down at her, a puzzled expression in his eyes. "You *are* lovely, Harry," he said again.

"Hmmm," she said, smiling, not wanting to spoil things by pointing out the obvious.

"I'll show you just how lovely you are," he murmured, lowering his mouth to her breast and kissing and licking until she was mindless with pleasure. He moved to her other breast and continued feasting upon her while his hand returned beneath her shift, sliding back to the place that ached for him and seeking out the source of her pleasure.

Harriet gasped and arched under his touch and Jasper murmured sweet things to her that she could not take in, too lost in the pleasure he gave her. He slid one finger into her slick heat and his own moan echoed hers.

"Oh, God, Harry, I want this. I want you. I've wanted you for so damned long, I thought I'd go mad. Tell me this means something, love, *please*."

Harry couldn't tell him anything, she was incapable of anything resembling speech, beyond thought or words, dazed with the pleasure he seemed to command from her body so effortlessly. She felt like an instrument that had been left to gather dust suddenly put in the hands of a master. How could he know her body, understand her pleasure, better than she had ever done?

"Jasper," she said, clutching at him as he raised his head, returning his mouth to hers.

"Tell me I mean something to you, Harry. It isn't just desire, is it?"

"Oh, Jasper," she said, wanting to cry, want to tell him not to talk, not to ask her such questions, questions that would leave her vulnerable and exposed far more than having his hands on her in such an intimate fashion. "Stop it, stop it."

He stilled at once and she wanted to scream with frustration.

"N-No... don't stop!" she wailed. "Just s-stop talking. I c-can't think. I don't want to think. Not now."

Jasper stared down at her. "Christ, Harry, you are drunk."

"I'm not!" she exclaimed, furious with him. "I told you, I only drank the punch."

"Oh, love," he groaned, resting his forehead upon hers. "That may be, but you're foxed, and I can't… damn it, Harry, I can't make love to you. Not now. I need to know you want this."

Harriet glared at him, outraged. "Jasper, we're naked, and your hand is… is *there*. I think you can safely assume I want this."

"Do you, Harry," he said, his voice low as he nuzzled her neck. "Do you really?"

"Jasper Cadogan, if you don't finish what you've started, I will kill you."

There was a low rumble of laughter and Jasper sighed. "All right, love. Don't fret, I'll put you out of your misery."

Chapter 4

No. I won't come back, and I certainly won't marry Gordon bloody Anderson. So there!

—Excerpt of a letter from Miss Bonnie Campbell to The Earl of Morven.

Still the night of the St Clairs' summer ball. 30th August 1814, Holbrooke House, Sussex.

Jasper could have cried. As it was, he would murder his bloody brother, for he didn't have the slightest doubt that it was Jerome who had been responsible for lacing the punch. Here he was, with the woman he loved in his arms, only to discover she was drunk. He'd suspected as much earlier but a) it had been impossible to believe Harriet was drunk, and b) she'd denied it so vigorously he'd believed her, or perhaps he'd wanted to believe her badly enough that he'd ignored the obvious. Either way, he couldn't pretend he didn't know now, no matter how much he wanted to.

Yet he couldn't leave her when he'd worked her to such a pitch. She was so responsive to his touch, far less shy and nervous than he might have expected. He wondered if that was the drink, but thought perhaps it was just Harriet. Before things had changed, she'd been bold enough in speaking her mind around him. It was only in crowds or before strangers she grew tongue-tied and unsure of herself. It always pained him to see it, making him wish he could hold her hand and reassure her.

She didn't need her hand held now, he thought wryly, as she pulled at his shoulders, tugging him back down to her, clutching at his hair until he kissed her again. He couldn't make love to her, not now, not when he was uncertain if she really wanted him to, but he could ease the aching he knew she felt.

He kissed her, slow and deep, savouring her, bewitched by the enticing taste of innocence and eagerness as she sighed against his mouth, and his hand returned to caressing her private flesh. It was no hardship to pleasure her, even though his own body ached with the desire to join with her, to make her his in every way, in such a way she could no longer deny she was his, or that they belonged together. As she came apart beneath his touch, arching and crying out, her fingers digging into his back, he stared down at her, his heart bursting with wanting, with loving her, and with the desperate desire to ensure this would be his and his alone, for always.

"Jasper," she murmured, sleepy now, her limbs pliant and heavy as the pleasure ebbed, leaving her boneless and sated.

"I'm here, love," he said, gathering her into his arms and pulling her against his chest. "I'll always be here," he added as her breathing deepened and she snuggled into his embrace.

***

"Congratulations," his mother said, her tone dry as she stared down at them.

Harriet was blushing with such ferocity he could feel the heat of it against his skin—his bare skin, as he was stark bollock naked, as was perfectly obvious to their audience. It was only Harry who was covering him, and he'd done his best to cover *her* with his coat.

Still, Jasper glowered at Mr Burton, Jerome, and his friends.

"Turn your backs!" he growled.

"I think we can do better than that," Mr Burton replied, his expression one of deep disapproval as he opened the door and indicated that everyone should leave.

They did, thank heavens. All except Jasper's mother.

"I should like to speak to you both back at the house as soon as...." She looked at the clothes scattered about the summerhouse and her lips twitched. "As soon as you are able. We have a wedding to arrange. I must say, Harriet," she added, giving into the urge to grin, "I couldn't be happier. Well, done, Jasper!"

She clapped her hands together with obvious delight and bustled out of the room.

Jasper held his breath.

Harriet was rigid in his arms and still turned away from him. She didn't move; he suspected she didn't even blink. She seemed too shocked to react. He listened to everyone moving away from the summerhouse, heard their voices receding as his mother ushered them away.

He took a deep breath, wondering what to say as his gaze fell on the smooth expanse of Harriet's shoulder. Unable to resist, he leaned down and kissed it. She gasped, and for just a moment he thought that a good sound, and that perhaps they could finish what they'd started, but then Harriet scrambled away from him.

"Going to be sick," she managed, and barely made it out of the door before he heard retching sounds from outside.

Perhaps not, then.

***

By the time Harriet had cleaned herself up and dressed, she wanted to die. She'd never felt so ill in her life, but she was almost grateful. It kept her mind off the disaster she'd just made of her life.

Don't panic, she instructed herself. *Do. Not. Panic.*

She was panicking.

Jasper kept trying to talk to her, but she just hushed him, holding up her hand and glaring. He shut up. She couldn't speak to him, not yet. Not until she figured out what had happened last night. It was all a blur, a hazy collection of half-remembered images and words jumbled up into a tangled mess. There was only one thing she could remember with any real clarity, and she really wished she could forget that bit. She flushed, turning her back on Jasper as she made a show of smoothing out her gown.

Don't think of it. Don't think of it. Naturally she could think of nothing else. Nothing else filled her mind but Jasper's naked body upon hers, his mouth fastened upon her breast and his hand between her legs, his fingers…. Her whole body heated as she remembered the exquisite pleasure of his fingers sliding inside of her, and the sounds she'd made as he'd given her the most incredible experience of her life.

"Harry," he said again, and she shook her head, fighting back tears.

Oh, Harriet, you fool.

She pulled open the summerhouse door and ran.

***

Jasper watched her go. More than anything he wanted to go after her, but now wasn't the time. He knew that much. Besides, he had a lifetime now, a lifetime to convince her that they were made to be together. He knew he ought not to feel so satisfied at the situation, especially when he'd trapped Harriet into it, albeit unwittingly. Yet, it was beyond him to feel sorry, to regret that it had happened. She would marry him—she had to—and she'd be his.

Assuming she ever forgave him, either for this or for whatever he'd done to hurt her in the first place.

With a sigh, he closed the door on the summerhouse and began to walk back to the house. He had just set foot in the gardens that lay directly behind the house when he caught sight of Harriet's brother, Henry. He was striding towards Jasper, a determined set to his jaw.

Jasper almost lifted a hand to hail him as he always did—considering Henry was his best friend—until he realised that he'd just ruined the man's sister, and there was a chance he wouldn't be thrilled about it.

"You bastard!" Henry shouted from halfway across the garden, confirming his suspicions.

"Henry," Jasper said, stilling and holding out his hands in a peaceable gesture. "Henry, let me explain, please—"

"Explain what, you blackguard?" Henry demanded, bearing down on him in fury. "How you got my sister drunk and seduced her? My God, I will thrash you within an inch of your life, you miserable cur!"

Jasper sighed and didn't bother trying to defend himself. He owed Henry the chance to vent his feelings. Even so, the thwack to his jaw came as something of a shock, more so as he stumbled back and landed on his arse in the middle of his mother's herbaceous border, the fresh scent of crushed lavender rising up around him.

"Christ," he muttered, touching a cautious finger to his jaw and checking for loose teeth with his tongue.

"Get up, so I can do it again," Henry growled.

"I love her, Henry," Jasper said, looking up at his best friend and hoping he could hear the truth of his words. "I've always loved her and, for the record, she's still a virgin and I'm going to marry her."

Henry stared down at him for a moment.

"Oh," he said, straightening and rubbing the back of his neck. "Well, I suppose that changes things," he said, his expression lightening. He reached out, offering Jasper his hand and tugging him to his feet. "Sorry about that," he said, gesturing to Jasper's jaw. "Had to be done, honour and all that."

"I quite understand, believe me," Jasper said. "And while we're about it, I didn't get her drunk, either. How could you think such a thing?"

Henry shrugged. "Didn't expect to hear the two of you had been found together in the summerhouse. I know Harry never drinks, though, and… well, I didn't know what to believe."

Jasper gave his friend an incredulous look. "You never realised?" he said, shaking his head in astonishment. "You never had the slightest clue I was in love with her?"

"No," Henry admitted, shaking his head. "Well, there was that summer, years back when you seemed to spend a deal of time mooning over her, and she blushed scarlet whenever you spoke to her. I thought then perhaps the two of you would get together, but since then… no. You're always taunting her and making her furious, and I thought she couldn't stand you truth be told."

Jasper let out a breath of laughter, though it was not an especially happy sound. "I think nothing's changed," he said bleakly. "Come on, I have to face everyone. We've a wedding to arrange."

***

Harriet dithered outside the door to the rose salon. Aunt Nell, Lady St Clair, and Jasper were all waiting for her inside. It was late in the afternoon and her headache had receded to a dull thud. The realisation that she'd been drunk had at least explained much of what had happened, and when she found out who'd poured whatever concoction had been in that punch, she would murder them. What a terrible coil she was in now.

She curled her fingers around the doorknob but couldn't seem to find the courage to turn the wretched thing. *Just go in, and get it over with*, she told herself. *You can do it.* Taking a deep breath, Harriet forced herself to move, and stepped into the room to find Aunt Nell and Lady St Clair all smiles, beaming at her. The urge to turn around and run out again was almost overwhelming.

"Harriet, darling," Lady St Clair said, holding out her hands. "I'm so happy. I confess I've been hoping for this day for such a long time. I've always considered you a daughter."

Oh, no. Harriet's heart sank. This would not be easy. She turned to see Jasper watching her warily. He'd washed and changed and looked abominably handsome. She, by contrast, looked how she felt. Utterly wretched.

"I'm so sorry, Lady St Clair," she said, forcing the words out. "B-But I'm afraid I will have to disappoint you. I can't marry Jasper."

Lady St Clair's smile faltered as Aunt Nell gave an audible gasp of shock.

"Don't be ridiculous, Harriet," her aunt snapped. "You *must* marry him. You're ruined if you don't."

Harriet steeled herself for the onslaught that was sure to follow her next words. "I don't want to marry Jasper, and I'm quite certain he does not want to marry me."

"Don't you dare put words in my mouth, Harry," Jasper said.

His voice was quiet, but his expression was thunderous. She could almost believe him, so intense was the look in his eyes. She could almost believe that the godlike figure by the window truly wanted plain little Harriet Stanhope, and not that he was being a gentleman and doing the right thing by his childhood friend.

"I do want to marry you, and you *have* to marry me, like it or not. I'm sorry if that's such a dreadful prospect, but you have no option."

"Actually, Jasper, I do," she replied, turning to look at him. "But either way, it's my decision, no one else's, so do be sensible. You must see that we'd be disastrous together."

"No," he replied, his tone clipped and angry. "I don't see that at all, and what the hell do you mean?"

"Harriet Stanhope, you've been caught in… in *flagrante delicto* with… *a man*," her aunt wailed, with such melodramatic fervour that Harriet almost expected to hear a clap of thunder to underscore it. None came, however, though her aunt turned a startling shade of scarlet. "You *must* marry!"

"I will marry," Harriet replied irritably, deciding she may as well get it over with. "I'm just not going to marry *him*!"

There was a ringing silence as everyone stared at her in shock, and then they all jumped as a knock sounded at the door.

"Go away!" Jasper bellowed, just as Lady St Clair invited whoever it was to come in.

The butler appeared, looking stricken and unsure of whether to close the door again.

"Yes, Temple, what is it?" Lady St Clair asked, as calm and poised as always.

"There is a gentleman here, my lady, a Mr de Beauvoir. He's asking for Miss Stanhope. He's most insistent that he see her."

All eyes swivelled to Harriet, who let out a breath of relief. She'd sent him an urgent message that morning but hadn't dared hope he could come at once, as she'd demanded.

"Show him in, please, Temple," Harriet said, ignoring the looks of disbelief being sent her way.

Temple looked to Lady St Clair, who nodded, then to Jasper, who looked as if he wanted to murder something. Temple retreated with haste.

"Who is he?" Jasper demanded, crossing the room to stare at her.

Harriet swallowed, a little unnerved by the depth of anger she could see in his eyes.

"Mr Inigo de Beauvoir," she replied, her voice not entirely steady. "My fiancé."

Jasper started as if she'd struck him.

"Your what?"

Harriet lifted her chin, trying hard to force the tears back. For a moment the temptation to throw herself into Jasper's arms, cry, and tell him she was sorry was almost overwhelming, but that was stupid and weak. She'd been perfectly correct before. They'd make a disastrous marriage.

"My fiancé," she said again, softer now as she realised his shock was palpable.

Poor Jasper, spoilt and adored his whole life. He never had got used to being told *no*.

She knew that marrying him would be perfect, her dream come true—at first. Jasper would be attentive and loving, and going on the way he'd made her feel last night she'd be putty in his hands. She'd not be able to keep the wall she'd built about her heart intact. Good Lord, he'd dismantled so much of it in the course of a few hours last night she knew she'd been right to keep him at bay for so long.

Jasper Cadogan was every childish romantic dream she'd ever had, but she'd not be made a fool of again. She would not open up her heart the way she had once before, only to be forgotten the moment she was out of his sight. As a young woman of sixteen she'd been shattered, but resilient enough to brush herself off and start over. As his wife, though, and the mother of his children....

What then would she feel when he was away from her?

What then would she feel when she heard the stories of his conquests?

No.

Jasper had never understood her in any case. He had no interest in her pursuits, no interest in learning of any kind, indeed he scorned it, and that she could not tolerate. Inigo did not love her, nor did she love him, but they both held a deep admiration and respect for the other's intellect, and that was a good basis for a happy marriage. Not only that, he would be loyal to her and never bring her misery with his affairs. What more could she ask for?

As if to answer her question, the door opened, and Temple appeared once more.

"Mr Inigo de Beauvoir," he said, before bowing and closing the door behind the new arrival.

Harriet let out a breath of relief at the sight of him. He was tall and lean, with a rather hawk-like profile. His hair was black, unfashionably long, and his eyes were an odd grey-green, cool and impassive under thick eyebrows. At thirty years of age, he looked older, mostly because he took very poor care of himself, sleeping little and working long hours, hence his decision to find a wife. In all, he had a rather sinister appearance, though Harriet knew better than to judge him by his looks. They had been corresponding in secret for some years now, and they had become friends and colleagues of a sort. He had encouraged her learning at every turn and was a firm believer that women ought to be educated in just the same way as men. Women were equals in his eyes, and only appeared stupid in comparison because they were taught that this was what was wanted from them.

"Thank you for coming," she said, moving to greet him.

He gave a formal bow, eyeing the rest of the room with his cool grey-green gaze. "Miss Stanhope, how may I be of service?"

Harriet flushed, realising she must explain exactly what had happened last night and wondering just how he would react. They did not love each other, but still, she had agreed to marry him and….

She swallowed.

"I… I'm in the most dreadful fix," she said, keeping her voice low and her back to the rest of the room. "Perhaps we could speak alone and… in private."

"There's no need for that, darling."

Harriet jumped as Jasper's voice came from close behind her.

"Mr de Beauvoir," Jasper continued smoothly, giving him a measuring look. "I'm St Clair. I'm afraid that Harriet and I were caught in a *very* compromising situation this morning. The news will be all over the village by now. We'll marry, at once." He paused, staring at Inigo. "You are at liberty to call me out, naturally."

"Jasper!" his mother exclaimed, putting a hand to her heart. "Oh, no!"

Inigo remained expressionless, save for the slightest quirk of one eyebrow. "Calm yourself, madam," he said, not looking away from Jasper. "I see no need for bloodshed, unless...." He looked to Harriet. "Were you forced?"

"No!" she exclaimed as Jasper stiffened in outrage. "No... I... I was drunk... at least, I didn't realise I was drunk. Someone put alcohol in the fruit punch, and it was such a hot night, and I was so dreadfully thirsty, and I drank a great deal and... and...." She trailed off as she realised she was babbling, before adding desperately, "I'm still a virgin."

Harriet had lived through many mortifying moments in her life. As a young woman who wore spectacles and was considered an oddity more often than not, it was inevitable, but never in her life had she experienced anything that made her want to curl up and die with quite such longing.

"I see," Inigo said slowly, pursing his lips. He regarded Jasper, who still looked as if he wanted to kill something, before turning back to her. "Well, Miss Stanhope, I see no reason for a great deal of fuss. It is clear you were inebriated, and I have no intention of punishing you for a silly mistake. My offer stands if you still wish to marry."

"What?" Jasper exploded, his outrage so fierce that Harriet leapt from her skin. "No reason?" he thundered. "We were naked together… *all night*! The *only* reason she's still a virgin and only just at that, is because I realised she was inebriated and called a halt, and I'm damn well going to marry her."

"*Jasper!*" Harriet and his mother exclaimed in horrified unison.

Aunt Nell made a groaning sound and collapsed into an armchair. Everyone ignored her.

"Well, can you deny it?" Jasper demanded, turning on Harriet. "Can you deny you wanted me, *begged* me?"

Harriet stared at him, furious and humiliated, *again.* How could he say such shocking things about her in front of everyone? The urge to cry made her chest tight and her throat ache but instead she turned and regarded Mr de Beauvoir, who had been watching proceedings with the detached interest of a natural philosopher watching the behaviour of some unknown species.

"If you can forgive my shocking lapse of propriety, I will be happy to continue our engagement, Mr de Beauvoir, though I should be grateful if we could speed up the proceedings."

"I think that might be wise," he said, one side of his mouth twitching a little in the first show of emotion she'd seen from him since he arrived.

"Harry, no!"

She gasped as Jasper caught her arm and swung her around, panic in his eyes. "Harry, for God's sake, enough. Enough of this ridiculous charade. You don't love him, and he sure as hell doesn't love you. Can you really marry a man who doesn't give a damn what we did together last night?"

"I know he doesn't love me," Harriet said, exhaustion tugging at her bones and making her long for an end to this ridiculous melodrama.

Her head was pounding, she felt sick, and she wanted to go away and have a good cry… but she had to get this over with.

"Our marriage would be based on mutual admiration and respect, my lord," Mr de Beauvoir said, with what Harriet had to admit was a rather condescending tone. "Love is an archaic and nonsensical idea driven by social mores to allow for physical passion. Indeed, marriage is an outmoded concept, however, we are not in a position to defy the world and so must conform. That aside, I greatly admire Miss Stanhope's mind. She has an astonishing intellect, and I think we could do great things together. Last night's—" He waved a hand nonchalantly. "—*indiscretion*… was brought on by alcohol and the attentions of a handsome man," he said, smiling a little. "Any inexperienced young woman would have her head turned by such an event."

Jasper stared at him as though he was speaking a foreign language, though his desire to break de Beauvoir's nose was coming across eloquently enough.

"Love is a nonsensical idea…?" he repeated faintly, too shocked for words. He shook his head and turned back to Harriet, his voice urgent. "Harry, love, I'm sorry for how this has come about, but I'm not sorry it happened. I wanted you last night and I want you now. I *want* to marry you."

Harriet swallowed hard and shook her head. "I don't believe you, Jasper. You've humiliated me today, and all because you can't have what you believe to be yours, but I'm not yours." *Not anymore,* she added silently, though her heart was shattering all over again. "I made a mistake, and I'm sorry, but I see no reason to punish us both further when there is no need."

"Harry, no…."

Harriet's heart clenched at the desperation in his voice. If only she could believe in that, believe that it was real, and not just for now, not just for a few weeks or months, but always. "You want me, I know you do. Don't deny it just because it scares you. Just… Just give me a chance. A few weeks… *Please.*"

"Stop it," Harriet begged, shaking her head and blinking back tears. She could hear his mother sobbing now too, and guilt and her own wanting was making her giddy and faint. "Please, stop it."

"No," Jasper said, shaking his head, clinging to her hands. "I can't, I *won't*!"

"Miss Stanhope." Everyone turned as Inigo spoke again, his calm, commanding voice cutting through the increasingly overwrought atmosphere.

Harriet turned back to him, grateful for his logical mind and detachment. She wanted to run away from all the upheaval and bury herself in books and research, and anything that didn't allow her to *feel* anymore. It was exactly why she had leapt at his offer in the first place.

"Miss Stanhope, upon reflection, I think Lord St Clair has a point. I have no wish to marry you only to discover you have regrets. In the circumstances, I think you need to get whatever this is between you and the earl out of your system. If—once you have purged whatever physical need you feel for the man—you still wish to marry me, I will be happy to continue with our plans."

Harriet gaped at him. Was he… was he actually suggesting…?

"Oh, there's no need to look so scandalised," Mr de Beauvoir said, clearly amused. "We have discussed such things in the past and you know my views on freedom of mind and body. I have no requirement for my wife to be a virgin. I don't, however, want any emotional scenes and outpourings of regret interfering with my work. I'd rather you get these physical urges out of the way now, rather than change your mind once we're wed. It's purely common sense." He glanced back at Jasper and looked him up and down with obvious contempt. "I feel sure a woman with such a brilliant mind will make the right decision."

"You cold bastard," Jasper said, his voice like ice.

For once, Harriet was tempted to agree with him.

There was a spectacular silence in the wake of this pronouncement, and Mr de Beauvoir chuckled as he looked from one shocked face to another.

"Shall we say a week?" he suggested before bowing over her hand. "I'm staying at the inn in the village should you have further need of me. Goodbye, Miss Stanhope. Lady St Clair, Madam, Lord St Clair, good day to you."

Chapter 5

Alice! Harriet's in the most dreadful fix! We must do everything we can to lessen the gossip. I won't be the least bit surprised if you've already heard, such news travels at lightning speeds as I know to my cost, but I'm afraid it's likely all true....

—Excerpt of a letter from Miss Matilda Hunt to Mrs Alice Hunt.

31st August 1814. Holbrooke House, Sussex.

"Leave us." Jasper's voice was hard and implacable, and he hardly recognised it, but his mother and Harriet's aunt had wit enough to leave quickly and without comment.

His heart and mind were being battered on all sides by so many conflicting emotions. It was all he could do to stay still and say nothing while they left. The urge to tear the room apart piece by piece was so tantalising he could taste it. He'd never in his life felt so out of control, so terrified, so bloody angry.

How dare he? How dare that man speak of Harriet in such a way? A man who thought himself worthy to be her husband, yet would hand her into another's bed until they'd wearied of each other.... Jasper felt sick. He also felt panic rising in his chest.

Inigo de Beauvoir was a name he was familiar with. Not out of interest, but because he'd heard him spoken of often enough. He was a member of The Royal Society, a Fellow of The Geological Society and often held lectures at The Royal Institution, which were so well attended people stood in the aisles to get the chance to hear him speak. Well, the bastard might have a brilliant mind, but he had a lump of bloody ice where his heart should be.

Yet, he was right. Harriet was frighteningly intelligent. She had a mind that Jasper could only admire with quiet awe and could not begin to compete with. Christ... he'd not even gone to university. If bloody Napoleon hadn't been causing chaos all over Europe, he'd have gone on a Grand Tour rather than continue the daily humiliation of being shown over and over that he was an idiot. As it was, his father had sent him to visit some maternal relatives in Russia, which Jasper had actually enjoyed, though he'd missed Harriet terribly.

Not that she believed that.

Why in God's name would she choose him over such a brilliant man? Yet... was such a loveless existence really what she wanted, what she needed? He didn't know if he could make her happy and keep her attention, but damn if he wouldn't die trying. It wasn't as if he resented her cleverness or would keep her from learning and spending time with likeminded people. Jasper couldn't discuss the things she was interested in perhaps, and likely he wouldn't even understand half of it, but he could give her every opportunity, and he *could* love her... he *did* love her.

Clever de Beauvoir might be, but he had miscalculated this time, for once Jasper had Harriet in his bed, he'd make damn sure she never wanted to leave it again. Maybe he was no intellectual giant, but he knew his way around a woman's body. Perhaps he was nothing but a pretty face, but that face would work in his favour now. He didn't care what he had to do, how dirty he had to play... Harriet would want him. She'd already admitted as much. She'd want him, flesh and blood and fighting for her. He'd make her need the heat, the passion, and the joy he could give her. Last night had been nothing, a sweet taste of what could be between them, a tantalising glimpse of what it would be like when he made her his. God help him but he would make her so crazy with wanting him she wouldn't remember her own name, let alone Inigo bloody de Beauvoir.

Once he had some semblance of control over himself, he turned to look at her. She was standing by the window, staring out over the gardens. Her shoulders were hunched, her arms wrapped about herself, the picture of misery.

"Do your parents know?" he asked. "About the engagement?"

She shook her head. "I'm of age," she said curtly. "They've taken little interest in my life to date. I see no reason why it should bother them now."

Jasper winced. For as long as he could remember, Harriet had longed for her father's attention. Another brilliant man with cogs and wheels instead of a heart. No matter how hard she'd tried—and she *had* tried—she could not impress him, for he did not believe the female brain capable of brilliance. Henry was a disappointment to his father in other ways. Oh, he was not stupid—he'd done far better than Jasper had, at any rate—but he couldn't hold a candle to Harriet. Not that her father ever deigned to notice.

"Do you mean to go through with it?"

"With the engagement?" she asked, her voice dull. "Why not?"

Jasper let out a breath, fighting for calm. "Because you don't love him, and don't give me some supercilious nonsense about social mores. You need to be loved, Harry. Everyone does. You deserve it."

"Perhaps I need to be understood more."

"A hit, Harry," he acknowledged, feeling the barbed edge of that comment sink into the exposed flesh of his heart. He seemed always to wear it on the outside of his ribs these days, open to attack. "Is that why you despise me, because you think me a fool?"

She turned at that, her surprise evident. "I don't despise you, and I've never thought you a fool. Quite the reverse. I'm just tired of being the subject of your derision, and I can't respect a man who despises learning as you do, who mocks me for everything I hold dear."

"But I don't, Harry," he ground out. "I've always admired you. Surely you know that?"

Her bitter bark of laughter startled him. "Oh, yes. You've always made a point of admiring my intellect. *My, my, the things you know, Miss Stanhope*," she mimicked, capturing his arrogant drawl with quite uncanny accuracy. "How many times have you humiliated me in public, Jasper? Would you like to count the occasions?"

Jasper flushed, knowing he'd deserved that. He had mocked her terribly for her intelligence, often and unkindly, and yes, in public, but only because he was so damned tired of being ignored. Better she hate him and lash out at him, than he cease to exist in her world.

"I didn't mean it," he said, knowing that was an inadequate reply, but he'd never been eloquent around her, and he didn't expect to manage it now. "I just…. Damn it, Harry, you make me so bloody wild when you ignore me!"

She laughed then, and it was such a tired and weary sound his heart ached. "I know," she said, the words almost soothing. "Poor Jasper. You've never been denied anything, have you? God, you were so spoiled. You and Jerome both. The apple of your mama's eye. It's a wonder you can dress yourself, oh, but… you have a valet, don't you?" she added, smiling.

"That's it then? You think me a pampered puppy with fluff between my ears?"

She shook her head and there was no malice in her words, no heat, but they burned all the same. "I think you've never had to work for anything you wanted. You've got a decent brain in your head, but you don't use it because you've never needed to, and you're too lazy to try to be more than you are."

That was so far from the truth he wanted to wail at the unfairness of it, except she didn't know that. No one did. She didn't know it had all been an act to disguise the truth, that he *didn't* have a decent brain in his head. It was so much better to be thought a rake and a libertine who didn't give a damn about his books and his schooling, than let anyone know he was an ignorant fool.

What would she say if she knew he could barely write, any attempt filled with spelling mistakes and odd sentence structure, and that reading was such a chore it made his head explode? Whenever he tried, the letters seemed to rearrange themselves and make no sense at all until he wanted to scream with frustration. He'd gotten by at school by getting the younger boys to read things for him and to write out his homework, learning as much as he could by heart. How could he tell *her* that? Bright, brilliant Harriet, whom he'd worshipped for so long, so in awe of her abilities… how could he tell her he was all but illiterate? Surely she'd despise him. He was the Earl of bloody St Clair and it took him hours to write the simplest of notes, which would still be barely legible. It was beyond humiliating.

Jasper forced down the knot in his throat. He couldn't confess the truth, but he could keep trying to make amends for taunting her.

"I'm sorry," he said, meaning it with such force the words sounded odd to his ears, his voice hoarse. "I'm sorry for all the times I mocked you and made you angry. I never meant it, Harry. I admire you so much, love. I swear I do. Please, don't refuse my offer without even thinking about it. We… We were close once, you liked me once. You even—"

"*No,* Jasper." She swung about and faced him, her eyes glittering and overly bright, but her voice even. "I'll marry Mr de

Beauvoir. It's for the best. You'll see that once I'm gone. The minute I'm out of your sight, you'll forget all about me."

Jasper's breath caught at her words. This was what she thought of him, that he was a shallow fool, callous and heartless? Hurt rose in his chest, hot and angry.

"And what about last night, Harry?" he demanded, his voice low as he stepped closer to her. "What about the fact you begged me to make love to you?"

Harriet's cheeks blazed scarlet, and she tried to turn away from him, but Jasper caught hold of her and pulled her into his arms. She gasped in shock and made a sound of protest until he kissed her, smothering it before she could tell him no. There was a moment of resistance and then she melted, opening her mouth to his and kissing him back. Jasper held her to him so tightly he must have crushed the air from her lungs, but she made no objection, her hands fisting in his hair and pulling, pain that sent desire surging through him, knowing they were both angry, but that she wanted him badly, even though she hated that she did.

"Deny that," he taunted breathlessly as he stared down at her.

She stared back at him, her dark eyes wider than ever behind her spectacles. They were all askew and she ought to have looked comical, but his heart clenched with longing. God, he was a fool. Of all the women to fall for. It wasn't arrogance to believe he could have almost any woman he chose with little more than a crook of his finger, it was the simple truth, and he'd fallen for the only one he could never hope to impress.

"I can't deny there is a… a physical attraction," she said, the words so cold and clinical he wanted to shake her. "Inigo… Mr de Beauvoir was correct."

"Oh, yes, love, he was correct." Jasper laughed, a dark, unhappy sound he didn't much like. "But I tell you now, if you think you can get me out of your system in a week, you're very much mistaken. Once I have you in my bed, you'll never want to leave."

Harriet stiffened in his arms and pushed at his chest, and Jasper released her.

"I have no intention of going to your bed."

"But you've been told to, Harry," he mocked, feeling sick to his stomach but unable to stop himself. He was desperate now, fighting for his future, and he'd do whatever it took, no matter how badly he had to behave. "Your husband-to-be wants to know you've purged me from your body and mind, and going on that little kiss you're a long, long way from doing that."

"Nonsense," she replied, but she sounded breathless and her eyes were still dark with wanting him. "Lust is a short lived emotion that does not endure. Once you're out of my sight, I'll not think on you again."

"But I shan't be out of your sight, Harry," he warned her. "So, don't think you can run away from this."

"What do you mean?" she demanded.

"I mean that I deserve a chance, damn it," he said, what remained of his composure cracking. "I have a week to win you, to make you see that it's me you want, and I'm not giving up without a fight."

Harriet swallowed and shook her head.

"What is it, love?" he asked, stepping closer to her. "Afraid you'll change your mind?"

"No!" she retorted, putting up her chin, her eyes sparkling with indignation. "I will not."

"Prove it."

"Fine!"

"Tonight."

"Yes!" Harriet glared at him, clenching her fists, utterly furious.

Jasper lunged for her and pulled her to him again, kissing her as if it was the end of the world, as if it was the last thing he'd ever know, and his heart sang with triumph as Harriet responded in kind, pressing herself against him with abandon, clutching at his shoulders.

Though it was the hardest thing to do, Jasper broke the kiss and stepped back, so quickly that she swayed. She was breathing hard, her lips reddened from his kiss, her expression a fierce combination of desire, indignation, and anger that he well understood.

"You know where my room is," he said, the words colder than he'd meant them to be. "I'll expect you after dinner."

She gave a taut nod and Jasper turned on his heel and left the room.

Chapter 6

Dear Prue,

I never got the chance to thank you for persuading Mama to let me stay on with Bonnie and Ruth. They're such fun and though I know I ought not say such a dreadful thing – it's so wonderful to be free of Mama for a while.

—Excerpt of a letter from Miss Minerva Butler to Her Grace, the Duchess of Bedwin.

31st August 1814. Holbrooke House, Sussex.

Matilda sighed and looked up at the dark clouds gathering overhead. She had better hurry back to Holbrooke House, she supposed, but she wanted to keep away for as long as possible. She'd made some excuse about needing to buy some new gloves and had walked into the village.

All other guests had left this morning as scheduled after last night's grand ball, but none of them had risen early and had so been in plenty of time to get all the salacious details of the newest and juiciest scandal. As the guests departed for their own homes, the gossip would go with them, it would be a matter of days before the story was common knowledge.

Ruth, Bonnie, and Minerva had left early, before Harriet's discovery with St Clair, and had gone to visit an aunt of Ruth's who lived an hour or so away. They'd return in the late afternoon, which left Matilda as the only remaining guest in the house, a fact which had made her feel awkward. This was undoubtedly ridiculous as you could lose an entire army in the cavernous place and not notice, but Harriet and Jasper needed time alone without worrying about guests poking their noses into their affairs, and Matilda didn't want to bump into them until they were ready to speak to anyone.

Lady St Clair had invited Matilda to stay for as long as she wished, and Bonnie and Ruth were not due to leave for a few more days. Prue and Bedwin had gone, as they had a prior engagement, much to Prue's anxiety. Prue had been quick to tell Matilda to assure Harriet that they would do all in their power to mitigate the worst of the gossip, though they both knew that would be a forlorn hope. Kitty had wanted to stay too and put off their return trip to Ireland to inform Kitty's parents of her marriage to Luke. Harriet had been adamant that she go, however; she didn't want her troubles clouding Kitty's happiness at her marriage. She promised to tell Kitty as once should she have need of her, and Matilda was touched by the way Kitty had vowed to return at a moment's notice. Kitty had meant it, and her sincerity had clearly moved Harriet.

Matilda was glad the girls had become friends, though they were terribly different. She hoped she could be a comfort to Harriet now, though, and that the girl might confide in her. That Harriet had been caught with Jasper of all people only proved Matilda's suspicions that there was far more to their relationship than Harriet allowed people to see. Had Jasper taken advantage and seduced her? Somehow Matilda didn't think so, but one never knew with men, and she vowed to give Harriet every chance to unburden herself.

Mr Burton had also been among the exodus of guests who'd left this morning. Matilda could not help the sigh of relief that escaped her at the knowledge, though she knew it was only a temporary reprieve. He'd made a point of telling her he'd call upon her as soon as she returned to town. That had been one reason she'd accepted Lady St Clair's offer with such alacrity. She had some hard thinking to do, and she was grateful for the open invitation to stay, not least because Harry would need her support now. She refused to admit to the added relief of having someone else's troubles to fret over. Her own could surely wait.

Matilda peered up at the threatening looking skies overhead and muttered an unladylike curse. It had been a lovely morning, but the excessive heat and humidity of the last few days had finally come to a head. Thunder rumbled ominously in the distance and Matilda hurried faster as the first fat spatters of rain smacked against the dusty road with surprising aggression. *Drat it all*. She was exactly halfway between the village and the house, and it made no sense to retrace her steps. It was only a distance of three miles back to the house and Matilda had been looking forward to a pleasant walk and the opportunity to stretch her legs. It appeared her optimism had been misplaced, and she let out a little shriek of dismay as the heavens open and the spiteful lash of rain soaked her muslin gown in a matter of moments.

Running as best she could with the wet material clinging to her legs, Matilda sought shelter under a huge oak tree as a clap of thunder rent the air directly above her. She jolted, and stared about her for another form of shelter, one less likely to get struck by lightning. Remembering that she'd seen what had perhaps been a shepherd's hut a little further up the road, she stumbled back out from under the oak tree and tried to ignore the freezing rain that stung her skin. A scream escaped her as another clap of thunder exploded overhead, so loud it trembled through the ground, vibrating in her chest and making her ears ring. As the sound diminished, another took its place, and it was a moment before she realised it was a horse shrieking in terror.

She turned and gasped as a massive bay horse reared up on the road close behind her, hooves flailing and showing the whites of its eyes as it fought against its rider's control. Matilda watched in awe and horror, unable to believe the man had stayed seated under such circumstances and brought the horse back under control. The beast was still wild eyed and terrified when another burst of thunder erupted above them, followed quickly by a lightning strike that hit barely ten feet away. The horse reacted at once, screaming with fear and rearing so violently she thought horse and rider would both plummet backwards, before it finally unseated its rider and plunged off along the road at breakneck speed.

"Good heavens!" Matilda exclaimed, and hurried to the man's side, praying he wasn't badly hurt.

As she drew closer to him her eyes registered a shock of white blond hair and her heart skipped in her chest as recognition dawned.

"Oh, no," she said, as the figure was too terribly still.

Sinking to the ground, she pushed the sodden hair from his eyes, which remained closed. The beautiful, arrogant profile was angelic when viewed this way, his thick eyelashes a darker gold against high cheekbones, and the mouth she'd always believed cruel far softer and surprisingly full in repose.

"My lord," she said, patting his cheek as her heart raced with fear. He couldn't be dead, not him. It wasn't possible. "My lord, wake up, please… *please* wake up."

He didn't stir and Matilda's heart clenched. *No, no, no you don't.*

"My lord," she said again, more urgently. "Oh, Montagu, damn you, *wake up!* Please, please…."

There was a sigh, and his eyelids flickered. Matilda held her breath as those startling silver eyes opened and found hers. For just a second he blinked, still hazy as Matilda let out a cry and put her hand to her heart.

"Thank God," she said, unable to hide the depths of her relief. "Thank God."

"Am I dead?" came a dryly amused murmur.

"Don't tempt me," Matilda muttered finding his eyes glittering and focused solely on her now. "You gave me such a scare."

"Ah," he said, his tone mildly curious. "I just wondered why you were thanking God so fervently. I'm relieved to discover it's not because you're finally rid of me."

Though the rain was still hammering around them, he did not try to move and she wondered if he was badly hurt.

"What's wrong?" she demanded, leaning him over as panic flared to life again. She stared at him, inspecting the length of his powerful body as she searched for any sign of blood or broken bones. The urge to run her hands over him and check thoroughly was something she fought to restrain. "Are you injured? Is anything broken?"

As her gaze returned to his face, she had a split second to register a look in his eyes that made her heart skip before his hand clamped at the back of her neck.

"Oh no!" she shrieked, smacking his arm away and scurrying backwards so fast she landed on her backside in a puddle.

Her heart was thundering in terror of his kiss, as she knew that was what he'd intended. She also knew that, if her mouth had met his any hopes she had for the future would be gone in the space between one heartbeat and the next. She could no longer deny his assertion that there was something between them, some powerful magnetic pull that didn't seem to care whether or not they actually liked each other. He'd been right, though she'd carry on denying it until her dying breath.

"A pity," Montagu sighed, sitting up on his elbows. "I thought you might be kinder to an injured man."

"Injured?" Matilda retorted, getting unsteadily to her feet and doing her best to glare furiously at him whilst wiping the rain from her eyes. It wasn't easy. "I'll do you a permanent injury if you try that again."

Montagu stared up at her, that arrogant tilt to his lips all too familiar. "Have no fear, Miss Hunt, I shan't try it again. Indeed, I think I prefer that you instigate our first kiss. It will be so much sweeter that way."

Matilda gaped at him. "You're insane."

He stared at her, the intensity of his gaze, that unwavering certainty that he was right giving her the maddening desire to look away, but she did not. "You know perfectly well that I'm not. You want to kiss me as badly as I want you to, but I'm a patient man, Miss Hunt. Now," he said, changing the subject as though they'd merely been speaking of the weather, and leaving Matilda reeling, "I'm afraid I shall have to avail myself of your aid. I believe I have damaged my ankle in the fall."

Matilda stared at him for a moment, torn between fervently denying she wanted to kiss him—even though she knew it was a lie and that she probably needed locking up for her own safety—and continuing to fret over how badly he was hurt.

"Is it broken?" she asked, moving back to him.

"No," he said, as she leaned down and put her arm beneath his to help lever him up. "I don't think so, only... *Christ*!"

Matilda exclaimed as the two of them nearly fell again, as she was unable to bear his weight. Somehow Montagu righted them both, and she stared up at him to discover his face was ashen.

"Are you quite certain it's not broken?" she ventured.

"Quite," he said tersely. "Sprained, I'd guess."

"At least the rain is lessening," Matilda said, trying to distract herself from the fact that the Marquess of Montagu's arm was around her shoulder and she was pressed tightly to his side. A low rumble of thunder grumbled softly, and she was relieved to know the storm was moving away. "What do we do now?" she asked, praying he'd not make some inadvisable remark as she was shivering, and she wasn't certain it was from the cold, though she would swear on her life it was if questioned.

He was so solid, though, far more muscular than she'd imagined beneath all that impeccable tailoring. She'd believed him tall and lean, but the body beneath her hand was hard and a great deal more powerful than she'd guessed. The heat of his body burned through his damp clothes and she was feeling quite giddy at his nearness. Perhaps she was coming down with something. She could only hope it was pneumonia and not something more dangerous.

Montagu didn't answer but looked around at the sound of horses' hooves.

"Thank heaven for small mercies," he said with a sigh, as whoever it was hailed them and drew to a halt, sliding from the saddle and running to the marquess.

"My lord!" the man exclaimed, eyes wide with concern. "Are you hurt, my lord? I left as soon as I heard the storm."

Matilda admitted to some surprise at the obvious concern in the man's expression. From his appearance, she assumed he was a groom or something of the kind, and he'd obviously left in a hurry without taking a coat, as he was in his shirtsleeves. Wiry and slim of stature, he was perhaps twenty years older than the marquess.

"Nothing of note," Montagu replied. "Thank you for coming."

The fellow belatedly swiped the cap from his head and astonished Matilda by muttering, "I tol' yer it were gonna storm."

"Noted," Montagu said, his expression both benign and quelling at one and the same time. She wondered how he did it. "I will relieve you of your horse and take Miss Hunt back to Holbrooke. Return to the inn, send my carriage for me, and get people out looking for Rhaebus. I pray he's not done himself an injury."

"Yes, my lord, at once."

"And how do you propose to get on a horse with a sprained ankle?" Matilda demanded, irritated.

Montagu returned a look of mild surprise as Thornton brought the horse closer. Matilda watched as the marquess grabbed a handful of mane with his left hand, put his right on the saddle and vaulted into place without ever touching the stirrups. Matilda's mouth went a little dry and she huffed, refusing to admit she was impressed.

"I can do it bareback too, if you like," he offered.

"Hardly the thing for the Marquess of Montagu," she countered, affecting a scandalised expression when in truth her imagination was already picturing it. "What would the *ton* say if they knew?"

"I expect all the young bucks would ride up and down Rotten Row with not a saddle between them the very next day," he said, his usual bored tone evident, though there was amusement in his eyes.

Matilda muttered something about pride coming before a fall, but otherwise refused to bite.

Montagu spoke a few words to Thornton before the man jogged off back to the village. The marquess moved the horse closer to her.

"Come along, Miss Hunt."

Matilda looked up, her eyes widening as Montagu reached down a hand to her.

"Oh, no," she said, backing off and shaking her head. "No, no. Indeed not. I thank you, but I shall walk."

"You shall not, you little fool. You're soaked to the bone and you'll catch your death. Besides which," he added, a wicked glint in his eyes that made her pulse flutter in a remarkably stupid fashion, "did you know that muslin becomes curiously transparent once wet?"

Matilda was suddenly a deal less chilled as her cheeks flared and she gave a little yelp of outrage. Her top half was at least covered by her spencer, sodden though it was, but from the waist down….

"Come, come, Miss Hunt. I'm a gentleman, after all. Surely you trust me not to look?"

"No," Matilda replied succinctly and began walking away, only to realise what kind of view that gave him. She cursed and swung back around, holding her reticule in front of her. "You go first," she ground out from between clenched teeth.

"Oh, no, Miss Hunt. I couldn't possibly."

Matilda narrowed her eyes at him and knew she wouldn't win. "You are, without a doubt, the most odious, arrogant, *irritating* man in the entire country."

Montagu tutted, shaking his head in dismay. "Oh, in the empire, surely? If a thing is worth doing etcetera…." he added, waving a hand nonchalantly.

Biting back the urge to growl with fury—he'd only enjoy it—Matilda stalked back to the horse. Montagu reached down before she'd prepared herself, and the next thing she knew she was sitting sideways in front of him. She gave a shriek, not least because the pommel was most uncomfortable, and almost slid off again, but a strong arm lashed around her waist, holding her in place.

"Calm yourself, you'll spook the horse," he replied, infuriatingly cool as Matilda stared at the ground, which seemed a dreadfully long way off.

"I don't like horses," she said, uncertain whether the proximity of the marquess or the lack of proximity to the ground was causing her the most distress. No. She wasn't the least bit uncertain. There was really very little option other than to plaster herself against him, given the lack of space. It was far too intimate, and it was playing havoc with her equilibrium.

"I have you," he said, his voice soothing, which disturbed her more than anything else he could have said or done.

The words slid over her skin like a caress and made her want to sink into his embrace. Instead she pushed away and sat up, as far away as was possible, rigid with anxiety as the horse swayed into motion. Alarmed, she grabbed at the nearest thing to steady herself and found herself clinging to Montagu's lapels.

He looked down and sighed. "Well, it was ruined anyway, I suppose, though I'd rather you'd put your arms about my neck."

"*I'd* rather die," Matilda said, willing her fingers to release his coat, but quite unable to do so.

She watched the ground passing beneath them as the horse strode on. They continued in this way for some time, Matilda rigid with tension, eyes fixed on the earth.

"Stop looking down," Montagu said, a note of amusement in his voice. "I promise I won't let you fall. I must confess, I am delighted to discover something that frightens you. I had believed you utterly fearless."

That was enough to make her look up and stare at him in amazement.

"What?" he asked. "There are many who fear me, who stammer and stutter in my presence, but not you. Not once. You've never feared me, not from the first."

It was said with no inflection, just an acknowledgement of the truth. Montagu was a powerful man with many interests. Love him or loathe him, no one could ignore him, and many feared his displeasure.

"You're wrong," Matilda replied, turning away from him.

She feared him, and she feared what path he could lead her down if she gave into temptation.

"What are you doing here, anyway?" she demanded before he could question her further, and more than relieved that Holbrooke House was in view.

The sooner she was out of his company, the better.

There was a short pause before he replied. "I had business in the area."

"With St Clair?"

"No, I.... St Clair invited me to the house party, but I had other matters that needed my attention. However, I was here for a few days, so I thought it polite to pay a call."

Matilda turned and raised an eyebrow at him.

"What?" he asked. "My manners are impeccable, Miss Hunt, ask anybody."

She made a sound that was not particularly complimentary and heard the low rumble of a chuckle. They rode on in silence for a while and Matilda concentrated her entire being on ignoring the hard male body so close to hers, the powerful thighs controlling the horse beneath them with ease, and the scent of him that rose from his damp clothes. Leather and horses, the subtle aroma of bergamot, and something hot and masculine curled about her. The desire to loosen her grip on his lapel and slide her hand up his neck was tantalising. She could sink her fingers into his hair and see the white blond locks tangle about them, watch those pale, silver grey eyes darken....

Stop it. Stop it. It would be like petting a cobra, she scolded herself. *Are you utterly insane?*

Utterly, undeniably, irredeemably, replied a wistful voice in her head that she refused to acknowledge.

"Have you thought any more about my offer, Miss Hunt?"

Oh, that was it.

"This is far enough," she said furiously as she gripped his arm and removed it from her person.

"Miss Hunt, have a care, you'll fall," he protested, but Matilda did not care.

With a muttered curse, she slithered from the horse in an unladylike heap before righting herself.

"Turn around and go back the way you came," she said, and flung her arm out, pointing him back towards the village.

Thank God, she thought, grateful for her anger, relieved it had saved her from making a fool of herself. She wasn't about to stalk off with him watching, however, not after the remark about her dress. Getting to her room unobserved would be challenge enough.

His expression darkened. "You act as though I offer you an insult," he said, his tone cool. "Yet you'd be one of the most powerful women of the *ton*. I've known women behave very badly indeed for the slightest opportunity to be considered as my mistress."

"Then go and bestow your *honours* on them, my lord," she said, sneering up at him, thankful for the reminder of exactly who he was and what he wanted from her. For a moment, in the relief of knowing he was alive, she'd forgotten, and that was an unforgivably stupid and dangerous thing to do.

He stared at her, and she thought he'd speak, but then his jaw tightened and he gave a barely perceptible nod.

"Good day, Miss Hunt."

Matilda watched as he turned his horse and rode away, ensuring he was out of sight before hurrying to the shelter of the house.

Chapter 7

Dear Aashini,

~~What is it about that dreadful man…~~

~~You never guess who I met today…~~

~~I'm such a fool.~~

I've been having a splendid time here at Holbrooke House, but I'm afraid poor Harriet is in rather a fix….

—*Excerpt of a letter from Miss Matilda Hunt to Lady Aashini Cavendish*

31st August 1814. Holbrooke House, Sussex.

Matilda stared into the flames that crackled merrily in her bedroom hearth. She was dry and warm, with a pot of tea on the table beside her and a plate of crumpets in her lap. The rain had started up again, but the sound of it pattering against the window glass was rather comforting when one was snug indoors. At least the storm had departed with as much speed as it had arrived. With an uncharacteristic surge of vindictiveness, she hoped that Montagu's ankle was very painful indeed, and then sighed as her eyes settled on the beautiful orchid he'd given her. She knew she didn't mean it. She ought to. If she had an ounce of sense, she'd wish it with all her might, but she didn't.

That she'd brought the blasted orchid with her rather than risk it dying in her absence said rather too much about her state of mind. Trust bloody Montagu to give her something so perfectly beautiful and horrifically expense that she'd feel like a monster if it came to any harm at her hands. She'd spent a fortune on books about its care, and hours reading about how to look after the blasted thing, for heaven's sake. It was pitiful. Why couldn't the man just send her roses and have done with it?

A knock at the door sent her thoughts scattering, and she put the plate of crumpets aside.

"Come in."

Matilda leapt to her feet as Harriet put her head around the door.

"May I come in?" she asked, her voice not entirely steady.

"Oh, love, yes. Yes, of course, come and sit down, Oh, Harriet…." she exclaimed as Harriet closed the door and promptly burst into tears.

Matilda rushed forward, hugging the girl tightly.

"There, there," she soothed. "Come and tell me all about it. I promise you'll feel much better when you've got it off your chest. I doubt it's half as awful as you think it is."

She guided a sobbing Harriet to the chair she'd just vacated and bustled about, allowing Harriet a moment to compose herself whilst Matilda stirred the fire and poured out another cup of tea. Once the girl had regained some semblance of control, Matilda shuffled the armchair on the other side of the fireplace closer to her friend and sat down.

"Now, then, darling. I think perhaps you'd better start at the beginning, don't you?"

Harriet looked at her for a long moment, her dark eyes owlish and vulnerable behind the dainty spectacles she wore, and then she nodded.

***

31st August 1814. Tunbridge Wells, Sussex.

"Heavens, but your aunt is dreadful," Bonnie said, as the carriage rumbled away from the neat little cottage where Ruth's aunt lived.

"Bonnie!" Minerva exclaimed, appalled, but Ruth only laughed at Bonnie's blunt assessment, a rather deep-throated chuckle that made Minerva smile despite her shock.

"Well, it's quite true, I'm afraid," Ruth replied, her lips still quirking as she turned to Bonnie. "All the Stone women are formidable, to put it mildly, but Aunt Ethel is one of the worst."

"I nearly upset my teacup when she asked if you were trying hard enough to catch a husband," Minerva admitted.

She'd been rather terrified by the old harridan, truth be told, and had been full of admiration for Ruth's quiet dignity. The young woman had not lost her temper once, despite some quite stunning provocations as to her lack of beauty and inability to catch a man, despite her outrageous dowry. Though, Ruth had also made it perfectly clear that she'd not be bullied.

Minerva wished she had that kind of strength of character. She had always feared she was shallow, and rather silly, and had always known that she wasn't terribly clever, not like her cousin Prue, who was a writer. That had rankled so much that she'd been quite foul to Prue, who'd always made her feel such a ninny, but only because Minerva feared she was right. Happily, they were close now, all such misunderstandings quite forgotten. Prue had even asked her husband, the duke, to give Minerva a handsome dowry and an allowance for both herself and her mother, such generosity that Minerva could never repay.

Before, she'd only had her looks to rely on, as she'd never been witty or popular, but at least now she had that to help things along. It was actually rather depressing, wondering if some chap would marry her for her money if nothing else, but… oh, well, her looks would fade one day, and she didn't want to live as her mother had for so long, scrimping and saving and worrying about bills. Her mother *appeared* blithely unconcerned by bills, but… one could never know if that was the entire truth. Minerva knew how to act, how to smile and laugh, and pretend one was having a jolly time when in truth you were tired, wretched, and wanted to go home.

She turned her attention back to Ruth and Bonnie and smiled. It was so lovely to have friends. Prue had done her the greatest kindness of all by inviting her to join the Peculiar Ladies, and Minerva felt a little rush of happiness as she watched Ruth and Bonnie laughing over Ruth's appalling aunt.

"I think we deserve a treat for withstanding such a dreadful ordeal," Bonnie said, looking out of the window as they passed through the smart and fashionable town of Tunbridge Wells.

"What did you have in mind?" Ruth replied, her eyes lighting up.

"Cream cakes," Bonnie and Minerva said in unison, Minerva knowing Bonnie well enough by now to know that was her idea of heaven.

Ruth laughed and gave a decisive nod. "Cream cakes it is, then."

***

After putting away a delicious and self-indulgent amount of tea and cakes, they pottered about the lovely shops on The Walks. Ruth bought a new bonnet, trimmed with fake cherries, which Minerva had tried tactfully to talk her out of as she thought it rather vulgar. Bonnie had been gazing so longingly at a length of dark blue ribbon that she could not afford but which Minerva, flush with her new allowance, had happily bought for her. There had been nothing that caught Minerva's eye, which struck her as odd as, previously, when she'd had very little spending money, there were always a dozen things at once that she'd longed for.

"Oh, a book shop," she exclaimed, tugging Bonnie by the hand.

"I never took you for a reader, Minerva," Bonnie said in surprise, hurrying behind her.

"Oh, I'm not," she said cheerfully. "I'm asleep after a couple of pages, but Prue adores books, and I'd like to get her a present."

"A lovely idea," Ruth agreed, as the three of them gathered to look in the shop window.

"Oh, look at that one. What lovely illustrations," Minerva said, pointing at a small book in the window, propped open to show the colourful pictures inside.

"A poetry book, I think," Ruth said, peering for a closer look. "Oh, drat. Look, that fellow is asking to look at it too. Come along, let's go in."

The three ladies hurried inside, just as the shopkeeper put the book into the fellow's hand.

"Oh, well," Minerva said. "I'm sure there's something else just as lovely. She turned quickly and walked straight into another customer who was balancing an uneven stack of books in his arms. He was a small, dusty looking man with the appearance of a scholar. Perhaps it was the books.

"Bloody hell," the fellow exclaimed, loud and irritated as the books in question tumbled to the floor, a rather large encyclopaedic looking volume hitting him square on the toe. "Damnation. You silly chit, don't you ever look where you are going?"

Minerva felt her face flame and gasped in shock, the sound echoed by Ruth and Bonnie behind her, all three of them too stunned to respond for a moment.

"That's enough," came a sharp voice from behind Minerva. "I saw what happened, and it was quite accidental. You've no business carrying so many books if you've not the wit to balance them properly, and certainly no business abusing this young lady."

Minerva turned and looked up… and up, at her defender. Her heart fluttered. *Good heavens.* She stared, astonished, not so much surprised at the rapid beating of her heart—which had never acted in such a peculiar fashion before—but by the cause of it.

He was as far from her vision of a romantic hero as she could imagine. Immensely tall and a little too lean with a sharp profile, he was certainly not handsome, until perhaps you got to his eyes. Those eyes were a deep slate grey with odd patches of green and utterly compelling. Minerva thought he was likely in his mid-thirties, an age she had previously considered ancient, but there was such vitality burning from this man that she shelved the notion at once. His coat was a little baggy, making her suspect he'd recently lost weight, and he needed a haircut.

Her heart did the odd little fluttering thing again.

How very strange.

Forcing her eyes away from the stranger lest she be seen to be staring, she turned back to the man who had abused her to discover he had turned a startling shade of white. She supposed she couldn't blame him. Her saviour had a rather forbidding aspect that would give any man pause.

"Forgive me, M-Mr de Beauvoir," the fellow stammered, looking up at the tall man with an almost deifying reverence. "I… I had no idea that… that…. *Sir,* please may I say how very much I admire and—"

"No, you may not. Go away."

Mr de Beauvoir made an impatient shooing gesture and the fellow flushed, mortified, before gathering up his tumbled books and hurrying away.

"Sycophantic fool," de Beauvoir muttered, irritated, before turning back to Minerva. "I'm sorry for any upset he may have caused you, miss."

"Oh, Miss Butler," Minerva said at once, though he'd not actually been soliciting her name. "And there's not the slightest need for you to apologise. I thought you were rather wonderful."

The fellow looked a little surprised, and possibly revolted at her praise. There was a slight sniggering sound from behind her that Minerva recognised as belonging to Bonnie. It was quickly smothered; no doubt Ruth's doing.

"It was my pleasure," he said brusquely, about to turn away until Minerva stalled him by laying her hand on his arm.

"But still, you didn't have to come to my rescue and… and I'm terribly grateful."

She sent him her most devastating look, perfected from hours before a looking glass, shy yet interested, all blue eyes from under long lashes. It had made many a young man sigh with longing.

Mr de Beauvoir wrinkled his nose.

"Good day to you, Miss Butler. Ladies."

He gave a rather stiff bow and Minerva watched as he left the shop. She let out a sigh as the door closed behind him.

"Minerva… oh, Minerva…?" Bonnie whispered, waving a hand in front of Minerva's eyes as though to bring her round from a trance.

"Oh, stop it," Minerva said, blushing a little.

"Only if you tell me what on earth is happening in that head of yours," Bonnie demanded, staring at her in wonder. "You looked at him like he was the sun and the moon and the stars all rolled into one, and he's not even handsome, besides looking poor as a church mouse. Did you see that dreadful coat he was wearing? It was all worn at the elbows."

"He needs looking after," Minerva said, nodding dreamily.

Bonnie pulled a face. "Blech," she said, looking at Minerva as if she'd run mad. "Ruth, you talk to her."

"What about?" Ruth replied, laughing now. "The fellow was very chivalrous, you have to admit, and there's no accounting for taste."

"Clearly," Bonnie replied, obviously bewildered.

"Oh, excuse me."

The two women looked around, astonished as Minerva waylaid the fellow who had abused her so rudely. The man started, almost dropping his now neatly packaged books for a second time.

"Please," Minerva said. "Could you tell me who that man was? You obviously admire him a great deal."

"*That* was Mr Inigo de Beauvoir," he said, with the same tone he might have said, *that was the Duke of Wellington*. There was reverence in his words, along with quite obvious contempt for her ignorance. "He's one of the brightest minds of our generation, a remarkable natural philosopher. I've listened to several of his lectures at The Royal Academy," the fellow added, as though this was some achievement, which perhaps it was.

He bustled off, looking as if he was bursting to tell someone exactly who had just torn him off a strip. Minerva wondered if the story would change somewhat in the telling.

"A natural philosopher," she said, or rather breathed, feeling thoroughly awed by such intellectual prowess. "How…."

"Dull," Bonnie muttered.

"Interesting," Ruth said firmly, whilst Minerva stared at the door, pondering why *wonderful* was the only word she could think of.

Chapter 8

Honestly, Kitty, I don't know what came over Minerva. If I was as beautiful as she is, I wouldn't waste it all on some fusty intellectual. He didn't look the least bit interested in her and how is that even possible? She's gorgeous, and besides that I doubt he's ever been to a ball in his life.

—Excerpt of a letter from Miss Bonnie Campbell to Mrs Kitty Baxter.

31st August 1814. Holbrooke House, Sussex.

"You spent a lot of time here as a child." Matilda guessed, watching as Harriet stared into the fire, the picture of misery.

Harriet nodded. "We practically lived here. The late earl and my father were very close friends, and my parents were often away with my father's work, researching some long dead Egyptian king or an illegible papyrus. Father could go away quite happily, knowing Lord and Lady St Clair would look after us."

There was a certain amount of bitterness behind the words and Matilda wondered how much Harriet and her brother had seen of their parents.

"So, you and Jasper were friends?"

Harriet let out a little breath of laughter and took her spectacles off to wipe her eyes with a handkerchief before looking back at Matilda. "I've loved him for as long as I can remember."

"Oh, Harriet," Matilda said, her heart aching.

Harriet's lip trembled, but she gave a resolute shake of her head. "No. Don't be nice to me or I shall start the water works all over again and I refuse to. I've spent too many years crying over that man, and I swore I'd never do it again. Not… Not again," she added, her voice quavering.

"What happened?"

It took a while for Harriet to reply and Matilda waited, allowing the girl time to gather her thoughts.

"He never saw me, not really. All the time we were growing up he'd drag me here and there with Jerome and Henry, but… but I always felt like I was a prop. You know, like a toy gun if they were playing soldiers, or a telescope or treasure chest if it was pirates. I was rescued, fought over, captured, and kidnapped more times than I can count. Always a passive role, naturally," she said rolling her eyes. "No matter how I protested. Not that it was so bad; I just took a book with me and learned to ignore all the shouting."

Matilda's mouth quirked with amusement, imagining an indignant little Harriet with pigtails and a boyish Jasper dressed as a pirate. Harriet caught her expression and laughed a little.

"It was all rather idyllic if I'm honest, though I seemed to spend an inordinate amount of time covered in mud or falling in the lake. At least they fished me out again, I suppose."

"And then…?" Matilda prompted.

"And then…." Harriet repeated, her eyes taking on a misty, far away expression. "I was sixteen, and more hopelessly in love with Jasper than ever before. Oh, Matilda, he was so beautiful, even then. Like some pagan god, all golden perfection. He was almost nineteen, and naturally a devastating hit with every female for miles around. They were all in love with him, from the kitchen maids to all the eligible young ladies. He need only crook his finger and they'd fall at his feet. They still do," she added with a sigh.

Matilda nodded, understanding how difficult it must have been for Harriet to watch Jasper grow up and grow away from her as he tumbled from one amorous adventure to the next. His reputation might not be the full truth of who he was, as his mother was adamant to prove, but neither had he gained it for no reason.

"He'd refused to go to university," Harriet said with a frown, her voice illustrating her perplexity.

Matilda could understand that too, though she held her tongue. Harriet would have given her right arm for such a chance, but such things were forbidden for women.

"His father was at his wits' end with what to do with him," she carried on. "He'd gotten into so much trouble during his last term and the earl worried what mischief such a young, handsome, and wealthy man could get himself into, if not given some guidance, something to occupy him. A Grand Tour was out of the question with the war raging, so he decided Jasper should go to Russia, to visit his mother's family. His grandmother was Russian, you see."

Matilda nodded, waiting for Harriet to continue, but the young woman was silent, twisting the handkerchief she held back and forth in her hands. At length she spoke again.

"I knew he'd be away for almost a year, which… well, it seemed like a lifetime. So, I spent the weeks before his departure trying to get up the courage to say… *something*. Only I couldn't. So, I did the only thing I could think of. I bought him a diary to record his travels in and… and I got a friend of mine to draw a likeness of me and… and stuck it between the pages. I thought at least that way he might be reminded of me, from time to time."

"That's sweet," Matilda said, smiling.

Harriet snorted. "It was pointless. I doubt he even knew it was there. To my knowledge he never wrote a word about his travels. Anyway…." she said, taking a deep breath. "It was the day he was due to leave, and I was beside myself. I thought my heart would break at having to be without him for so long, and… and I knew he didn't even care, except…."

"Except?"

"He was travelling to the port with another young man he knew from school, who was calling for him later that morning. I pitied him that. According to my brother, Peter Winslow was a vile, sneaky creature, but his father was travelling with Jasper as his guide because he had business interests in Russia, and Jasper was staying at their house overnight before he sailed. Happily, Peter wasn't going; his mother said his constitution wasn't strong enough to endure Russian weather. Just as well, as he'd have made Jasper's life intolerable… such an oily creature he was. Anyway, I told Jasper that I had a gift for him, and we went for a walk, down to the summerhouse. I made some excuse about having left it there but in truth I wanted to be alone with him…."

Matilda waited, leaning forward with anticipation as she realised she was dying to know what had caused this terrible rift between the two of them, hoping that if she knew she could help them mend it.

"And he was so pleased, far more than the diary warranted and… and the next thing I knew he… he kissed me." Harriet swallowed, her eyes filling with tears. "It was such a kiss, Matilda, so… so tender, and he told me not to go marrying anyone else while he was gone." She gave a mirthless laugh and wiped her eyes with the mangled handkerchief. "As if anyone would ever ask *me*!"

Matilda reached out and took Harriet's hand, giving it a squeeze.

"Anyway," Harriet said, shaking off her misery and straightening her spine. "Winslow arrived, and we had to go back to the house. Jasper couldn't say anything more to me with everyone was around, and I convinced myself that was the only reason he said nothing more. I asked him to write to me and let me know how he was getting on, and I promised to write in return."

Matilda waited as Harriet gathered her thoughts once more.

"His mother and father were travelling down to wave him off, and Lady St Clair is dreadfully forgetful. Just as they were due to leave, she remembered she'd left the book she'd wanted to take, inside on the consul table. Well, of course she would have asked a maid, but I was getting tearful and trying hard to hide it, so I ran back inside for her to take a moment for myself. As I came back, Jasper and Peter were on the doorstep and the door was ajar, they didn't know I was there."

Matilda waited, a sudden tightness in her throat.

"Peter made some remark about me being a strange creature, about me having always followed Jasper about like a puppy and asking if he had any interest there and Jasper, he... he gave this odd laugh, as though Peter were mad for thinking such a thing. Then he looked back at Peter and his voice was so cold, his expression full of disgust. *Don't be ridiculous*, he said, *as if I'd be interested in Harriet*, and he walked off down the stairs."

"Oh, Harriet." Matilda got to her knees in front of her and held her hand as the girl dissolved into tears.

With a tremendous effort of will Harriet calmed herself once more.

"I'll never forget the way he said it, Matilda. With such disdain! As though Peter was a fool for even considering he could have any interest in me. I told myself that he hadn't meant it, though it certainly sounded like he had. I told myself that he was just irritated with Peter, and I waited for him to write to me. If he felt anything for me, surely he'd write, wouldn't he?"

"One would imagine so," Matilda agreed, nodding.

"I waited and waited, determined that I'd not write to him until he'd sent me a letter. If he wrote to me, I'd reply and ask him why he'd spoken so to Peter, but he never did, Matilda. Not once. He was away almost a whole year, and he never once wrote to me… but that wasn't the worst of it."

"Oh, Lord," Matilda said with feeling.

Harriet returned a wan smile. "I saw Peter two months later. He was full of news of Jasper, having heard from his father, you see. He seemed to delight in telling me how popular Jasper was with the ladies, and some truly shocking stories about him, things one ought never discuss with a lady, but it was certainly clear that Jasper was not pining away for me."

"I'm so sorry, Harriet."

Harriet shrugged. "At least I knew. Better that I'd discovered it then, rather than sitting about waiting for him to come home and ask my father's permission to court me, when that was clearly not on his mind. By the time he returned, I'd resolved to forget him and concentrate on my studies. As far as my father would allow me, anyway." She gave a heavy sigh. "Now I think perhaps Jasper thought he was being kind," she said, her expression perplexed. "Kitty made me reconsider his actions and I've been trying to do as she asked. With the benefit of hindsight, I've come to believe he thought it was a sweet thing to do, giving me my first kiss, for I never knew him to be cruel before that, and surely he knew I was infatuated. Perhaps he thought it a good moment, when he would be gone for so long. I've been trying to forgive him for it. He wasn't to know how badly he hurt me, how many nights I cried myself to sleep after he'd gone."

Matilda's heart twisted at the confusion in Harriet's eyes, knowing the poor girl had been thinking about this and puzzling it out for years and years.

"And when he returned?"

Harriet looked away, staring at the fire. "I avoided him. I went to visit my aunt in Scotland a few weeks before he was due to return. Everyone assumed I'd be back for the big event, but I pretended to be ill, and my aunt is rather a hypochondriac herself, so it wasn't hard to persuade her I was too unwell to travel. I didn't see him for months after that, as we were both away for various reasons, and when I finally saw him I all but ignored him and... and we ended up as we are now."

"But did he never ask you why?" Matilda demanded.

"Of course," Harriet said, nodding. "But I could never bring myself to tell him I'd heard what he said. I'd been so humiliated, knowing he'd just been playing with me. God, he must have been amused by how I fell into his arms. I practically swooned. So, I pretended it had been a silly infatuation and that I'd grown out of it."

"But it wasn't silly, was it, Harriet? And you're still in love with him."

Harriet closed her eyes and nodded. "I tried so hard, Matilda. I tried so hard to stop loving him. He's not the boy I fell in love with any longer, is he? He's a grown man and I don't know him at all. We don't have the least thing in common. I'm plain and I love learning, he looks like a fallen angel and despises it. Why on earth would he want me? Why do I want him? He hurt me so very badly and I've hated him for it, and I don't understand how I can hate someone and love them at the same time. It's illogical."

Matilda gave her a wry smile. "Illogical it may be, but not impossible, I assure you."

Harriet returned a quizzical look and Matilda hurried the conversation on. "So, what happened last night?"

There was a heartfelt groan of misery, and Matilda waited for what would come next.

"I allowed myself to soften a little, to accept Kitty's advice and put the past behind us, to forgive him, and that—together with the brandy soaked punch and that stupid bloody dare—well...." Harriet threw up her hands in despair. "And just look at the mess I'm in now!"

***

Jerome watched his brother as he poured himself another drink. That had to be his second in ten minutes, which was most unlike him.

"Steady on, Jasper," he said, amused at being the one to have said it. The boot was generally on the other foot.

His older brother turned and glared at him but said nothing, raising the glass to his lips.

Jerome shrugged. "It doesn't bother me if you're foxed at dinner, but Mother will be furious, and I'd say you're in enough trouble."

"Well, I figured it was my turn," Jasper muttered, giving Jerome an impatient glance before turning away.

"Can't deny it, I suppose. You're dashed near respectable these days. A regular dull dog. Well, until this morning's excitement, anyway. Such a scandal, Jaz, really! I didn't know you had it in you, and with Harriet, of all people."

"What do you mean by that?"

Jerome paused, taken aback by the fury of his brother's words. "Well," he said carefully, watching Jasper with interest. "If it had been Miss Hunt or Miss Butler, I'd not have been so surprised, but Harry? She's—"

"She's what?" Jasper snapped, his posture rigid.

Jerome blinked, startled. "Sensible," he said at last. "A bluestocking, and practically our sister. What were you thinking?"

Jasper's jaw tightened and Jerome didn't think he'd answer.

"She's *not* our sister," he replied tersely, but at least looking less as if he would give Jerome a black eye.

"Well, no, not technically, but… but if she's already engaged to this de Beauvoir fellow, and he doesn't care what's gone on, why are you fighting so hard to marry her?"

"Because he's a cold bastard who only cares for what Harriet can do for his career. He'll never give a damn for her besides whatever that terrifying brain of hers can do. He'll never look to her comfort, never worry if she's happy or not. I won't stand for it. She deserves better."

"Isn't that her decision, though?" Jerome pressed, looking at his brother anew. "And since when do you care? The two of you have been at daggers drawn for bloody years. I thought it was your life's work to antagonise her, and now you're so worried for her happiness you're ready to marry her? My God, Jasper, you'll kill each other within a sennight."

"Shut up, Jerome. You've no idea what you're talking about."

Jerome shrugged. "No surprise there, but I wish you'd explain it to me all the same."

"I tell you what. I'll explain what's going on with Harriet, if you tell me what you're playing at with Bonnie Campbell."

The dinner gong sounded at that precise moment and Jerome let out a breath of relief and sprang to his feet.

"Saved by the bell," he said with a smirk, and hurried out of the door towards the dining room.

Bonnie was not a subject he wanted to touch on with his brother. Jasper was reading far too much into it. Bonnie was a lively girl with a smart mouth and a nose for trouble. She was also a great deal of fun… more so than anyone he'd ever met. He wasn't offering anything but friendship, though, and she knew it as well as he did. He'd been very upfront about it and she'd laughed and told him she knew exactly what he was offering and what he wasn't. She'd even made a great joke about how scandalised the *ton* would be if he married a little Scottish nobody with no breeding and worse manners.

So, why shouldn't they enjoy each other's company? Especially now, when everyone was gone and there were no old tabbies disapproving of the two of them… well, apart from Jasper. Once upon a time, Jerome had idolised Jasper and very much modelled himself upon his big brother. He was the life and soul of any party, beloved by all—except the masters at school—and a devilish one with the ladies.

In recent years, he'd become increasingly circumspect, with only occasional glimpses of the outrageous young man he'd once been. On those occasions, Jerome had the unsettling feeling that Jasper was at his most unhappy. Not that they'd spoken about it. One didn't talk to one's brother about… about *feelings*. God forbid. Still, there was a nagging sensation tugging at him and Jerome wondered if it might be his conscience. He wasn't entirely certain, because it rarely troubled him, but perhaps he ought to find out what was wrong with Jasper. After all, the fellow seemed to delight in sticking his nose into Jerome's affairs.

He saw no reason at all not to return the favour.

Chapter 9

What on earth have I done?

Why on earth did I let him rile me?

I should never have agreed to this ridiculous... outrageous... <u>scandalous</u> idea.

Oh, heavens. What am I to do? I can't back down, but if I go...

—Excerpt of an entry from Miss Harriet Stanhope to her diary.

31st August 1814. Holbrooke House, Sussex.

"Of course we'll not say anything," Ruth said, though her eyes were still wide with shock.

Minerva didn't blame her. Harriet and Jasper? She thought Harriet loathed Jasper. Though, thinking about it now, she supposed that *could* be the spark of attraction.

"We'll pretend we don't know what's happened," Minerva agreed, giving Matilda a reassuring smile as they pulled on their gloves and prepared to go down to what was bound to be a very awkward evening.

"What on earth is the point of that?" Bonnie said, rolling her eyes. "They'll all know we *do* know. How could we not? I'm not saying we should speak about it, but we can at least show Harriet our support, not pretend we're blind to the mammoth-sized scandal sitting on the doorstep."

Matilda nodded her agreement. "Yes, Bonnie is correct. There's no point in pretending you don't know, only do try to be discreet. Poor Harriet is so upset. I don't think she'll come down for dinner in any case. She certainly didn't intend to when I saw her earlier."

"Imagine, though," Bonnie said, her eyes twinkling with mischief. "A night with Jasper Cadogan. Lucky girl."

Minerva bit her lip as Ruth gasped with shock and Matilda glowered a little.

"Not entirely appropriate, Bonnie."

"Sorry," Bonnie replied, looking quite unrepentant. "But you said she was engaged to some other chap? Who is he? Do we know him? And why hadn't she told us?"

"I believe she only accepted the engagement a few weeks ago, though he offered for her last summer. Apparently, they've been corresponding for almost three years."

"Goodness, Harriet *is* a dark horse," Bonnie said with approval.

Matilda shook her head and gave Bonnie a despairing glance. "These were not *billet doux*, but an exchange of intellectual ideas and theories. There was nothing the least romantic about it, from what Harriet said."

Bonnie grimaced. "Well, what's he like, then?"

"I've no idea. I was out when he visited the house this morning."

"Oh, yes," Minerva put in. "Henry said you came back looking like a drowned rat. Did you get caught in that dreadful storm, you poor thing? Happily, it had finished by the time we left Ruth's aunt's house."

Matilda flushed for no reason Minerva could fathom. "Oh, I got a little wet. Nothing to signify. Now, then," she continued, gesturing for them all to hurry. "There goes the dinner gong, so we'd best go down."

The ladies made their way down the stairs, and Minerva admitted to some trepidation for the meal ahead. She hated it when there was tension in the air but the talk was all polite nothings, and no one dared say anything of consequence. Still, she was hungry and there was little point in pretending otherwise. She'd finally taken Prue's advice and stopped dieting so drastically, and it was so lovely to enjoy a good meal and not watch everyone else tucking in while she barely touched her own. Besides which, Bonnie was right. They ought to support Harriet, whether or not she was there, and they could not do that if they did not appear.

Lady St Clair greeted them all warmly, as if there was nothing at all the least bit wrong, and they seated themselves for dinner. They were eating in the small dining room this evening, the one the family used when they were not entertaining, which was a relief. It was rather more intimate and a deal less intimidating.

Lady St Clair took her seat at one end of the table whilst St Clair sat at the other. There were no formal seating arrangements, and everyone just sought a chair and then stopped in their tracks as Harriet appeared. She was pale and stiff, but she stood tall and held her head high as she walked to the table. She took the nearest chair by Lady St Clair and to Minerva's left, as far from St Clair as she could get.

Good for you, Minerva thought, and reached out a hand under the table to take Harriet's and squeeze. She didn't know Harriet terribly well, but she hoped the gesture might give the young woman courage. To her relief, Harriet squeezed back before letting her hand go.

"Did I tell you I had a letter from Jemima?" Matilda said to Bonnie, her voice bright and cheerful as she broke the rather stilted silence.

"Oh, no," Bonnie said, rising at once to the bait, to everyone's relief. "How is she? Has she explained her disappearance?"

Minerva vaguely remembered Jemima, though she'd only seen her once or twice. She was blonde and pretty in a fragile, somewhat ethereal way. Minerva mostly remembered noticing that the dress she'd worn was several seasons out of fashion, rather too big for her, and had clearly been altered several times already. It occurred to her that perhaps the girl could no longer afford to attend such lavish *ton* events if she was forced to make do and mend. No doubt she'd been sneered at by many who would look down on her for such things. Minerva felt a swell of relief that she'd not been one of them. She'd acted badly during the earlier part of this season, mostly from desperation, but she had no desire to compound her shame by remembering any unkind words she'd given. At least she was not guilty of that with Jemima.

"She says her aunt has been ill, and she's been looking after her. They're very close, I believe?"

Bonnie nodded. "I think she lives with her aunt, does she not?"

Matilda nodded. "Yes, that's right. Anyway, I must call on her when I return to town."

"I wish I could go with you," Bonnie said, her tone wistful.

"Are you returning to Scotland, Miss Campbell?" Lady St Clair asked, with what Minerva suspected might be a hopeful tone.

"I imagine so," Bonnie replied, returning a smile that was quite obviously forced. Minerva felt a surge of pity for her, more so as Bonnie's gaze moved to Jerome and settled there.

"Did you hear the news?" Lady St Clair asked, drawing Bonnie's attention away from her youngest son as her voice vibrated with suppressed excitement. "The Marquess of Montagu was coming to visit us this afternoon when he got caught in that dreadful storm. He was thrown from his horse."

"Couldn't happen to a nicer fellow," Jerome quipped, earning himself a snigger from Bonnie and a glare from his mother.

"Did you not see him, Miss Hunt?" Lady St Clair asked, turning to Matilda. "He must have been travelling the same road as you at the same time."

Matilda's cheeks flamed as all the Peculiar Ladies present looked up to stare at her with identical expression of enquiry.

"I-I-I," she stammered.

"It's a long road, Lady St Clair," Harriet blurted, taking everyone's attention from Matilda. "And Matilda got soaked, but she returned home long before the storm was over, didn't she, Henry?"

Henry stared at his sister for rather too long a moment before he spoke. "Yes. Yes, indeed. I saw her, you see. Wet. Very wet, but… but it was still storming, thundering, that is…. Lightning, too."

"So, Montagu was likely miles away from her, still at the other end of the road," Harriet added, with a tad too much force.

"Oh," Lady St Clair said with a nod, and returned her attention to her soup.

Henry cast his sister a *what the devil was that about* look, but Harriet ignored him. Matilda concentrated on her own bowl and did not look up. Minerva wondered what Matilda was hiding. Was there something going on with her and Montagu? Surely not. Not after what he did to her.

"Is he badly hurt?" Henry asked, as everyone looked back to Lady St Clair once more.

"A sprained ankle, I believe," the lady replied. "Painful, but not serious."

"Pity," Bonnie murmured under her breath as Minerva tried not to choke on her soup.

"Lady Helena was lovely, wasn't she?" Lady St Clair said, changing the topic once more.

"Oh, yes," Minerva said, glad to have something to contribute. She knew Lady Helena well now, since Prue had married her brother, the Duke of Bedwin. "She *is* lovely, so vivacious, and always on the move. I swear she's never tired. I never met anyone so full of energy, and so sweet natured too."

"Yes, exactly as I found her." Lady St Clair nodded, pleased, before turning to her son. "Did you not think so, Jerome?"

Jerome, who had clearly not been attending the conversation, looked up from his dinner.

"What's that?" he asked, whilst pulling a bread roll in half.

"Lady Helena," his mother said patiently.

"What about her?" He stuffed a large chunk of roll into his mouth and chewed while he waited.

"Honestly, Jerome, I may as well talk to the wall. Do attend the conversation, dear. What did you think of Lady Helena?"

"Oh," Jerome said, swallowing. He paused, giving it some thought. "Which one was she?"

Bonnie snickered, and there was a flash of impatience in Lady St Clair's eyes. "Never mind," she said, giving up on the conversation.

Minerva bit her lip and applied herself to her soup once more, until everyone had finished and the staff cleared the table and brought in the next courses. Though it was only an informal dinner, the table was laden. A fish dish Minerva could not identify was served alongside roast beef, several roast chickens, pigeon pie, harrico of mutton, veal collops, an almond tart, and several dishes of vegetables.

With a happy little sigh of anticipation, Minerva accepted servings of the pie, roast chicken, and a good helping of vegetables.

"It's good to see you eating properly," Bonnie murmured to her. "The first time I saw you at dinner I worried for you. You didn't eat enough to keep a sparrow alive."

Minerva grinned at her, then took a deliberately large mouthful of roast chicken and gave a contented sigh. Bonnie laughed and followed her example. Minerva looked around the table to see if everyone else was tucking in, and noticed Harriet picking at her dinner with a distinct lack of enthusiasm. A glance down at the other end of the table confirmed that St Clair was doing little better. His hand rested on the stem of his wine glass which he was twisting back and forth as he studied the contents with an inscrutable expression.

Minerva sighed and hoped the two of them could sort their problems out. It *was* possible. Bedwin and Prue had been in a terrible fix once the duke had discovered who had written that salacious story about him. Surely if they could overcome such problems, St Clair and Harriet could find a way forward.

Wistfully, Minerva's memory returned to the book shop and the rather unnerving grey-green stare of the man she'd met. They must have more hope than she did, at any rate. For there was no earthly reason a man considered *one of the great minds of our generation* would take a second glance at a pretty little ninny like Minerva.

With a dejected sigh, Minerva returned her attention to her dinner and tried to put him out of her mind.

***

Jasper didn't exactly run from the room the moment dinner was over, but it was a close thing. It had been an interminable evening, made worse by Harriet's pale, troubled expression as she stared at her plate and barely ate a mouthful.

Was this what the coming night meant to her? Was it an ordeal to be got through? His heart plummeted to his boots. If it was, he wouldn't be able to go through with it. He'd never taken an unwilling woman to his bed, and he wasn't about to start now. Yet, she'd not been unwilling when he'd kissed her earlier, any more than she had been last night, and this morning she'd been perfectly sober. The moment he had her in his arms she'd become all heat and pliant limbs, her desire quite unmistakable. Well, she'd obviously changed her mind. She'd not come tonight, so he may as well not get his hopes up.

Not that he was giving up—far from it—but if he couldn't get her into his bed, he had to acknowledge that his chances were diminishing. Even if he managed it, he had to admit his problems might have just begun. What would happen when the novelty of bedding him diminished? What if that was all they could find in common? He loved her company, loved to hear her talk so passionately about whatever new thing she was interested in, no matter if he understood it or not, but what about her? What happened when she grew tired of him and he could not capture her interest anywhere else but in bed?

Still, he couldn't help but listen for every creak and footstep as he prepared for bed and dismissed his valet, assuring the man he'd not be needed again and could retire for the night. Jasper moved to the bed and sat down at the edge of the mattress, remembering a time when Harriet had looked at him as if he'd hung the moon for her alone. The year she'd turned sixteen he'd bathed in that adoration, even as he'd feared putting it to the test. What if he let her in and she saw how far he really was from the ideal she'd fallen for? What if she saw the truth of him and changed her mind? Seeing that adoration turn to regret—or worse, pity—would be appalling. The fear of it had nearly killed him. Yet it had happened anyway.

He remembered all the evenings they'd spent together when Harriet had read to them, Jerome, Henry, and he gathered about her in front of the fire as she weaved a magical tale. Jasper had loved those evening most of all. He'd loved to hear stories as a child but, as he'd grown older, he could ask no one to read him a bedtime story for fear of being thought a baby. Reading himself was such a chore it took any pleasure from the story, and so he'd given up, but Harriet would read to him whenever he asked and seemed to enjoy doing so. His favourite had been *The Arabian Nights Entertainments*. They'd been romantic adventures, full of danger and intrigue, love and betrayal, and to hear Harriet read them had made the stories come alive. She must have read that book a dozen or more times, and even though their brothers objected and demanded she read something else, she'd just smile, take the book from his hand, and begin all over again.

Jasper rubbed the heel of his hand over his heart, trying to shift the ache that had settled there. She'd loved him then. She'd loved him for so long, and then it had stopped. Harriet had stopped looking at him with adoration. She'd stopped looking at him at all. She'd not talk to him unless spoken to, and then she was polite and distant. He'd been cut from her life and he'd not understood it. The pain of it had made him angry and he'd lashed out, mocking her in front of friends when she was clever, taunting her for being more interested in books than real life. She borne it at first, with all the quiet dignity she was capable of, but he'd kept on until she'd retaliated, until she hated him for it. He'd watched her retreat from the world, knowing it was his fault and hating himself for it, but unable to stop. If he stopped tormenting her he'd cease to exist in her world. She would forget him utterly, and that felt like dying.

So there was no point in sitting here waiting for her to come. He'd destroyed his own happiness and, even if Harriet still wanted him physically, she was far too clever to give in to such shallow desires.

With a sigh he pulled open a drawer on the nightstand and took out a battered little book. He carried it with him wherever he went. No matter if it was just a few days away, or a month, the book came too. It was a diary, or ought to be. The fact that he'd never written a word in it made his chest tight. How he wished he could. He'd wanted to tell Harriet about all the extraordinary and wonderful things he'd seen when he went to Russia. He'd longed to write to her, too, and had been torn between praying she'd write to him and praying she wouldn't. For there were no little schoolboys to read to him or help him write out a reply, and even if such a thing could be had, he could hardly have anyone else read such a personal letter, nor write a reply. He'd been stuck. Nowadays he got away with it by acting the part of lofty nobleman, too high in the instep to be bothered with reading correspondence, let alone replying, but it had been harder then.

So, he'd watched the arrival of the post with anxiety. Letters arrived from his parents every few weeks or so, and he spent hours labouring over them to decipher anything of importance he needed to know… or any mention of Harriet. At least they never expected a reply. The family joked about what a terrible correspondent Jasper was and believed him too lazy and tied up with his own affairs to bother to reply. Besides, his guide, Mr Winslow, had been tasked with reporting back to his parents.

At least since he'd become earl, he'd employed a secretary, ostensibly because he was far too self-important to read or write for himself, but in truth because it was the only way he could manage. It didn't help with personal affairs, though.

Anyway, Harriet had never written to him. Not once, and the hurt of that been worse than he'd imagined possible. He'd thought the kiss they'd shared had been special, perfect. It had been for him. He'd not been slow in taking up a young man's interest in amorous adventures, and by that time he'd learned enough to know that kiss had been out of the ordinary, that Harriet was out of the ordinary. She'd been there, right in front of him all that time, but it was only that summer that he'd truly seen her for what she was, and had fallen for her, hook, line, and sinker.

Jasper smoothed his hand over the worn leather of the binding and tilted it slightly, so it fell open at the only page that mattered. A neat little pencil drawing of Harriet met his eyes, the picture so familiar he knew every line, every shaded contour. She was younger in the image, naturally, but she'd changed very little, her expression as serious as ever. He drew in a deep breath and wished he knew how things had gone so wrong. For a while he'd believed it was because he'd never written, and he'd tried to speak to her—prepared to humiliate himself by explaining, if that was why she was so hurt—but either she lied very convincingly or there was some other, deeper reason for the way she'd cut him out of her life.

He would know, he promised himself. He'd get to the truth, and then he'd do whatever it took to make it right, no matter what he had to say, what he had to do. The idea of his life, of his home, without Harriet in it, was too bleak an image to contemplate.

There was a quiet knock at the door and Jasper almost dropped the book, he was so surprised. All at once his heart was thundering in his ears and he put the book back in the drawer and hurried to the door, pulling it open.

"Jaz, can I borrow that green waistcoat of yours…?"

Jasper glared at his brother, torn between breaking his nose again and howling with despair.

"Fine, yes, whatever. I'll have Merrick bring it to you in the morning."

"Jolly good, thanks, old man, oh, erm… Jasper…?"

"Yes, what?" he practically snarled, wanting his brother gone at once.

"Oh, well," Jerome hesitated and then reached out an awkward hand and patted Jasper's shoulder in the most uncomfortable show of familial affection it had been Jasper's misfortune to witness. "I just… well, I hope. You're all right, aren't you, Jasper?"

Despite Jasper's irritation, his brother's concern was touching. "I'll do, Jerome. There's no need to fret, I've no intention of throwing myself off a cliff and landing you with the earldom, if that's what's bothering you."

"Oh, thank God," Jerome said with obvious relief. "I mean, that's not why I was worried," he added in a rush. "Not the earldom bit, I mean."

Jasper snorted, knowing that was entirely true, but also that his brother would rather die than become earl. Far too much responsibility. "I know, Jerry. Don't fret. Thanks for troubling yourself, though."

"Oh, well, you're my brother, Jaz. Don't like to see you so Friday faced."

Jasper nodded and made a shooing motion. "Away with you, nodcock. I'm devilish tired and will be in no better frame of mind if you don't let me sleep."

Jerome grinned, nodded, and bade him goodnight, obviously quite as anxious as Jasper was to let the conversation lie. With a heavy sigh, Jasper shut the door and leaned back against it. Bloody fool. Of course it wasn't Harriet. It would never be Harriet. She had more bloody sense than that. Good heavens, the woman had a brain the size of England… what on earth would she want with him?

The knock that sounded was so faint he might have missed it if he hadn't been leaning against the door. As it was, he jolted in shock and yanked the door open so fast that Harriet leapt back with a squeal.

"Were you waiting by the door?" she demanded, pressing a hand to her heart.

"No!" Jasper retorted, a little too quickly and with too much force, before realising she ought not be seen outside his room and opening the door wide for her to enter. "I… I was just passing the door when… when you knocked," he said, wincing inwardly as he sounded like a complete idiot. Nothing new there, then.

Harriet entered his room and Jasper closed the door, staring at her in wonder. She'd come. He couldn't believe it. She'd actually come to him. His throat went dry as he looked at her. She wore a simple white cotton nightgown and wrap. No frills or lace, nothing the least bit provocative about it. How very Harriet, and how very unlike every other woman he'd ever bedded, who'd been all silk and seductive techniques. Yet Jasper had never felt longing the like of which rose inside of him at the sight of her.

She clutched her arms about herself, obviously nervous, and Jasper's heart ached.

"I didn't think you'd come," he admitted.

She shrugged as though it was nothing of import, but it was a stiff movement. "I said I would."

"I know, but...." He hesitated, wanting to be honest with her, and wanting her honesty in return. "I was afraid you wouldn't, all the same. I'm so glad you did."

"Let's just get this over with, shall we?" she said, tugging at the ties on her wrap with unsteady hands.

Jasper felt the words like a knife but just took a deep breath and stepped closer, stilling her hands with his own. "Harry," he said softly. "Look at me."

She shook her head, and he put his hands on her shoulders to find she was trembling.

"Don't be frightened, love. Not of me. I'd do nothing you didn't want, surely you know that? I'd not hurt you for the world."

She snorted at that, and he swallowed.

"I know I have hurt you. I know that, but you have to believe me when I tell you I don't—"

Before he could finish the sentence, Harriet reached up and put her hands to his head, pulling him down to her and kissing him, ending any further discussion. Heat erupted between them and he pulled her into his arms, sighing against her mouth at the rightness of it.

This was where she was supposed to be, where she belonged; with him, and he would never let her go.

Chapter 10

Auntie was in fine form as always and sends her best love to you. I am having a lovely time here at Holbrooke House. Bonnie and Minerva and Matilda and Harriet are so kind, and Lady St Clair is very welcoming, making us all feel quite at home.

Yes, the earl is still every bit as handsome and charming as he is purported to be, but no, father, he really won't offer for me. Not even if you double my dowry. I believe he has fixed his interests elsewhere already.

—Excerpt of a letter from Miss Ruth Stone to her father.

The night of the 31st August 1814. Holbrooke House, Sussex.

Jasper drew back, feeling a little dazed as he broke the kiss.

"Where are your spectacles?" he asked, touching his finger to the bridge of her nose.

"I left them in my room," she said, blinking up at him. "I assumed I would not require them."

"That depends," he said, a stupid smile curving over his mouth. "Can you see me?"

Harriet rolled her eyes at him. "I'm not totally blind, you know."

"I know. I just don't want you to miss anything." Jasper's smile widened with delight as she blushed scarlet. "Besides, I adore your spectacles."

"Oh, please," she said, and he knew she was dying to roll her eyes once more. "No one loves a girl in spectacless."

"I do," he murmured, ducking his head to press a kiss to the side of her neck and loving the sound of her breathing hitch as he did so. "I always have."

"Don't," she said, pushing him away. "Don't do that."

Jasper frowned, staring back at her. "Do what?"

"Don't... make love to me, or say things that aren't true. I've said I'll go to bed with you, but... but it's physical. Nothing more. We just need to get it out of our systems, that's all."

He stared at her for a long moment, wondering if his heart could stand much more of this jolting back and forth between happiness and misery.

"Go, then," he said, the words not entirely steady. He turned away from her, knowing he couldn't stand to watch her leave.

"But...." Harriet said, so obviously perplexed that he wanted to cry.

"I can't do it, Harry," he said, too much emotion in his voice to hide it as he turned back to her. "You tell me not to say what isn't true and to keep it purely physical, but I can't do both. The truth is that I love you, and if I take you to bed, I'm going to make love to you because I can't do anything else. That would be a lie, Harry, and there have been too many of those between us."

He stared at her, seeing the confusion in her eyes, knowing that she didn't believe him.

"Very well," she said, her voice not entirely steady. "Do that. Make me believe it."

Jasper's breath caught. Now, that he could do.

He closed the distance between them and hauled her back into his arms, the tension leaving him as her fingers wound into his hair and she melted into him. Jasper smiled against her mouth as her hands slid down his neck and chest, to the belt on his dressing gown, tugging it free before she reached up and pushed it from his shoulders. He released his hold on her to allow it to fall to the ground. There was nothing beneath the robe and he held himself still, giving Harry the time to look him over.

Her eyes widened and her breath caught, and every nerve ending in his body leapt to attention as she reached out a tentative hand and touched his bare skin.

"You've seen me before," he reminded her. "Twice, apparently."

She blushed and gave him a pert look. "Once from a distance and the second time is a little… hazy," she admitted.

"Well, you'd best take a good look this time. I'd like to leave a lasting impression," he said, though he had no intention of giving her the slightest opportunity to forget him.

"Like David," she murmured, trailing a finger through the coarse hair on his chest.

"You've never seen David," he replied, the words breathless.

"I've seen pictures, and a life size copy," she said, somewhat defiantly. "Though there are… some differences," she allowed.

Jasper smirked. "Yes, I always thought him rather poorly endowed myself."

"You might be right," Harriet murmured, staring down at the part of him that was clamouring for her attention. "But other than that…." Her finger traced a path down his abdomen, making the muscles twitch and leap until she reached his hip bone. She looked up at him. "You're the most beautiful thing I've ever seen."

Jasper's throat tightened. He knew he was handsome, of course he did. Women had told him often enough, and behaved shockingly to get him into their beds, but never had the words meant anything to him. He couldn't hold a candle to Harriet's mind, could never entertain her with his cleverness, but this... he could give her this, as shallow as that might seem in comparison.

"I think that's supposed to be my line," he said, trying to smile but finding he was too overcome to manage it.

She huffed out a little laugh at that. "We said the truth only, remember."

He frowned and reached out, capturing her face in his hands. "I don't know what you see in the mirror, love, nor what anyone else sees, but I see *you*, Harriet, and you *are* beautiful."

Harriet stared up at him, her eyes misty with tears, with the longing to believe him, though he knew she didn't. Not yet, but she would. If it took him a lifetime, she would come to believe she was beautiful and loved, by him.

He moved closer, touching his mouth to hers, softly, tenderly, putting all his hopes and dreams into the touch of his lips against hers. Harriet sighed and reached for him, pressing against him and desire flamed again, stronger than ever. It was the hardest thing to hold himself back, to keep his touch slow and gentle.

Reaching for the ties she'd half undone, he finished the job, pushing the wrap to the ground before undoing the neck of her nightgown and pulling it open until it slid down to the generous curve of her hips.

His breath hitched as he pulled back to look at her and he caught her hands when she would have covered herself.

"You've seen me before, too," she complained as he held her hands out of the way.

"And yet you still take my breath away," he said, meaning it. "Oh, love."

He bent his head and kissed first one breast, then the other, returning to toy with the tightly puckered nipple, circling it with his tongue before sucking gently. Harriet gasped and clutched at his hair, holding him in place.

"Lovely," he murmured. "So perfect."

He stood and looked at her, finding her eyes darker than ever, her cheeks flushed. He smiled and kissed her nose before pushing the nightgown from her hips.

"Come to bed with me, Harry. Please," he added, still a little uncertain despite the look in her eyes.

She nodded and moved ahead of him, climbing onto the mattress and lying down, stiff as a board. Jasper lay beside her, his head propped on his arm and a ridiculous smile on his face.

"What?" she demanded.

"Nothing," he said, still smiling like an idiot. "I'm just happy, that's all. You make me happy."

"No, I don't," she countered, looking away from him. "I make you angry."

"Only because I provoke you and you retaliate. *Then* I get angry."

She huffed out a breath. "True. So, why must you provoke me?"

"Because it's better than being ignored, Harry. If you don't see me, I... I feel like I might disappear entirely."

Harriet's gaze snapped back to his, intent and questioning, that fierce brain turning over his words and weighing each one. She looked away again, still quizzical, but he knew she'd not ask whatever questions were burning inside her. If she couldn't puzzle it out herself, she'd leave it unanswered, too proud to ask him to explain.

"Shouldn't you... do something?" she asked, sounding rather impatient.

"Perhaps," he said, lying on his back, his hands behind his head. "But I think you should go first this time."

"What?" Harriet sat up and stared down at him.

"Come on, Harry. You always loved a puzzle." He swept a hand down the length of his body. "Figure me out."

Her brows rose but he could see the flicker of interest in her eyes.

"How…?"

"However you want," he said, his voice huskier now. "Touch me wherever you want, however you want."

She swallowed, and he waited, the anticipation killing him. After what seemed an eternity, she shuffled closer and put her hand flat on his chest, over his heart. It thudded beneath her palm, fast and erratic.

"Not dead, then," she said, the glimmer of a smile at her lips.

"Very much not dead," he murmured.

Harriet licked her lips and moved her hand to touch his nipple, her fingers brushing the sensitive skin until it was a hard little nub. "I like these," she said. "They're so neat."

Jasper snorted.

"When… when I do what you did to me, with your mouth… does it feel the same?"

"You've done it before."

"Yes, but you never told me how it felt, and I can't remember…."

He tutted. "You are never to come to bed drunk again," he muttered. "Why don't you try it and find out?" At the determined look that flared in her eyes Jasper wondered how much he could endure of her investigation, thinking he might have made an error in judgement. No. She was fascinated, and he'd deny her nothing, even if it killed him.

Harriet bent, looking a little awkward and frowning with concentration as she ran her tongue over his nipple. Jasper's breath caught, and she looked up, a glimmer of satisfaction in her eyes. She did it again, harder this time, circling with her tongue before closing her mouth over him and sucking a little.

Jasper let out a little huff of breath as she repeated the action on the other side.

Harriet sat up.

"It does feel the same," she said, sounding rather smug.

He closed his eyes and laughed. "Oh, yes, it does."

When he opened his eyes again, she was looking him over, her gaze travelling to his cock, which glistened at the tip, wet with anticipation. Jasper held his breath as she shifted down the bed and ran an experimental fingertip down the length of him.

His cock leapt beneath her touch and Jasper cursed under his breath.

Harriet snatched her hand away.

"Don't stop," he ground out. "Do it again."

She did and his breathing grew ragged, which was ridiculous, she'd barely touched him, but this was Harriet, and he'd wanted this for so long, for a bloody eternity.

"Can I kiss you here too?" she asked, her tone so matter of fact, Jasper was momentarily stunned into silence.

"Yes," he croaked, before covering his face with his hands. "Oh, God, yes. Yes, please."

He couldn't watch her, afraid he'd spend the moment she touched him with her mouth if he saw her do it. Instead he screwed his eyes shut and held his breath and nearly died with wanting at the first warm flutter of her breath against his belly.

There was nothing for a moment, just the soft susurration of her breathing rushing over him and he was on the brink of pleading for mercy when he felt the flicker of her tongue against his cock. She trailed over the length of him and Jasper groaned, the sound deep and heartfelt. Harriet must have taken it for the sound of approval it most definitely was as she repeated the action and then pressed damp little kisses along the path her tongue had taken. She reached the head and her tongue swept over him again. Then he heard a sound of surprise.

"Salty," she said, and her fingers caressed the sleek head, smoothing the moisture there over him. "What is this?" she asked, her question not the least bit self-conscious, only curious. "I know conception is caused by the male ejaculation of sperm, but this isn't the same, or is it?"

Jasper made a choked sound somewhere between amusement and despair. "No, love," he said, his voice strangled. "N-Not the same. It's my body telling you that you're driving me out of my mind, and it wants to be inside you, very badly indeed." He dared to look up at her and found her nodding, her expression still serious.

"This is physical evidence of desire, then?"

She looked back at him and Jasper nodded.

"There's something similar isn't there?" she asked, her gaze direct. "For me?"

Jasper nodded again, beyond giving an explanation. "Lay back."

She did as he asked and Jasper turned onto his side again, sliding a hand up the outside of her thigh. Harriet watched him and he leaned down and kissed her, pleased when she sighed and opened to him at once. As they kissed, he gently parted her thighs and returned to stroking up and down, aware of the quickening of her breath. He broke the kiss as his fingers sought the feathery patch of curls, wanting to watch her, needing to be certain of her approval.

"Here is your evidence, love," he said, parting the delicate folds and seeking the wet heat within as he dipped a fingertip inside her.

Harriet's breath caught. "Yes," she said. "Oh, yes."

Jasper bent his head and kissed her again as he continued to caress her, his finger sliding a little deeper as his thumb circled over the little hidden bud with care. Harriet arched, a soft cry torn from her that made his body tighten with need.

"D-Do I…?" Harriet began before his touch made her arch again and the words were lost.

"Do you what?" Jasper asked, nuzzling at her neck and tugging gently at her earlobe with his teeth.

"D-Do I…?" she began again, and he looked up watching her as she asked with typical solemnity. "Do I taste salty too?"

Jasper stared down at her, wondering for a frantic moment if she was doing it on purpose, for she was shredding his self-control. He swallowed and tried to find his voice.

"Why don't we find out?"

He moved down the bed, delighted and astonished when she parted her legs wider for him, giving him access. She sat up, propped on her elbows and staring down at him.

"Do you want to?" she asked, frowning a little. "I never thought to ask if—"

Jasper gave a slightly hysterical laugh. "Yes. Yes, I do want to. More than anything."

"Good," she said, apparently satisfied as she lay down again.

His lips quirked. God, she was wonderful. Utterly unique, truly herself. There was not another woman in the world like her, and he could not afford to let her go. With that in mind he settled to his work, determined to please her, to bring her such pleasure that she'd never be able to forget it, or to forget him.

The sound she made as he parted her curls and licked would certainly be burned into his mind until the day he died. It was at once wanton and all surprised innocence and, when he did it again, there was such approval in the breathless gasp she gave, he'd have purred if he was capable of it.

"Oh," she cried, reaching down to tangle her finger in his hair, arching her hips to give herself more fully into his reach. "Oh, Jasper."

The sound of his name spoken with such husky desire sent a bolt of need straight to his groin and it took every ounce of concentration not to give into the desire to sink into her there and then. He'd not be selfish in this. Though he'd never bedded a virgin before, he knew that her first time might not be everything he wanted for her, but there was no way she'd leave his bed without knowing how much pleasure there was to be found there.

"How do I taste, Jasper?"

Jasper chuckled against her skin, amused she still wanted to know. "Sweeter than honey," he murmured. "Sweet and tart and utterly delicious."

She sighed, satisfied, and gave herself over to the pleasure he gave on her. To his relief, it didn't take long before he sensed her climax at hand. Not that he wanted to stop, far from it, but he didn't think he could wait much longer. Beneath him he was aware of her body growing taut, of the tightening of her fingers in his hair and her stuttering breath as she grew closer to the edge.

Jasper hummed with approval as he sucked gently on the delicate bud of her sex and she shattered, her cry loud and raw enough to make him extremely glad his rooms were far from anyone else's. Pleasure thrummed through him as he guided her, easing every ounce of delight to be had from her body before he finally moved to take his place between her thighs. He couldn't wait any longer. It would kill him.

"Harriet," he said, staring down at her as she blinked hazily up at him. "Please," he added, wondering if that was coherent enough as he was beyond words now. He slid his cock over her slick flesh and she gasped and then wrapped her legs about his hips, arching to meet him.

"Yes," she said. "Yes."

That was all he'd needed, and he pushed inside, watching her face for any sign of pain or distress.

"Is it…?"

"Yes."

He bent his head, resting his forehead against hers and sliding deeper, closing his eyes as the exquisite heat of her engulfed him like a velvet glove.

"How does it feel?" she asked.

Jasper forced his eyes open again and stared at her, dazed with pleasure. "Like heaven. Like nothing on earth but you, Harry." He thrust deeper, and she gave a startled little cry. He stopped at once. "It hurts?"

Harriet shook her head. "No, at least… only for a moment. It's… strange, that's all."

"And now?" he asked, withdrawing and sliding inside her again.

"It's fine," she said, closing her eyes as he did it again. "Fine…. Oh."

He smiled at that little oh of pleasure and kissed her forehead as he slid a hand between them and found the secret place that had loved his tongue so very much.

"And now?" he asked, touching her so very gently.

"Oh, yes," she said, sighing and wrapping her arms about him, pulling his head down and seeking his mouth. "Yes, yes," she whispered.

From the point of view of a man who believed himself an experienced lover, it was an embarrassingly short time before Jasper felt his own body tighten.

"Harry," he said, staring down at her.

"Yes," she said, staring up at him and smiling, actually smiling at him, such a soft look in her eyes that his heart soared. "Oh, yes."

He shuddered as waves of pleasure crashed over him, holding Harriet to him and crying out, unable to contain his joy in the moment as he said her name.

"Harry, oh, yes, Harry. I love you. I love you."

Chapter 11

My dear Miss Hunt,

I do hope that you are well and no worse the wear for your exposure to the inclement weather this morning. I should be glad to have my physician attend you should you have need of him.

My ankle is sprained, as suspected, but I can report there is no permanent or serious damage. I inform you only to save you the trouble of enquiring, as I have no doubt you were about to do. I should not like you to worry yourself unduly on my behalf.

Happily, Rhaebus was recovered, unharmed.

I predict the next time we cross paths – or swords – will be no less dramatic. In anticipation…

M

—*Letter from The Most Honourable, Lucian Barrington, the Marquess of Montagu to Miss Matilda Hunt.*

The night of the 31ˢᵗ August 1814. Holbrooke House, Sussex.

"Argh!" Matilda crumpled the note in her hand and was on the brink of tossing it in the fire but found herself compelled to uncrumple it and read the blasted thing again.

"*As I have no doubt you were about to do,*" she read bitterly, before adding, "Over my dead body."

Of all the smug, irritating, self-important….

Grrrrr.

She paced her bedroom, beside herself with frustration. If only she were at home and could pick a suitable missile to hurl across the room and vent her feelings. He knew as well as she did that she hadn't had the slightest intention of enquiring after his bloody ankle. Whether or not she'd wanted to, it would have been quite inappropriate… especially as no one knew about their meeting. Her friends had clearly gained the notion that something had gone on, though. That was beside the point, however. The very idea that she was fretting herself to death on his behalf was laughable.

Admittedly, she had wondered if he was well, but only so she could enjoy the vague hope he'd broken the blasted bone. Oh, that wasn't true either, but neither had she been *worrying herself unduly.*

The note had been slipped under her door and she'd found it after dinner when she'd returned to her room. She had no idea how he'd done it, or rather, had arranged for it to be done. She wasn't about to contemplate the possibility of Montagu creeping about Holbrooke House to deliver her a note, even if his ankle wasn't damaged. No doubt he had trusted servants to do such sneaky work for him.

> *I predict the next time we cross paths – or swords – will be no less dramatic. In anticipation…*

What the devil did he mean by that?

Matilda flounced into the chair by the fire, glaring at the note she still clutched. The handwriting was predictably elegant and precise, like the man himself. Even the flourishing M at the end was arrogant. Still seething, Matilda willed herself to consign the aggravating note and any thoughts of the man to the flames. She couldn't make herself do it, which only incensed her all the more. Instead, she got to her feet, stalked to her bedside table, shoved the note between the pages of the book she was reading and slammed the drawer shut again.

The orchid on her nightstand trembled with the force of the movement, the delicate flowers swaying.

Matilda muttered a curse under her breath and blew out the light.

***

Harriet stared at the rich colours of the canopy over the bed, trying to comprehend the events of the past few hours. Nothing had gone as she had imagined it would.

It had taken every ounce of courage she possessed to walk the dark corridors of the vast house to Jasper's rooms. Of course, she knew where they were, knew this great behemoth of a house every bit as well as the family did, better even.

She'd remembered the story of the ghost and wondered if she'd see it on the way. She never had done before and was rather ambivalent about the idea of seeing it or not. Whilst it would be unpleasant, it would be interesting to have proof of such a phenomenon. At this point, she'd realised she was trying to distract herself from her current purpose, not terribly successfully either. She was all a-quiver, her heart thudding in her chest so furiously she considered it perfectly loud enough to summon the dead.

Then Jasper had been there, waiting, and… the things he'd said, the way he'd touched her… it had made her hope and dream and….

How could she dare to believe it?

She turned on her side, no easy feat as Jasper had slung an arm and a leg over her. He was sleeping now, not exactly snoring, but breathing heavily. Harriet studied him, pleased with the opportunity to do so at close quarters without scrutiny.

His eyelashes were a darker shade of gold to his hair and ridiculously long. Any woman would kill for lashes like those. He looked boyish and untroubled in sleep, the worry lines she'd noticed around his eyes earlier this evening smoothed away. There was also a very faint scattering of freckles across his nose she'd never noticed before, and which she found perfectly charming. His hands were similarly marked where the sun had browned him, and the knowledge made her smile.

He'd said he loved her. It had sounded as if he'd meant it, too. It had sounded that way all those years ago, though, when he'd asked her not to marry anyone else. Well, she hadn't, not that anyone had asked. Not until Inigo.

What ought she to do? Being with Jasper, having a life with him, was every dream she'd ever had until he'd broken her heart. Could she really risk it again? Would it not be safer to return to Inigo? They had so much more in common, so many shared interests. Except now there was a new problem.

As she knew he was fully aware, Jasper had not withdrawn at the crucial moment. Which meant there was a chance, slight as it was, that she was carrying the future Earl of St Clair. The idea that he would allow her to marry Inigo now....

Not that it was his choice, but....

She sighed. If she hadn't been trapped before, she certainly was now. The troubling thing was that she rather thought she might be glad. Perhaps she wasn't brave enough to trust him again, to allow herself to love him as she had done once, but she could simply let it happen. Now the choice had been taken from her.

What to do about Jasper Cadogan.

Good heavens.

How much of her life had been wasted contemplating that very question? Except it didn't feel like a waste at this moment.

Jasper sighed. His arm, which was a heavy weight across her middle, tightened, drawing her closer, and he made a sound of contentment.

"Are you asleep?"

"Mmmm," he mumbled.

"I should go."

His arm tightened further, and a scowl marred his handsome face though his eyes remained closed. Harriet reached out, smoothing the furrows. "I can't be found in your rooms, and I'm tired. If I fall asleep, I'll be here until morning.

His eyes flickered open, and she was dazzled all over again by their remarkable colour, that pale blue-green that was not quite either and yet both at once.

"I rather think that horse has bolted," he said, a wicked grin flickering at his lips.

"That doesn't mean I want to start another round of gossip. You know how servants talk."

Jasper shook his head. "Not Merrick. He hates gossip. He'll take my secrets to the grave."

"Hmmm," Harriet said, not liking the sound of that. "Have many dark secrets do you have exactly?"

"Only one worth a damn," he said, reaching out and tracing the line of her jaw. "And it's becoming rather less of a secret by the minute."

She stared at him, torn between hoping he'd say it and hoping he wouldn't. How much more could her heart withstand before it capitulated entirely and dissolved into a puddle at his feet?

Forestalling the question entirely, she kissed him. He pulled her to him, deepening the kiss, and awakening all sorts of sensations as her body responded at once despite her fatigue.

"Stay," he said, such pleading in his eyes she couldn't refuse. Not when she wanted to do as he'd asked, anyway. "Please," he added. "I want to wake up with you."

With a sigh, she moved closer and put her head on his chest, closing her eyes as he stroked a lazy hand down her back.

"Very well," she said, closing her eyes. "I'm too tired to argue."

"Miracles do happen," he murmured and, for once, she let him have the last word.

***

The next morning dawned with the fresh vivacity that always followed a summer downpour. The sun-parched earth had soaked up every drop and the grass was brighter, the colours more dramatic, as though Mother Nature was having one last burst of glory before the approaching autumn stole summer's thunder.

Minerva looked out of her bedroom window with a burst of anticipation. There was a trip planned today, to Tunbridge Wells. Though she'd stopped there with Bonnie and Ruth, they had by no means seen all there was to see, and she was very much looking forward to exploring a bit more. If she was honest, however, her main reason for wanting to return was the very slim chance of bumping into Mr de Beauvoir for a second time.

Why she was so struck with him, after such an inauspicious meeting, she hadn't the faintest idea. It had occurred to her that perhaps it was some perverse desire to thwart her mother, who had been aggressively in search of a titled husband for her daughter since the moment she'd come out. Minerva had been bullied and forced to this and that social event, told what to do, what to say, how to act, when to smile… until she was dizzy and sickened by the whole affair and had forgotten who she was and what she wanted for herself. With Prue's help she had changed that, and had promised herself she would make her own decisions from now on. The intriguing Mr de Beauvoir would be everything her mother would abhor. He was not titled or rich, had no charming manner or handsome face to recommend him and, heaven forfend, he was an *intellectual*.

If her dear mama had the slightest inkling of Minerva's thoughts, she'd probably suffer a nervous collapse.

Nonetheless....

Minerva still hoped she would see him again. Chewing at her lip, she considered what to wear that would show her in her best light, and then she considered what might actually impress him, as she doubted it would be her dress.

"I wonder if Harriet has any interesting books I could borrow?" she wondered aloud.

If she could show him she was attempting to expand her brain, perhaps that would impress him. Minerva pulled a face and sighed. Only if she could talk about said book with any conviction, which she felt unlikely. Still, it was the only thing she could think of.

***

Jasper blinked, staring at the woman sleeping next to him with the dazed disbelief of a man waking from a dream. For a terrible moment dreams and reality overlapped, and he feared it had been nothing more than his imagination, but then she made a little snorting sound, somewhere between a snore and a huff, and his mouth curved into a grin.

The sound woke her and she blinked in the dim light of his room, eyes widening with shock as she saw him.

"Oh," she said in surprise, and then let out a breath. "Good morning."

"Marry me," Jasper said, unable to keep the words back any longer. "Please, Harry, say you will."

He watched her brow wrinkle, saw the troubled look enter her eyes.

"I'll make you happy. I swear it."

She sighed and turned onto her back. "We can't spend our lives in bed, Jasper. There's more to a marriage than that."

"I know," he said, reaching out and cupping her face, turning it back to look at him. "But bed is more important than I think you realised. Could you really marry him now? Won't you be thinking of me whenever he touches you? For it won't be like it is with us, Harry. I promise you that."

The words had sounded a little harsher than he'd intended, fuelled by jealousy. He didn't think his heart would survive if she chose de Beauvoir over him.

She said nothing, just stared up at him, her dark eyes solemn. Panic rose in his chest. Why would she choose him? She thought he was a brainless fop, and he didn't know how to convince her otherwise, not when he feared it was true. One day soon he'd have to tell her the truth, he owed her that much, but the idea made him feel sick. What if she was appalled by him, embarrassed even, or worse, what if she pitied him? How would he bear it?

"You have to marry me now, anyway," he said, sounding far harsher than he'd intended, unnerved by her silence, lashing out as he always did when she unsettled him and dented his confidence. "You could be carrying my child."

"Yes, I realise you made sure that was a possibility," she said, her voice cool and direct

Jasper flushed, torn between wishing he had done it on purpose and mortification. Good God, why did she always make him feel like such a foolish boy? "I didn't do it on purpose," he said stiffly. "I... I just didn't think, *couldn't* think. I lost control."

"I could wait until I'm sure there's no child," she said, and though it was gently said the words struck at his heart. "It's unlikely, you know. Some people try for years before they conceive."

This was too reasonable and Jasper had gone far beyond reason. He moved on top of her, pushing her legs wide and fitting his body intimately against hers. "Then I'd best give myself a better chance, hadn't I?" he growled.

Harriet gasped as he slid his arousal between her legs, but she made no complaint, lifting her hips towards his, putting her arms about him.

"Would you really do that to me?" she asked, gazing up at him. "Force a child on me to make me do as you want?"

Jasper closed his eyes and swallowed as shame washed over him. He shook his head. "No," he admitted, daring to look at her. "Though I fear how far I would go. I can't lose you, Harry. I love you," he said, staring down at her. "And I think we could be happy. I know I'd do anything to make you happy."

There was fear in her eyes, but there was want too, he was certain of it. She wanted to believe him, and that was more than he could have hoped for.

"Harriet." He breathed her name against her neck as he pushed inside her body, pleasure unfurling through him as she gasped and held him tighter, welcoming him in. "Don't refuse me, love, please. Say yes."

"I... I can't think when... *Oh*...."

"Harry?"

"I'll think about it, Jasper, I promise. Just... *later*.... Give me a little time."

It wasn't a no, at least, and that was more than he'd had yesterday. He said nothing more. He could give her time, and during that time he'd make certain she'd never be able to look at another man, not when she wanted him so badly.

Chapter 12

My lord,

I am truly and deeply sorry for your loss and though I doubt you'll believe me I don't mean to cause you any further distress. However it makes no difference to me if Gordon Anderson is now your heir. I wouldn't care if he were the next King of Scotland. I won't marry him. You'll not have any problem finding a girl who would leap at the chance to marry him now, so why not find one? Just not me!

— Excerpt of a letter from Miss Bonnie Campbell to The Right Honourable William Douglas, The Earl of Morven.

1st September 1814. Holbrooke House, Sussex.

Harriet thanked her maid and dismissed her, reaching for her spectacles. She had made it back to her room unseen, thanks to a detailed knowledge of all the hidden passages and hidey holes that ran through the vast building. Merrick had, as Jasper had suggested, not so much as blinked an eye at her being in his master's chambers, and had treated her with all the respect due the future countess.

She gave a heavy sigh and got to her feet, staring out of the window. How lovely it would be to live in such a splendid place, and with Jasper as her husband. It was the embodiment of her every dream, and yet she wasn't sure she was brave enough to reach for it. Last night, and this morning—she recalled with something of a blush—it had been so easy to be with him. She'd been so overwhelmed by how he made her feel that it had been on the tip of her tongue to just agree to anything he wanted, yet she feared deciding anything at such a time. Desire was no basis for a marriage, not when she was still so unsure of his motivation.

She could not pretend that she believed his declarations of love to be sincere. Not that she thought he was lying to her; he clearly believed it himself. Yet, Jasper was so damned stubborn, and she'd been refusing him for so long, that she could not help but suspect it was just a case of wanting what he couldn't have. Surely, once his satisfaction at having won was over and done, he'd realise he'd married a dull little bluestocking, and not a very pretty one at that. She remembered again the lush beauty of his last mistress, Mrs Tate, and the comparison to Harriet's own limited charms seemed mean indeed. He'd regret it in time, when he realised his wife would rather sit at home with her nose in a book than go out to whatever party or social event seemed to fill his calendar.

Wouldn't it be better for her to marry Inigo and have done with it? It would save them both a great deal of heartache when Jasper awoke to the mistake he'd made. Harriet reached up and massaged her temples. Her head was pounding, though she didn't think it was only her anxiety over the decision she faced. She felt hot and her throat was scratchy. No doubt she'd caught some ghastly cold and would soon have to face Jasper with the added indignity of a red nose and watery eyes. How revolting. She resolved to ask for some willow bark tea when she went down, and to eat a hearty breakfast. Perhaps she'd not succumb to it if she put it from her mind.

Harriet's thoughts scattered as someone knocked at her bedroom door, and she opened it to find Minerva waiting for her.

"Hello, Harriet," she said, and for just a moment Harry felt a surge of jealousy.

This was the kind of girl who ought to be the next Countess St Clair. She was lovely, with thick blonde hair and quite startling blue eyes. For a moment, Harriet pictured her with Jasper, and acknowledged what a handsome couple they would make. Jealousy tore through her, almost stealing her breath.

"Minerva," she said, her tone rather frosty.

The girl hesitated at the unfriendly greeting and Harriet cursed herself for being so stupid and unkind.

"Forgive me," she said, sighing. "I have a bit of a headache and it's making me tetchy."

"Oh, you poor thing," Minerva said sympathetically. "Shall I have someone fetch you some willow bark tea?"

Harriet smiled and nodded, feeling worse than ever. "Yes, I'm sure that's just the thing. That and some fresh air will do me the world of good. Are you ready to go down to breakfast? We'd best hurry if we don't want to keep everyone waiting."

"Oh, yes, I am, but… I was wondering if… if you might lend me a book, please?"

Harriet blinked at the girl, rather surprised. "Certainly, though… I don't read a great many novel as a rule. At least, I don't have any with me. I expect Matilda does, though, if—"

"Oh no," Minerva said, her cheeks flushing a soft pink which made her look lovelier than ever. Harriet held back a sigh of frustration. "I don't want a novel. I… I'd like something educational."

Minerva put up her chin, a slightly defiant glint in her eyes that assumed Harriet would judge her too stupid to read such a thing.

"Of course," she said, smiling at Minerva. It was a wonderful thing if the girl wanted to use her brain and Harriet would be happy to encourage her. "What subject did you have in mind?"

"Erm…." Minerva said, looking a little panicked. "What is there?"

"Well," Harriet mused, opening the lid on a case that held the books she'd brought with her.

"Good heavens!" Minerva exclaimed, staring down in astonishment. "You brought all those to a house party?"

Harriet pushed her spectacles up her nose and shrugged. "I like to read. Now, then," she said, looking down at the books. "I only have a limited selection here, but there's philosophy, physics, natural sciences, chemistry…."

"Oh, um…. Chemistry, perhaps?" Minerva ventured, looking very uncertain.

"Oh, well, in that case, I shall lend you this," Harriet said, selecting *Conversations on Chemistry*, the book Inigo had sent her. "I've read it myself, though I need to read it again as I was rather er… *distracted* and I don't feel I appreciated it as I should. The author is a woman, though she's not credited, but I have a friend who knows her and thinks highly of her. I thought it an interesting read for a beginner to the subject. It was very well and clearly written."

Minerva took the book from her with a daunted expression suggesting she believed it would bite her.

"Don't look so terrified." Harriet smiled. "It's not in Greek, I promise. Just try small sections at a time. If they don't make sense, why not come and ask me and we'll talk about it? Not that I can claim to be anything of an expert, far from it, only it is a subject that interests me, and I would like to learn more."

"Is there any subject that doesn't interest you?" Minerva asked, still looking rather intimidated.

"No," Harriet said with a sigh, frowning at her book collection. "That is my besetting sin. I can't settle to one subject and do it justice. I just enjoy learning, and if something new is set before me, I want to know about it. So I never really learn anything in sufficient depth, which I fear is a dreadful weakness."

"But you know quite a lot about many things. I mean... I know nothing about... about *anything*! Unless you count knowing which dress to wear to what occasion, how to curtsey to a duke or a viscount, how to make tea, embroider, or a dozen other useless talents."

"Minerva!" Harriet said, appalled. "That's not the least bit useless. Those are things we need to know to navigate the world we've been born into, and consider why you know nothing else? You've never been to school, have you?"

"No, of course not."

"Well, how ought you to know anything at all? Women are kept in ignorance to keep them docile and easy to control, if you ask me. Many men fear an educated woman as they might just discover we're every bit as intelligent and capable as they are. Not all men," she added, for fairness, for Inigo had encouraged her studies without hesitation.

Minerva stared down at the book in her hand and took a deep breath. "Well, I shall try, Harriet, and I shall come and talk to you about it if I can't make head nor tail of the dratted thing."

Harriet smiled at her. "Well, that's a good start, and I shall look forward to having someone to talk to about it, I can tell you. Now, come along. We'd best hurry."

***

Minerva travelled with Harriet, Lord St Clair, and Matilda, with Bonnie and Ruth following in Ruth's carriage with Henry and Jerome. They arrived in Tunbridge Wells in good time, with the carriages setting them down close to The Walks. The general plan seemed to be to look at the shops, visit the nearby Chapel of Ease, King Charles the Martyr, have something to eat and then walk it off in The Grove park afterwards.

"Are you going to take the waters?" Harriet asked Matilda, who pulled a face as they passed by the Chalybeate spring.

The water had stained everything it touched a vivid orange, it was so rich in iron. A lady stood with a dipper at hand which you had to pay for the use of. The water itself was free, but if you wanted to drink it in a genteel fashion you paid for the privilege.

"No, I thank you," Matilda said with a shudder. "I'm fit as a fiddle. If I was ailing, perhaps I'd force it down, but not if I don't have to."

"Agreed," said St Clair with a smile. "Perhaps if they served it with brandy...."

Everyone laughed and moved on.

"Do you think it will rain again?" Harriet asked, looking up at a pale blue sky tumbled with an increasing number of fluffy white clouds. Darker, heavier clouds were visible coming in from the west, though.

"Well, I brought my umbrella, so it ought not," Matilda said with a wink.

"Oh, Bonnie, let's go back in here," Ruth said, tugging at Bonnie's arm as they passed a shop with its window bursting with hats and lavish bolts of fabric in all the latest colours. "This is where I bought that dear little hat."

Bonnie and Minerva exchanged a glance. Minerva shrugged and returned a rueful smile.

"Jasper!"

Jasper turned as his brother hailed him, having come across a man they appeared to both know.

"Good heavens, it's Rothborn," Jasper exclaimed in surprise.

"Solo Rothborn?" Matilda enquired, looking over at the man with interest.

Minerva followed her gaze but could see nothing but the back of the man's head. He was tall and broad shouldered with light brown hair, but nothing more of note.

"Who is he?" she asked, curious why it was such a surprise.

"Solomon Weston, Baron Rothborn," Matilda said as Jasper excused himself to speak with his friend. "He's a recluse, hardly ever seen in public. That's why everyone calls him 'Solo' Rothborn."

Minerva turned back to Harriet who was eyeing the bookshop two doors down with a longing expression. "Shall we go in?" Minerva asked, hopes fluttering.

Harriet flashed her a grateful smile. "Why not?"

Minerva held her breath all the way around the bookshop, which was sadly devoid of any evidence of her quarry. Harriet had settled in a corner with some formidably sized text book that made Minerva's head hurt to even contemplate, so she wandered the aisles alone. She smiled, delighted to discover copies of Prue's book, lovingly bound in scarlet leather, and spent a while browsing the novels before returning to Harriet, who was still ensconced with her tome.

"I... I think I'll wait outside," she offered, to which Harriet lifted a hand, not looking up. Minerva gave a rueful smile and went back outside. She found Lord St Clair heading towards her as she exited.

"Have you seen Miss Stanhope?" he asked as he drew closer. "I've been looking everywhere."

"Yes, with her nose in a book," Minerva laughed, gesturing behind her.

Jasper smiled, and Minerva's breath caught at the look in his eyes. "I thought as much," he said ruefully, before hurrying inside.

Lucky Harriet, Minerva thought with a sigh. How might it feel to have such a man so in love with you? Harriet was a fool if she didn't snatch him up. Minerva turned back towards the shop Matilda and the others had gone into, wondering if they'd be anywhere near finished yet, and then paused as she saw the face she'd been searching for.

"Mr de Beauvoir!"

Minerva's breath caught as she realised what an outrageous thing she'd just done. She'd never been properly introduced to him and here she was in the street, to all intents and purposes alone, and hailing a man she hardly knew.

The man stopped, his dark brows drawing together as he looked at her without the slightest trace of recognition.

"I'm afraid you have me at a disadvantage, Miss...?"

"Butler," Minerva said at once, feeling her cheeks heat with embarrassment. "We met in the book shop. The one over there," she added, gesturing to it as his expression showed no sign of his remembering her. How humiliating. It wasn't like it had happened weeks ago! "The fellow shouted at me when he dropped his books, and you very kindly defended me and told him it was an... accident," she trailed off, feeling increasingly mortified.

De Beauvoir grunted, which Minerva took to be a sign he'd finally placed her.

"I did not realise I was speaking to such a celebrity," she added, forcing a sunny smile, desperate to find something to say to him. "I understand your talks at The Royal Academy are highly thought of."

"You are interested in chemistry, Miss Butler?" he asked, looking a little sceptical.

"I... I don't know," Minerva admitted. "I have this though," she added hurriedly, fishing in her reticule for the book which was weighing it down. Harriet had given her a funny look when she'd stuffed it in her bag—it wasn't exactly *light* reading, after all—but she'd hoped… well, for a scenario like this one. She showed him the cover and his eyebrows went up in surprise.

"Indeed," he said with approval. "I know the lady who wrote it. You could not do better for an introduction to the subject. How are you finding it?"

"Oh," Minerva said, feeling colour rise to her cheeks. "I only got it this morning, so I… I've not…."

"Well, I'm sure you'll find it illuminating. Now, if you would…."

Damn, he was going already.

"Oh, are you here to buy more books?" she asked, wondering why she was prolonging this agony when he couldn't wait to be rid of her.

"Er… no, not this morning. I—"

"De Beauvoir!"

He turned around, not looking especially pleased as he was hailed once more, this time by a group of fashionable people who were heading towards them.

"Oh, bloody hell," he muttered, glowering. "Miss Butler," he added, *sotto voce*. "Could I trouble you to remind me of an urgent appointment in precisely two minutes?"

"Oh!" Minerva exclaimed, delighted to be given the opportunity to be of use to him. "Indeed, you may."

She turned her attention to the newcomers with interest. There were three men, one of an age with de Beauvoir, and the other two young dandies. With them was a stunning, exquisitely dressed woman also of around thirty years of age, and a lady Minerva took to be her maid.

"Lord Havisham," Mr de Beauvoir said, acknowledging the older man before turning to the woman with a frown. "Ah, and Mrs

Tate. Good afternoon." His words were perfectly polite, but his reluctance to stand and speak with them was palpable.

"De Beauvoir," said Havisham, either ignoring or blithely unaware of de Beauvoir's indifference. "Tried to see that last talk of yours. Couldn't get in the bloody door. Wanted to ask if you'd come and do it again for me and some friends. Clever chaps, all of them. Know you'd like them. Feed you, of course, and plenty to drink. In fact, come for the weekend!"

"A kind offer," de Beauvoir replied, looking as though he believed it anything but. "I'm afraid I have work commitments."

"Oh, nothing that won't wait, I don't doubt," Havisham replied, waving this away with the careless indifference of a man who'd never worked a day in his life.

"Oh, Mr de Beauvoir, do forgive me for interrupting," Minerva said, sensing him bristling with irritation, "but you do have that appointment…."

"Yes," de Beauvoir agreed, snatching at the exit she offered him. "Quite right, Miss Butler."

"What appointment would that be, Inigo?" the woman who'd addressed him as Mrs Tate purred. She gave Minerva a pointed look and smirked. "I'm sure they'll wait a few more minutes, for a price."

Minerva gasped in outrage.

"You overstep, madam," de Beauvoir said, his voice so coldly furious that Minerva felt the chill of it even when it was not directed at her. "The appointment is with my solicitor. I was merely walking Miss Butler back to her companions. If you would excuse us."

He held out his arm to Minerva, who took it with alacrity, sent a look of sheer triumph towards the vile Mrs Tate, and stalked away with him, nose in the air.

Once they were out of earshot, de Beauvoir let out a breath.

"Miss Butler, I must beg your pardon for having subjected you to such a scene."

"Oh, please don't apologise, I was never more entertained," Minerva said, grinning up at him. "And it appeared you really needed an escape route. I was only too happy to provide one. What a ghastly woman."

He nodded. "I cannot disagree. It's a strange thing, but some women seem to take a man's disinterest in them as a personal affront, especially if they are considered beautiful."

Minerva nodded, understanding how a glamorous woman like Mrs Tate would be irritated by de Beauvoir not giving her a second glance. It had rankled Minerva that he'd not remembered her after all.

"Yes, well, for some of us our faces are our fortunes. Take that away and… and I suppose it's rather frightening to contemplate what's left. If there *is* anything left," she added, feeling a twist of anxiety knot in her stomach.

It was a moment before she realised de Beauvoir had stopped and was staring at her rather intently. Minerva gasped, realising she'd spoken carelessly and practically admitted she was an empty-headed pea hen. Well, and so she was for having spoken without thinking, she thought with a surge of irritation.

"And what do you think you'd find, Miss Butler, if you were not blessed in such a way?"

Minerva swallowed, put on the spot by the rather forthright question. Oh, well, she'd likely blown any chance of getting to know the man better; she may as well speak her mind. "Not a lot," she admitted. "I… I've always been rather frightened of clever people. My cousin Prue is terribly clever. She's a writer," she added, giving a wistful sigh. "I hated her for a long time because she made me feel stupid in comparison, but I know it wasn't her fault now, it was my own lack that made me angry with her."

She looked up and found herself the subject of those intense grey-green eyes. Heavens, but they were forceful. Minerva had the strangest feeling he could see right into her brain… and wasn't that a terrifying thought?

"I think, Miss Butler, that you are a great deal more intelligent and perceptive than you give yourself credit for."

"Oh," Minerva said, glowing with pleasure at his words.

"If I were you, I'd read that book. I think you might surprise yourself."

"I-I will," she stammered, finding her heart thudding rather too fast in a not altogether unpleasant fashion. She stared up at him, drinking in his rather uncompromising features. It was a harsh face, to be sure, but one that she felt engraved upon her soul, unforgettable. He hesitated for a moment and then seemed to come to a decision.

He reached into an inside pocket and took out a small silver case, which he opened. "My card, Miss Butler," he said, handing it to her. "If you find the book of interest, or have any questions, you may write to me."

Minerva swallowed and took the card from his hand, wishing she wasn't wearing gloves as their fingers brushed. "Thank you so much," she said, her voice rather faint. "I shall do so."

He nodded, put his card case away, and gave her a slight bow. "Good day to you, Miss Butler."

"Good day, Mr de Beauvoir," Minerva said, still feeling a little dazed.

She watched him stride away, his tall and rather gaunt frame disappearing into the crowds, as she clutched the card tightly in her grasp.

Chapter 13

My dear Harriet,

How are you? What is happening with St Clair? Are you to marry?

I feel like the most abominable friend for leaving you alone at such a time. I ought not to have allowed you to have talked me into leaving. Dearest Harry, do please tell me everything, and you need only say if you want me to return. You may rely upon me to do so at once.

*— Excerpt of a letter from **Mrs Kitty Baxter** to **Miss Harriet Stanhope**.*

1st September 1814, Holbrooke House, Sussex.

Harriet looked up, the discreet cough beside her ear jolting her out of her reading.

"Oh, Jasper," she said with a sigh. "You startled me."

"Really?" he replied, looking sceptical. "You were so engrossed I'm fairly certain a meteorite could have fallen on the Wells and you'd not have batted an eyelid."

She gave a little huff of laughter and shook her head. "True enough. How long have I been here?"

"Half an hour at least, I'd say."

He gave her a fond smile which did odd things to her stomach.

"Did you know, natural philosophers used to believe meteorites came from volcanoes on the moon, or were caused by lightning or condensation in clouds? That is, until a fifty-six pound meteorite fell in a field by Wold Cottage in Yorkshire. It fell out of a clear blue sky and left a crater twenty inches deep! What a shock that must have been."

"I didn't know that," Jasper said, grinning at her. "But I can't tell you how much I love that you do."

Harriet flushed, wondering if he was teasing her, but he seemed sincere.

"Come along," he said, taking the book from her hand.

"What are you doing with that?" she protested.

"Buying it for you, naturally."

She stared up at him, a strange feeling in her chest which was at once alarming and inevitable. "You don't need to do that."

He gave her an odd look, then leaned towards her and pressed a kiss to her forehead. "I promised to make you happy, Harriet. If books make you happy, I'll spend every penny I have on them."

"Jasper," she said, uncertain of what she wanted to say, but the words died at the look in his eyes.

"As long as you remember to look up from time to time and remember I'm there, it will be money well spent."

Harriet sighed and contemplated the likelihood of being able to withstand Jasper's brand of sweet-natured charm for more than another few hours without caving in and agreeing to anything he wanted. The blasted man was a menace, and yet a little flutter of something warm and hopeful unfurled in her chest and she could not help but smile at him.

"Thank you, Jasper. You're rather hard to forget, you know."

She knew; she'd tried often enough and for more years than she cared to contemplate.

"I should think so," he retorted, before going off to buy her book.

Harriet stared after him, the stupid smile still pasted to her face.

"Miss Stanhope, I'm hardly surprised by your looking like the cat that got the canary. I must congratulate you on a job well done."

Harriet turned, her heart plummeting as she found herself eye to eye with Mrs Tate, the glamorous widow who'd been Jasper's most recent paramour.

"I can't think what you mean, and I don't believe we've been introduced, madam," Harriet replied, the words crackling with all the ice she could muster though her cheeks were aflame, for she knew exactly what the wretched woman was implying.

"Well, if I'd known he'd fall for such an obvious tactic, I might have tried it myself," the lady said, her catlike green eyes glittering with malice.

"Oh, but you need a spotless reputation in order to be ruined, Mrs Tate," Harriet flung back, a little startled by her own audacity, but her temper had been lit and she was damned if she'd allow the woman to know just how inadequate she made her feel. "I'm afraid, in your case, that ship sailed a long, *long,* time ago."

To her irritation, Mrs Tate just laughed, a deep, rich sound that only made Harriet feel increasingly gauche.

"Touché, Miss Stanhope. Well, I really did mean it as a compliment you know. What a coup, for...." Mrs Tate gave Harriet a gesture that took her in from head to toe. "Someone like you," she said in wonder, shaking her head as she looked Harriet over with a rather pained expression.

In that moment, Harriet was all too aware of how she looked next to this woman. Her plain muslin gown was last season's, as she'd dressed in too much of a hurry and had taken little note of what she'd picked out. It was of the best quality, but simple and dreadfully immature when set against Mrs Tate's stylish ensemble in midnight blue. She looked ravishing, as well she knew.

Harriet's breath caught as Mrs Tate leaned in and she was assailed with the scent of ambergris. "I'll get him back, you know," she said, in a sultry undertone. "He'll marry you for his heir, but once that's done... he'll come back to me. They always do."

She drew back and winked at Harriet, who felt sick, hot and cold and nauseated all at once. There was the defiant urge inside of her to tell Mrs Tate she didn't want Jasper and she was welcome to him, but it would be too obviously a lie, and a wretched thing to say. If Jasper heard her say such a thing it would hurt him, no matter his true feelings, and she knew too vividly what that felt like to speak without thought of the consequences.

"Harriet."

She turned then as Jasper approached. There was fury in his eyes as he looked at Mrs Tate, and Harriet felt just a little bit better.

"Is everything all right, darling?" he asked, sliding a possessive arm about her waist.

Harriet looked up at him. "Quite all right, thank you, Jasper. Mrs Tate here was just explaining how you're only marrying me because you must, because you need an heir. She was telling me how you'd be back in her bed the moment that had been accomplished."

Harriet turned and gave Mrs Tate the sweetest of smiles, experiencing a momentary surge of triumph at the panic in the woman's eyes, before turning on her heel and walking away.

***

"You bloody bitch."

Mrs Tate stiffened, but put up her chin. "It's nothing but the truth. The girl may as well know it. Cruel of you to lead her on, you know, darling." Her expression changed, a sly look he knew all too well creeping into her expression as she moved closer and slid a hand down his chest. "We were so good together. Don't you remember how good?" she purred.

Jasper slapped her hand away in disgust and took a step back.

"You're a fool, Jenny," he said, wondering what in the name of everything holy he'd been doing toying with her at all. He must have been bloody desperate. "I'm in love with her. I've always loved her. It's me that trapped her into marriage, if you must know, and if you so much as speak her name, I'll make sure no one ever wants to dally with you ever again. There will be no more wealthy protectors, not once I'm done."

She glared at him, her eyes furious though her complexion was leaching colour.

"I treated you well," he said, beside himself with the unfairness of it. "You did handsomely out of me, but that's not enough, is it? You wanted my heart on a platter like every other poor fool you've ensnared. Well, I'm sorry to disappoint you, but interfere in my life again, and I'll make you regret it. Are we clear?"

Mrs Tate gave a taut nod, and Jasper turned, hurrying out of the shop and after Harriet. He looked up, irritated to see the sky was growing dark as the rain clouds gathered overhead. A fine drizzle began, swirling in the cooling air and clinging to his hair and clothes as he set off in search of Harriet.

It took him the best part of an hour to find her and, when he did, his heart sank. She was huddled on a bench in a quiet corner of the Grove. It was a small wooded area, surrounded by heathland on Mount Scion and a lovely place to stroll on a sunny day. With the weather worsening by the moment, the area was deserted, and Harriet looked small, alone, and deeply unhappy. Not to mention wet. The tree canopy overhead had saved her from the worst of the weather, but her clothes were damp already and the rain was falling harder now.

Jasper cursed Mrs Tate, and then himself for ever having had anything to do with her. He'd been winning Harriet over, he'd felt certain of it, but now....

"Harry," he said, approaching her as he might a skittish horse, afraid she'd bolt at the least provocation. "Harry," he said again, his heart clenching as she didn't answer him, but just stared straight ahead.

"It will always be like this, Jasper," she said, her voice expressionless. "No matter how you feel now, whether or not I believe you are in love with me, there will always be women like Mrs Tate."

"N-No, Harriet, I wouldn't...."

She lifted a hand, silencing him. "Even if that's true, I will always wonder." She looked up at him and he could see she'd been crying, her eyes wider than ever and reddened behind her spectacles. "You're handsome and rich and powerful, and beautiful women will always put themselves in your path. Far more beautiful than me. The kind of women who can be witty and amusing and please you in the bedroom. Can you honestly tell me you'll never be tempted, in five years, in ten... when whatever novelty there is in having such an odd bookworm for your wife has worn off?"

"I don't want anyone but you, Harry," Jasper said helplessly.

"But don't you see?" A tear slid down her cheek. "Even if that's true, I'll always wonder. I'll always be frightened that the next time you might be tempted, and I think that might drive me mad, Jasper. It's certainly not fair on you."

"No," Jasper said, shaking his head. He got to his knees before her, unheeding of the dirt or the fact that the rain was falling more heavily by the moment, soaking into his coat and running down the back of his neck. "I'll never be tempted, Harry, because there's only ever been you."

She gave an impatient little huff of laughter. "You mean like the day you left for Russia, when you kissed me and asked me not to marry anyone else, and not twenty minutes later I heard you tell Peter Winslow not to be so bloody ridiculous when he asked if you were interested in me? Is that your idea of devotion, Jasper? For I tell you now, it isn't mine."

Jasper stared at her in shock, astonished that he'd understood it at last and that it was so outrageously bloody senseless.

"That's why...?" he said, his voice hoarse. "That's why you've hated me all these years? Because...." He stared at her, unsure of whether to laugh or cry.

"Partly," she agreed with a stiff nod.

"Oh, Harry. Oh, love, if only you'd said, dear God." He put his head in his hands and took a deep breath before he was calm enough to speak again. "Harry," he said, his voice not entirely steady. "Peter Winslow was a spiteful little prick, and I hated him, and he me. He's been jealous of me since... since I can't even remember. If he'd known you were important to me, he'd have ruined it. He'd have whispered malicious gossip in your ear or...." He paused as the shocked expression that had entered her eyes at his words deepened. "Christ," he said, shaking his head. "The little shit. I'll bloody kill him. What did he say, Harry?"

Harry blinked hard, her eyes too bright and her voice thick. "He... he said he'd heard from his father who'd written to tell him how popular you were and how... how all the women were fawning over you. He said you were—"

Jasper felt rage surge through him and promised himself the pleasure of putting an end to Peter Winslow's chances of fathering a child any time soon.

"I can imagine what he said," he growled, beside himself with frustration and bitterness that so much bloody time had been wasted. His anger mounted, his voice growing strident. "It wasn't true, Harry. There was no one. Good Lord, that was likely the only period of my life when I returned home and saw how pleased my father was with me because I'd behaved myself and not caused any trouble, *and it was all for you, Harry*!" he shouted this last, overcome with emotion.

Harriet stared at him. "I... I can't believe it," she said, staring at him through rain speckled spectacles, her hair dripping as the rain came down and neither of them moved. "Y-You never wrote to me, Jasper, not once. Not once in a whole year—"

"You never wrote either!" Jasper snapped back, too aware of how he could have resolved everything with such ease if he'd only been able to write to her. If he'd written to her, reassuring her of his feelings, she'd never had doubted him, but he'd been too aware of how a letter from him would look, how stupid it would make him appear to someone as clever as Harriet. His stomach churned with guilt and regret. "For God's sake, Harry. We can't talk here; you'll catch your death."

He pulled her to her feet, tugging her with him, intending to take her back to the carriage. They'd have to endure a bloody carriage ride in company, but the minute they got back he was taking her to his bed and leaving her in no uncertain terms of his feelings.

At that moment the heavens opened, the rain falling in sheets and Jasper guided them under the relative shelter of a huge oak tree.

"Thank goodness there's no thunder this time," he said, turning to look at Harriet, and finding such a look in her eyes that his heart did a strange little somersault in his chest. She reached for him, grabbing at his neck, pulling his head towards hers and kissing him as if the world was about to end. There was desperation in the way she clung to him, as if she couldn't ever get close enough.

"Harry," he said between kisses, his heart soaring because she wanted him, damn it, but his head was telling him she was wet and cold, and they needed to get warm and dry as soon as they could. He tried to pull back. "Harry, love…." he protested, but Harriet's mouth was hot and urgent and then her hand reached between them, cupping him through his breeches.

Jasper's breath caught in his throat, sense going out of the window on a rising tide of desire. He pulled her closer, his hands cupping her behind as she tugged at his buttons, freeing him.

Jasper hissed with a combination of pain and pleasure as her cold little hand curled about his overheated flesh. They were hidden beneath the trees here, at least, and no one was mad enough to be out walking in this weather. Besides, they were marrying now, no question. There was no other possible outcome. He tugged at Harriet's skirts, aware they were damp and clinging to her, but too far gone to care. Hiking them up, he backed her up against the tree, lifting her until her legs wrapped around his waist. He drove inside her in a swift movement that made them both cry out.

She clung to his neck, feverish with excitement, clutching at his hair as he thrust into her over and again.

"Yes," she cried, the breathless sounds of her pleasure driving him on as the sheer mad, reckless joy of it overtook him.

After so long of wanting, of believing he'd lost her, she was here and mad for him, and he was losing his bloody mind.

"Jasper," she said, the sound of his name filled with the same combination of wonder at the sheer lunacy of what they were doing. "Jasper," she said, again, his name lost against the noise of the wind and the rain as her body began to tighten around him, sending him towards the edge. She jolted in his arms, clinging to him and crying out as Jasper swallowed the sound of her pleasure and followed her into ecstasy.

Chapter 14

Dearest Alice,

It was so lovely to hear from you. I am glad to know you and Nate are so happy, though I'm hardly surprised. I am sorry to hear about the morning sickness, but I'm so excited to be an Auntie I'm afraid I can't be <u>that</u> sympathetic, I'm too pleased by the idea of a niece or nephew to fuss over. I will be sure to visit you when we are both back in town and look forward to discovering if you've grown frightfully fat!

— *Excerpt of a letter from Miss Matilda Hunt to Mrs Alice Hunt.*

1st September 1814. Holbrooke House, Sussex.

Harriet endured the carriage ride home in a kind of daze. Jasper sat close to her, the warmth of his thigh burning against hers, but she was chilled to the bone. The heat of their lovemaking had long since faded, though her cheeks felt warm enough if she considered what she'd done. Heavens, she must have been mad. In The Grove of all places, in public! What kind of licentious creature was she becoming?

She slanted a glance at Jasper, well aware of why she was suddenly capable of such wanton behaviour. The man was like a drug; the more you had of him the more you needed. No wonder Mrs Tate had been so miffed to lose him. Harriet pushed thoughts of Mrs Tate away with irritation. She believed Jasper had no interest in the woman, but her words had been true, too. There would always be the Mrs Tates of this world, trying to steal her husband away from her.

Well, let them try. The thought was raw and savage, and she knew she'd made her decision. She would marry Jasper, and pray it didn't end in tears. It was all she could do, for she could not bring herself to walk away from him. If she did, she would always wonder *what if* and that would make her more miserable than anything else. If their marriage failed, at least she'd know she'd tried, and she'd always have her work, and maybe there would be children too.

Harriet smoothed a hand over her belly and looked down, wondering if even now his seed was growing inside of her. She looked up, aware of eyes upon her, but Minerva and Matilda were both dozing as the carriage made its way back to Holbrooke House. Turning, she found Jasper staring down at her, such a soft look in his eyes as he regarded the hand that lay upon her stomach, she knew he'd guessed her train of thought. He reached over and took her hand, raising it to his lips and kissing her fingers.

"Harry, darling, you're frozen," he said, shaking his head.

He'd already stripped off his coat and put it around her shoulders, but now he put his arms about her and tugged her close.

"I'll have a hot bath drawn for you as soon as we get in. Then, something to eat and a tot of brandy… and straight to bed," he murmured in her ear, the words making her shiver harder. "And I'll make sure you're warm all the way through."

"Jasper!" she whispered, scandalised that he should say such things with Minerva and Matilda in the carriage, even if they were asleep.

He chuckled and leant down to kiss her temple. "I love you."

Harriet smiled up at him, longing to say the same in return, for she did, there was no point in denying it. Yet, it didn't seem right to say the words now, not until she had seen Inigo and explained that she wouldn't be marrying him. Once she was free of their engagement, she would tell Jasper that she loved him, that she had always loved him, and she always would, and then... then they would see where that led them.

As soon as they arrived home, Harriet rushed upstairs but asked her maid to delay the bath Jasper had ordered for her with regret. It sounded a wonderful idea, as she was chilled through and the headache that had plagued her all day was worsening steadily. Instead, she sent her maid off, asking that a carriage be readied for her at once. Harriet changed her sodden clothes, her skin prickling with gooseflesh even as she stood before the fire. Once she was dressed in warm clothes, she redid her hair as best she could and hurried back downstairs.

The weather had improved none in the time it had taken Harriet to change and rain hammered on the roof of the carriage, making her feel she was sitting on the inside of a drum. She closed her eyes against the din that did nothing to ease her aching head and tried to ignore the fact she was bone-weary and her throat was sore.

It was only a journey of half an hour to the inn where Inigo was staying, but the place was bustling. Outside, three carriages took up all the available space as they'd stopped as close to the entrance as possible to allow the guests to enter without getting drenched.

Harriet cursed; she had no choice but to make a run for it. She jumped down, and her feet were immediately soaked. The ground was saturated and the rain still fell heavily. Skirts in hand, she ran pell-mell for the door but, by the time she reached it, she was drenched to her shift for the second time that day. Shivering, she hurried inside and asked for Mr de Beauvoir.

The inn was so overrun with unexpected guests driven in by the terrible weather that it was a while before anyone found the man in question. When he appeared, he looked at Harriet in dismay.

"Miss Stanhope," he exclaimed, looking her over. "My word, you're wet through. Come into the parlour before you catch your death."

Harriet did as he asked, grateful to stand and warm her hands by the fire; they were blue with cold and she felt quite unwell now. "I'm s-sorry to arrive unannounced like this," she stammered through chattering teeth, "but I had to speak with you."

"Well, it must be urgent to bring you out on a night like this," he said, shaking his head.

"It is," Harriet agreed. "I felt I must tell you at once that... that I intend to marry Lord St Clair."

"Ah."

Harriet let out a sigh as he smiled at her. Thank goodness he wasn't angry.

"Well, then let me be the first to congratulate you."

"You're not upset?" she asked, relief washing through her.

"Well, I am disappointed, naturally. But we are friends I hope, Miss Stanhope, and I see no reason for that to change?"

"Oh, I'm so glad," Harriet said, pushing her wet hair from her forehead. "I just... I felt I must tell you at once. It seemed wrong otherwise."

"I quite understand. He's a very handsome and charming man, not to mention titled and rich. Any woman would be tempted, I'm sure."

Harriet stared at him, suddenly rather angry, though she wasn't entirely sure why. Jasper was all those things, but that wasn't *why* she loved him. In some ways she loved him despite those things, as his beauty and charm terrified her the most, and made her fear she would lose him in the end.

"That's not...." she began, shaking her head as her brain seemed suddenly full of fog. "That's not why," she said, determined to get her point across. "I love him. I always have. Ever since we were children. He says it's the same for him, too." She smiled at Inigo's bemused expression and her anger faded as she realised he didn't understand. "I think you are without a doubt the most brilliant man I have ever known. However, even brilliant men make mistakes. You are wrong about love, Inigo. There is far more to it than you suppose. I hope you discover that for yourself one day."

His bemusement turned to a frown, and he shook his head, the movement curt and decisive. "I have no time for such fancies. My love—if there is such a thing—is for my work alone. You understood that which was why our arrangement suited me. There is no space in my life for a romantic attachment, certainly not for love, even if I acknowledged such a sentiment. I could certainly never love a woman who was not my intellectual equal. What a pitiful excuse for a husband I would make if I even tried, which I have no desire to do. It would be a cruel thing to marry a woman who had no interest in my work and was destined to be ignored, as she would always come second to it. No. If you have any kindness for me at all, you would do well to wish me to find a likeminded lady, whose passions are reserved for science, or to remain a bachelor, content with his lot."

"As you like, Inigo," Harriet said with a smile. She was feeling a little dazed now and not altogether as though she could remain standing much longer. "I'd best leave you now, before I'm missed."

"Yes, you must get home and get warm, Miss Stanhope. Whilst I appreciate the sentiment, I cannot help but feel you would have done better not to have come. You don't look terribly well."

Harriet nodded and mumbled something, she wasn't entirely sure what, and then waited while Inigo searched for an umbrella so she didn't get even wetter on her return to the carriage. Once inside, Harriet put her head back against the squabs. She felt distinctly odd, exhausted and cold to the bone, her body wracked with shivers. Succumbing to the desire to sleep, she slid down so she could lie across the seat and closed her eyes.

***

Jasper took out his pocket watch and frowned at it. He'd had supper sent to Harriet's room, but he'd imagined she'd be finished by now. Deciding there was very little point in bothering with propriety after this afternoon's little escapade—especially given he could trust all the remaining guests—he went directly to her room.

He'd just raised his hand to knock when a commotion in the hallway downstairs drew his attention and he moved back along the corridor until he could look over the bannister. There were shouts and exclamations and Jasper frowned, moving towards the stairs and hurrying down in case he was needed.

"What is it, Temple?" Jasper called, and then stopped in his tracks as a footman carried something into the house. No, not something, *someone*. A woman.

Oh, God.

Jasper raced down the stairs, staring at Harriet. She was flushed, feverish, and wet through once again. What the bloody hell had she been doing?

"Harriet!" he exclaimed, putting his hand to her face and finding it hot beneath his touch. "Give her here," he said, taking her from the footman. Harriet mumbled something and turned her face into his neck. "Temple, fetch my mother, and send for Doctor Haysom at once."

"Yes, my lord," Temple replied, barking instructions and sending the staff running.

Jasper carried Harriet back up the stairs. "What have you been playing at, you little fool?" he asked, wanting to shake her. "You were supposed to be having a bath and getting warm, not going out in the rain again."

He kicked at her bedroom door, bringing her maid running to open it. The girl exclaimed with alarm as Jasper barged through, carrying Harriet in his arms. He deposited her on the bed.

"She needs these wet things taken off at once," he instructed, taking off Harriet's shoes and tossing them to the floor while the maid gaped at him in horror.

"Don't just stand there!" he shouted. "Get her clothes off."

"B-But, my lord," she stammered, staring at him with wide eyes.

"Oh, for heaven's sake, girl!" Jasper snarled, too impatient to deal with such inanity. "We're to be married, assuming she doesn't catch her death whilst you're dithering."

"Jasper! The girl is quite right. Out with you."

Jasper turned, at once relieved and incensed to see his mother arrive and take over.

"But…." he began, but his mother took his arm and gave him a warm smile, reaching up to pat his cheek.

"Just think how mortified Harriet will be when the gossip goes around the servants. Now, you leave her to me, and you can come in once she's comfortable. Away with you, now."

Jasper cursed, but the only important thing was that Harriet be cared for at once, so he waited outside. He paced up and down, wondering what had been so terribly important that Harriet had gone out again in such weather. What had been so urgent that she'd had to deal with it immediately, and risk making herself ill?

"Temple!" he shouted over the bannister. "Temple!"

He ran down the stairs to find his butler hurrying towards him. "My lord?"

"Where did Miss Stanhope go this evening?"

"I'm afraid I cannot say, my lord. Would you like me to ask the driver?"

Jasper nodded, frowning, before dismissing his butler and heading back up the stairs.

Chapter 15

Mr de Beauvoir,

It was so lovely to see you today, despite the odious Mrs Tate. I haven't yet begun reading the book we spoke of, but I intend to start after dinner this evening... providing I can stop daydreaming about your eyes, and the piercing way you have of looking at me. How I wish you might remember me this time, perhaps even think about me, as I am thinking of you....

— **Excerpt of a letter from Miss Minerva Butler, consigned to the fire.**

2nd September 1814. Holbrooke House, Sussex.

Matilda hurried along the corridor towards Lord St Clair, who had just exited Harriet's bedroom.

"My lord," she called after him, noting the fact he was wearing the same clothes he'd been in last night, and that he'd not yet shaved.

He looked tired and dispirited and, on seeing her, he stiffened, his expression wary.

"I can assure you there is no impropriety," he said, the words brittle. "Her maid is with her and my mother has been coming and going since daybreak."

"Oh, Lord St Clair, as if I give a hoot about such things," she said, shaking her head at him. "Me, of all people? I only wanted to enquire how she was. Is there anything I can do, anything at all?"

He sighed, rubbed a weary hand over his face, and shook his head. "Forgive me, Miss Hunt. I'm tired and… and scared to death, if you want the truth. She's burning up and…." He swallowed. "My father died of pneumonia."

"Oh, my lord," Matilda said, her heart clenching at the fear glittering in his eyes. "But surely Harriet is not at risk of…?" She stopped, unable to put it into words.

She watched St Clair swallow. "No," he said, his tone decisive. As though it would be because he decreed it, and that was that. "No, she is not. She is dreadfully unwell, but it is not yet pneumonia, and she has the best care, and… and I won't let her, damn it. Not now."

Matilda reached out and put her hand on his arm. "I thought Harriet looked happy yesterday, on the way back home. The way she smiled at you, I hoped—"

"So did I," he replied, the words edged with desperation. "But last night, instead of getting herself warm and dry, she went out again, into that bloody deluge. She went to visit Mr de Beauvoir, Miss Hunt. Now tell me, why would she do that?"

"I…." Matilda began, halted by the look of devastation in St Clair's eyes. "I'm perfectly sure there is a very good explanation," she said firmly. She stared at him, willing him to believe her, for she knew Harriet would not play either him or Mr de Beauvoir false. She was too inherently honest, to her own detriment sometimes. "Harriet is the most decent and loyal person I have ever known, and she would never treat you so shabbily. Surely you know that?"

St Clair swallowed hard and then gave a taut nod. "Yes. I do. I keep telling myself that and most of the time I believe it. Only…" He sighed and raked a hand through his hair. "I'm afraid I can't think very clearly at the moment. If you'd excuse me, Miss Hunt. My mother has refused to let me back in the room until I've bathed and changed."

"Of course," Matilda said, her heart full of sympathy for the poor man as he strode away from her.

***

Jasper looked up as he heard the bedroom door open, and sighed as he saw the maid tiptoe out for a moment. Not that he'd be left alone with Harriet for more than a few minutes; her bloody maid guarded her like a dog with a bone. The poor girl would probably die of outrage if she knew what they'd done in the park yesterday, in the rain....

God damn him for a bloody fool.

Guilt ripped through him. Harriet had been chilled to the bone then, and he'd known it, but he'd been too bloody consumed with his own needs to consider anything else. What the hell had he been thinking? Taking her up against a tree like a common strumpet, and in the pouring rain, too. He was a bloody filthy satyr, and if anything happened to her....

Anguish closed his throat, and he shied away from the idea, unable to finish the thought.

He would not watch Harriet slip from his grasp as his father had. It was just a fever, nothing more. It wasn't pneumonia, the doctor had said so. Yet, her hand was hot and dry when he reached for it and he lowered his head, pressing a kiss to her fingers.

He looked up as the door opened and his mother appeared. Jasper blinked hard and looked away. He heard the rustle of expensive fabric as Lady St Clair moved to stand beside him.

She laid her hands on his shoulder and pressed a kiss to the top of his head. "Stop fretting so, dearest. She's a strong young woman, and she has a great deal to do. Not to mention, she's one of the stubbornest creatures that was ever born. She's not going anywhere, I promise you, and Dr Haysom agreed there was no undue cause for alarm, did he not?"

Jasper looked up into his mother's beautiful face, filled with the childish desire to believe her without question. Her expression was serene; she clearly believed it, and the doctor *had* said as much.... Something in his chest unwound just a little, and he took her hand and held it to his cheek. "Thank you."

"Of course, my darling boy. Now, I am going to sit with my soon-to-be daughter-in-law, and you will have something to eat. Merrick tattled on you, I'm afraid, so don't tell me you had a hearty breakfast, for I know you did not. There's not a bit of use trying to convince me that half a slice of toast is sufficient for a man of your size, so... run along now."

She made a shooing motion and Jasper knew better than to argue. With a long-suffering sigh, he cast one last look at Harriet and got to his feet.

"You'll call me, if...."

Lady St Clair gave him a look that told him he was an idiot.

"Yes, of course you will. Thank you, Mother."

She inclined her head graciously and seated herself in the chair he'd just vacated, so Jasper had no choice but to leave her to it. Once outside, he realised he really was famished, and he was halfway down the stairs when Temple showed a visitor into the grand entrance hall.

"You!" Jasper growled.

Whether it was a sleepless night sitting by Harriet's bedside whilst she sweated out a fever, or simply the fact he'd been longing to knock the fellow's block off since the first moment he'd seen him, Jasper wasn't entirely sure. He certainly didn't care. All he knew was that he was simmering with too much pent-up emotion and the safety valve had failed. He exploded across the hallway, grasped Mr de Beauvoir by his none too tidy cravat, and hit him.

***

Minerva frowned down at the book in her hand.

Much to her astonishment, she discovered she had been entirely absorbed in it for over two hours. Two hours! Not only that, but it had been written in such a way that she didn't feel like a brainless ninny. In fact, the book was laid out in the manner of a conversation between three women, Caroline and Emily—who began with every bit as much trepidation on the subject of chemistry as Minerva had herself—and Mrs B, their instructress. The first conversation—that on the difference between decomposing a body and merely chopping it into bits—had shocked Minerva to her bones in the most delightful manner, and now she was riveted. She had already learned that 'we *decompose* a body into its *constituent* parts; and *divide* it into its *integrant* parts' and was feeling very pleased with herself.

Now, however, her stomach was growling, and she began to wonder what time it was as she uncurled herself from the delightfully comfy chair she'd been glued to in the library. Setting her book to one side, she stretched and sighed, then got to her feet and retrieved her shoes from where she'd kicked them off. Her hand was on the doorknob when she heard the crash.

It was followed swiftly by raised voices, and Minerva flung open the door to see... good heavens! St Clair and Mr de Beauvoir on the floor... *fighting.*

For a moment, St Clair seemed to have the upper hand as de Beauvoir's nose was bloodied, and it looked as if the earl was about to get in another blow when his opponent raised his knee in a sharp movement than even made Minerva wince.

St Clair doubled up, groaning, allowing de Beauvoir enough time to get to his feet, though his relief was short-lived. Lord St

Clair scrambled up and would have lunged for de Beauvoir again, except….

Minerva gasped, staring up at St Clair's wild turquoise eyes as she put herself between the two brawling men.

"M-My lord," she stammered. "S-Surely there is some misunderstanding?"

"Is there?" St Clair growled, chest heaving. "Then why was Harriet with him last night? Why did she go out in the bloody rain for a second time? Why is she in her room burning up with fever, tell me that!"

"Oh, for the love of…!" de Beauvoir exclaimed, accepting the handkerchief Minerva handed him to stem the flow of blood. "She came to tell me she was in love with you, you blithering imbecile," he said, the words slightly muffled. "Not," he added with fury, "that I can think of a single reason why such an intelligent woman would do something to patently idiotic. However, she seemed to think you were worthy of her and had decided to marry you instead of me. Being a scrupulously honest sort, she felt the need to tell me at once that she'd made her decision and you were her choice. You must forgive me, *my lord*," he sneered, "if I suspect she's made a grave error in judgement."

Minerva stood between the two men, feeling a little like a defenceless bunny keeping two wolves apart, until the prickling tension between them dissipated.

"Oh," Jasper said, clearly at a loss for anything more eloquent.

"*Oh*," de Beauvoir mimicked, which Minerva had to admit wasn't terribly helpful.

She might have tried harder to make peace between them, but she was still reeling from the idea that de Beauvoir had been engaged to Harriet and she'd not known. Good heavens, she'd been dreaming of her friend's fiancé! The idea made her feel nauseous until she reminded herself that they were no longer engaged, and that de Beauvoir didn't seem terribly distraught about it. Then she compared herself to Harriet, and the nauseous sensation returned with a vengeance.

"De Beauvoir, I... I owe you an apology," St Clair said, running a not entirely steady hand through his hair. "The truth is Harriet arrived last night, soaking wet and out of her head with fever, and... and I've been up all night worrying and I think perhaps I lost my mind."

Minerva watched as de Beauvoir's face tensed with anxiety. "How sick is she?"

St Clair shrugged. "I'm advised by the doctor that she should make a good recovery, only...." The earl let out a breath. "My father died from an illness that began very much like this, and—"

De Beauvoir nodded. "There's no need to explain, and I accept your apology. I only came to assure myself that she was well. I could see she wasn't herself last night, and I told her it was a damn fool thing to have done. Confound her, she could have very well waited until the morning, but... well, she's a stubborn woman."

The earl smiled and nodded. "That she is."

"Jasper!"

Everyone looked up to see Lady St Clair leaning over the balcony. "Oh, good day, Mr de Beauvoir," she said, before crooking a finger at her son. "Jasper, there's someone who wishes to see you."

The earl let out a breath and didn't even stop to make his excuses. He bounded up the stairs, two at a time, and never looked back. This left Minerva and Mr de Beauvoir alone together, the servants having made a discreet exit once they were certain their master would not do murder before their eyes.

Minerva dithered for a moment before summoning a footman. "I need warm water, tincture of arnica, and some clean cloths brought to the library at once, if you would, please. Oh, and bring some tea and sandwiches too. Mr de Beauvoir has had a trying morning, I fear."

"If you'd like to come through, Mr de Beauvoir," she said, smiling at him as her heart thudded with delight at the unexpected prospect of playing nursemaid to his wounds.

"There's really no need, Miss Butler," he said, hesitating.

His dark brows were drawn together, and he was looking at her as though he suspected her of having ulterior motives. He really was clever.

"If you could see yourself you would think otherwise," Minerva said, taking his arm and guiding him to the library. Though she was rather surprised by her own boldness, being alone with him was far from the rigorous notions of propriety she'd always followed, after all, but she would not let the fellow get away that easily. "I'll ask Temple if a clean cravat can be found. Yours is covered in blood. And we must get something on that eye; it's swelling at quite a rate."

De Beauvoir grunted, but seemed to recognise a lost battle when he saw one, and allowed Minerva to bear him off to the library.

She settled him in a chair by the fire with a plate of sandwiches and a cup of tea and then drew up a footstool, arranging the bowl of water and other items on a small table beside her while he ate. Minerva shot him a sideways glance as he inhaled the sandwiches and she wondered when he had last eaten. His large frame was far too gaunt.

Once her supplies were in order, and he'd finished eating, she set to work.

"I can manage perfectly well," he insisted, trying once more to avert the ministrations of his angel of mercy, but Minerva just rolled her eyes at him.

"You can't see the damage. I can," she remonstrated. "So do stop being such a baby."

"I am not...." he began indignantly before recognising the teasing look in her eyes and giving a huff of resignation. "Why is it women feel the need to tend a fellow's wounds? I'm perfectly capable, I assure you."

"We feel the need because we know quite well that you'll just wipe off the blood with your handkerchief and leave whatever injury is left to fester. Just like you've left that button on your coat hanging loose. It's about to fall off, you know," Minerva added, shaking her head at him.

"My buttons are my own affair," he muttered, looking so adorably sulky that Minerva had to bite her lip to stop from laughing.

"Don't you have a housekeeper, at least?" Minerva enquired, beyond curious to know more about him.

He frowned—which seemed to be his natural expression—and looked vaguely uncomfortable. "She gave notice and left six weeks ago. I've not had the time to engage another," he added, crossing his arms tightly as Minerva wrung out a clean cloth and began dabbing at the blood on his face.

"Ow!" he said, jerking away from her.

Minerva tutted and took hold of his chin with her free hand, holding him in place. "Why did she leave?" she asked, having to expend considerable effort to keep her voice even and not all breathless and bothered as it ought to be, because she was.

She could feel the prickly rasp of whiskers along the uncompromising line of his jaw, and it was doing odd things to her heart.

"There was an... explosion," he admitted.

Minerva looked at him. "An explosion," she repeated, amused at the flash of guilt in his eyes, as if he'd just admitted to kicking a ball through a window.

"It was *supposed* to explode," he said, clearly irritable, which for some bizarre reason only made Minerva want to hug him. What was wrong with her? "I just forgot to warn Mrs Thompson that there might be a… a bang, and she pitched a fit. The ridiculous woman accused me of trying to blow her up and said…." He stopped and then huffed as Minerva waited for him to finish. He rolled his eyes. "She accused me of being some manner of warlock."

Minerva sniggered.

"Oh, dear," she said, failing to keep her voice entirely even. "What a trying time you've been having of late, and now you've lost your only hope to the call of her one true love."

That was clearly too much, and he batted her hand away. "Please," he said, revolted. "They are two attractive, healthy adults. It's nothing more than lust, a chemical reaction; a primitive desire to procreate. No more, no less."

Minerva felt her colour rise at his words and saw a glimmer of satisfaction in his eyes at having shocked her. Something devilish stirred in her chest as her temper flickered to life. The desire to show him that he may well be a brilliant man, but he was also remarkably stupid was irresistible.

"So, it would be that way between any man and any woman?" she asked, looking at him with wide eyes.

He frowned, apparently giving the question due consideration. "No," he allowed, shaking his head. "There are preferences, I'll grant you. For example, I cannot compete with St Clair's looks and I shouldn't pretend to, nor his money," he added. "Physical appearance weighs heavily with most people, naturally. The prettier the female, the more popular she is and vice versa. Though men are a deal less picky than women until they are forced to wed."

Minerva nodded gravely.

"Yes, I see." She pursed her lips, considering his words and wondering how best to go about riling him. "So, when a man and a woman kiss, there is a chemical reaction between them that women wrongly identify as love, when it is nothing but lust. Is that correct?"

He shifted in his seat, clearly a little uncomfortable with the turn the conversation had taken, which was entirely his own fault.

"Not just women. I've known perfectly rational men become similarly afflicted by overwrought emotions."

"So afflicted that they hurried down the aisle?" she guessed, her tone innocent as she suppressed a smile.

"Quite."

"But a man of science, a man such as yourself, you must be far more objective, I imagine. You could never confuse attraction, or lust, for anything other than what it was?"

"No, of course not."

"But what about me?" she asked, and it was no effort to make her voice low and breathless for her chest was tight with anticipation. "How can I tell the difference between love and lust? For… I believe I may be in danger of making a dreadful mistake."

His expression darkened and what little remained of her breath was trapped in her lungs as those piercing grey-green eyes focused on her. "Is some blackguard toying with your affections, Miss Butler? If so, you need only tell me his name and I shall send him on his way. I hope… I hope you've not been *indiscreet*?" he asked, and Minerva was gratified that there seemed something like concern in his expression.

"Not yet," she murmured, staring at him and wondering if she'd entirely lost her mind. "But… But I'm fascinated, and I think… I think I could fall in love very easily indeed."

"It is not love, Miss Butler," he insisted, the words harsh. "At best, it is nothing but a brief infatuation. It will pass, and I implore you not to do anything foolish—"

"Too late," Minerva said, and leaned in and kissed him.

For a moment his lips were warm beneath hers, and impossibly soft. How odd. She'd not expected that, and then he jerked away from her and stumbled to his feet, staring at her as though she were some manner of venomous snake.

"I'll not play the fool for you, Miss Butler, if that was your aim," he said with icy disdain, practically vibrating with fury. "Did you think I would fall at your pretty feet? Try your wiles on another man, one more receptive to such lures, for you'll not reel me in. Good day to you."

With that he stalked from the room, slamming the door behind him.

Minerva jolted as the sound reverberated around the room and then touched her fingers to her lips. *Well, at least he thinks my feet are pretty*, she thought with a sigh.

Chapter 16

Mr de Beauvoir,

I am so sorry that you met with such a violent reception when you came to visit me. I know Lord St Clair regrets his actions but please understand it was out of worry for me. I hope you can forgive us both. I am making a good recovery and will resolve not to stand in the rain again any time soon.

— **Excerpt of a letter from Miss Harriet Stanhope to Mr Inigo de Beauvoir.**

2nd September 1814. Holbrooke House, Sussex.

Harriet smiled as Jasper hurried into the room and sank to his knees beside the bed.

"Harry," he said, taking her hand and holding it to his lips. "God, Harry, you gave me such a scare, love."

"I'm sorry," she said, meaning it.

She knew how his father had died and remembered the days it had taken him to pass, with each breath more difficult and excruciating to endure, and the violent cough that had made him cry out with pain. The late earl had been a larger-than-life figure, a charming rogue, yet devoted to his wife and children. His death had devastated all of them and had hit Jasper especially hard. Despite the front he put on for his mother's sake, she'd suspected he'd felt himself ill-equipped to take on the earldom at such a young age.

"Don't frighten me like that again, please," he said, closing his eyes and letting out a breath. "I… I'm afraid I might have gone a little bit mad."

Harriet frowned at him, wondering what he meant. Her head ached, her eyes were sore, and she felt as if she'd swallowed broken glass.

"What?" she asked, which was as much effort as she could manage.

"They carried in you from the carriage last night," he said. "Soaked to the bone, *again*," he added, glaring at her. Harriet might have blushed with remorse if she hadn't already been feverish. "Then I discover you'd been to see de Beauvoir."

Harriet's heart skipped. Oh, good Lord, what had he done? Visions of pistols at dawn and heaven alone what else filled her fever dazed brain. "N-No, Jasper, you don't understand…." she rasped, forcing the words past her sore throat.

"Hush," he said, smiling at her. "I do understand. De Beauvoir told me why you'd gone to see him. Sadly, he didn't manage to say it before I knocked him on his arse."

Harriet groaned.

"It's all right. I apologised," Jasper said, grinning at her. "I don't think I'm his favourite person, but he won't call me out."

She let out a huff of laughter, which quickly turned to a hacking cough, and Jasper fussed over her, plumping her pillows and helping her sit up before he fetched her a glass of water.

"Better?" he asked anxiously, when the coughing fit had subsided.

Harriet nodded, sighed, and lay back against the pillows.

"What did he tell you, Jasper?" she asked.

Jasper took her hand again and laid it against his cheek, before turning his head into it and pressing his lips to her palm. Harriet shivered.

"I think you know," he said softly.

He looked up at her and her breath caught. He was so beautiful it hurt to look at him, and it was so hard to believe she could hold on to such a man. Yet here she was, feverish and ill—heaven alone knew what state her hair was in, she must look an utter fright—and he was still looking at her with adoration. His brain must be addled, she decided, and tried to remember if Lady St Clair had ever mentioned that he'd been dropped on his head as a child.

"I love you," she said, because she had to, because he deserved to hear it after all this time.

To her astonishment his eyes grew bright, and he blinked hard before giving a rueful little laugh.

"Thank God," he said, his voice almost as rough as hers. "Thank you, God, and thank you most of all, my darling girl. I love you too, and I shan't let you down. I promise."

Harriet nodded as exhaustion tugged at her eyelids. She was so very pleased to have pleased him and, with a contented sigh, she went back to sleep.

***

7th September 1814. Holbrooke House, Sussex.

Jasper made a nuisance of himself for the next few days, driving Harriet's poor maid to distraction as he fussed and rearranged everything she'd already arranged perfectly well, but he felt as if he'd go mad with nothing to do.

Harriet slept a great deal at first but, as the days passed, she improved, the fever abating and a healthier tinge returning to her cheeks. This morning, when he entered her room, she was sitting up in bed and looking far brighter.

"Good morning, love. How are you feeling?"

"Bored," Harriet said with a huff. "I want to get up, but that stupid doctor says I can't, until tomorrow at the earliest."

"You're adorable when you're grumpy, did you know that?" Jasper said, smiling as he bent to kiss her forehead.

"I'm never adorable," Harriet replied, wrinkling her nose.

"I beg to differ. Now," he said, pulling up a chair and sitting down beside her. "We have a wedding to plan."

Harriet groaned.

"Well, that's the kind of thing that can hurt a fellow's feelings, love," Jasper said, shaking his head at her, well aware it wasn't the marriage she objected to now, just the fuss.

"I didn't mean it like that," she said quickly and then caught the amusement in his eyes. "Oh, Jasper, I can't bear it. All those people staring at me and wondering how I trapped you into it."

Jasper felt his temper rise at the idea. "I have already made it very clear to anyone who cares to listen, that *I* trapped *you*," he said, which was perfectly true, but Harriet just snorted.

"Oh, they'll just think you're being a gentleman and saving my reputation," she said irritably.

"Not when they see how devoted a husband I am, trailing around after you like a little lamb."

Harriet snorted again, though she looked amused this time. "You? A little lamb?"

"Baaaa."

She snickered and shook her head. "Foolish man," she said, but with such affection in her tone that Jasper felt his heart swell. She loved him. It seemed utterly impossible, but she'd said so, and Harriet never lied.

Don't mess it up, St Clair, he warned himself.

"How about a private wedding, in the chapel here? Just you and me, our brothers I suppose," he added with a long-suffering sigh. "And whatever peculiar women you wish to invite."

"Peculiar Ladies," Harriet corrected sternly, before sighing and reaching out to take his hand. "Oh, Jasper, that sounds perfect, but don't you mind? Won't your mother be dreadfully disappointed? I imagine she's been longing to arrange some grand affair."

"I'll talk to her," he said, smoothing his thumb back and forth over her hand, still finding it hard to believe that she had reached for him, that she *wanted* him.

Anxiety lingered in his heart, the fear that she wanted him against her will, that she knew as well as he did that she'd likely grow bored with him. *No, she loves me*, he reminded himself, and not just for his handsome face, not just because of how he made her feel in bed, there was more to it than that, wasn't there?

An unpleasant thread of panic uncoiled in his belly and he swallowed it down.

"I want to marry as soon as we can arrange it," he said, assuring himself he wasn't saying it to tie her to him, to ensure she couldn't ever leave him, wouldn't have time to come to her senses and change her mind.

"I think we must," she said with a sigh. "I can only imagine what's being said about me."

"No one will say a damn thing," he assured her. "Not if they know what's good for them."

She sighed and pressed a hand to her heart. "I do love it when you're all masterful and growly."

Jasper snorted, aware he was being teased. "Wretch."

Her face softened and there was an odd quivering sensation in his heart.

"I love you, Jasper. I always have. You do know that, don't you?"

He swallowed hard, still unused to this extraordinary revelation, but he nodded, too overcome to speak.

"I can't wait to get out of this bed," she said, closing her eyes for a moment.

"I can't wait to get you back in mine," he countered, finding his voice again and enjoying the bloom of colour in her cheeks.

She ignored the comment, though her lips twitched.

"I must warn you that Mother is making plans for a grand ball for our engagement party," he said, smiling at her appalled expression.

Harriet shrugged, her lips quirking. "Oh, well, I owe her that much, if she's not getting the big wedding she hoped for," she said with a sigh. "Tell her I approve everything, whatever she wants. I'm in her hands."

"That will please her," Jasper said, nodding with approval.

She sighed and turned to look towards the window and the little patches of blue sky visible outside. "I'm so bored," she complained, the closest thing to a whine he'd ever heard from her. "I can't even read because it makes my head hurt."

"Poor darling," he said, his voice soothing as he leaned over and pressed a kiss to her nose. "You should rest."

"I don't want to rest," she muttered, "I want to do something. Oh," she said, brightening and sitting up straighter. "You could read to me. Please, Jasper, or I think I'll go mad."

Jasper knew a moment of sheer panic. He grew hot, then cold, and then a clammy combination of the two settled over his skin.

"I-I...." he stammered, terrified that she'd discover his secret at last. He knew he had to tell her one day, *must* tell her, but he hadn't been prepared to do it so soon, not before they were married at least. He wasn't ready.

His panic was such that it sent any possibility of coming up with a reasonable excuse vanishing in an unlikely puff of smoke, like a bad magician. All at once, he was eight years old with his tutor breathing down his neck and telling him not to be so bloody absurd, telling him he was doing it on purpose when he discovered the notes Jasper had struggled over for hours were a splotched mess, and many of the words or letters were back to front.

The man had been furious with him, thinking he'd been messing about, and Jasper had been so sick with humiliation and frustration that he'd snatched up the ink pot from the stand and hurled it to the ground. There had been something satisfying in the crash it made, and the way the black ink had splattered everything, covering his tutor head to foot in black splotches and speckles.

That had been the beginning of a lifetime of bad behaviour, of shunning his schoolwork and pretending he didn't care, when he cared more than anyone could imagine.

"I can't...." he said, pushing to his feet. "I... I must do... *something*. I forgot, sorry, darling... I'll come back later...."

Feeling like a cad and an utter fool, Jasper rushed from the room. Once outside he leaned against the wall, his stomach tied in such a knot he thought he might be sick. *Oh, God. Oh, God.* She would find him out. She would realise he was a bloody half-wit and then she'd refuse to marry him. What if their children inherited his brains instead of hers? What if....

Stop it, he told himself, forcing the panic down again as he'd taught himself to do. He'd get around it. He always got around it. Perhaps he could memorise the first chapter of a book by heart. No, there wasn't enough time. It would take him ages, and the only way to manage it was by getting someone to read him the piece over and over as he pictured the words in his head until he could recite it back. He'd managed many awkward situations in such a way over the years, but Harriet would be long recovered by the time he could do it with confidence.

He ran down the stairs and headed outside, running to the one place no one ever disturbed him.

It was quite a walk to Jasper's sanctuary, which lay on the farthest edge of the home farm: a large, well-lit space in one of the many outbuildings required to serve an estate as vast and opulent as Holbrooke House. This place was strictly out of bounds to everyone, and Jasper had never even let a maid in to clean or sweep, preferring to do such tasks himself. The windows were high on the walls, giving plenty of light but allowing no one to look in, or Jasper to look out.

He let out a breath as he closed the door behind him and leaned against it with relief. The sweet scent of sawdust and drying wood filled the air, and eased the panic that was clawing at his chest and making his throat tight. Taking a moment to lock the door, Jasper removed his perfectly tailored coat and reached for a lightweight, loose fitting version that reached to his knees and covered his expensive clothing. His boots would get covered with dust, and poor Merrick would sigh reproachfully, but there was no help for it.

Jasper moved into the workshop, his hands trailing over chisels and tools the like of which the Earl of St Clair ought never to touch. He turned his hands palm up, amused to see the calluses there, like any common workman. This was where he came when he needed to get away, when his frustration with his own inadequacies left him feeling like a failure, and when his longing for Harriet's approval bit too deeply.

With a sigh, he selected the chisel he needed, and went to work.

***

Harriet regarded the door Jasper had just gone through—practically at a run—and frowned.

Her first reaction had been one of profound hurt and indignation that he couldn't be bothered to sit and read to her to alleviate her boredom. Yet, he'd sat with her for hours, seemingly perfectly content to keep her company, even when she was sleeping. No, it wasn't unwillingness to entertain her or stay in her company. So, why had he run as if the room was on fire? She'd seen the panic in his eyes when she'd suggested he read to her; it was the closest thing to terror she'd ever witnessed in her life.

The idea unsettled her. What on earth should make Jasper feel so afraid? Try as she might, she couldn't understand it. He'd tormented her for years about her cleverness, though she understood now that he'd done it for her attention, idiotic as that seemed to her. Men were odd creatures and no mistake. Yet, he'd said he loved her for her cleverness, loved the strange things she knew. He said he'd spend every penny he had on books for her.

If she hadn't already been madly in love with him, that single statement would have been enough to have her falling head over ears. In Harriet's opinion, that was the single most romantic thing that anyone had ever said in the history of the world. Why then, if that was so, would he take to his heels when she suggested he read to her? It didn't make a lick of sense. No doubt there was some cork-brained *male* explanation that would make her head hurt, but she couldn't see it.

Sighing, Harry closed her eyes and wished her brain was functioning at its usual speed. Currently, it felt sluggish and full of cotton wool and unequal to the task, but she would figure it out. She would figure him out, puzzle of a man that he was, eventually.

Chapter 17

Dear Mr de Beauvoir,

Please forgive me for my shocking behaviour when you visited Holbrooke House yesterday. I might say that I don't know what came over me, but I'm afraid I do.

I regret to inform you I am infatuated.

I promise you that the kiss was not planned — how could it have been? — and that there is no plot to entangle you in my snares. Indeed, I am as perplexed by my reaction to you as you appeared to be revolted by it. I might inform you that my mother expects me to marry a titled and wealthy gentleman and, if she had the slightest inkling of my behaviour, she'd likely lock me up.

As a man of science and reason, please explain to me what I must do. How do I rid myself of this silly longing for someone who clearly holds me in contempt — as I always knew you would?

Please advise me, Mr de Beauvoir, for I fear making a fool of myself if ever we meet again.

Yours in admiration,

Miss Minerva Butler

PS. I am very much enjoying the book, as you predicted.

— *Letter from Miss Minerva Butler to Mr Inigo de Beauvoir.*

8th September 1814. Holbrooke House, Sussex.

Harriet was more than relieved to have finally made it down the stairs. Tucked up before the library fire, she was trying and failing to read the book she'd brought with her. She'd not seen Jasper again yesterday, or this morning, either, and though she still felt tired and sluggish, her mind was not as foggy as it had been yesterday.

"Do you prefer pink or yellow roses?"

Harriet turned towards the desk, where Lady St Clair was happily ensconced, surrounded by lists and planning her and Jasper's engagement party with the same determined *mien* Wellington must have worn before going into battle.

"Pink," Harriet replied absently. "Where's Jasper?"

Lady St Clair looked up, frowning. "I have no idea," she said. "Though I'd take a guess he's probably in that workshop of his."

"Workshop?" Harriet echoed. "Jasper… *works*?"

There was a trill of laughter from the desk. "He's not the idle fop everyone thinks he is, Harriet, dear. I thought you of all people knew that."

Harriet blushed, wondering what she knew about Jasper, about the man he was now. She had misjudged him badly these past years. What else had she got wrong? Once upon a time she'd known him as well as she'd known herself, but they'd been children then, and there had been so many years since their estrangement. He'd become a man during those years, a beautiful man, with a reputation for wild living and womanising. Though even she had noticed he'd calmed down a great deal over the past years, his reputation still clung to him. A workshop, though?

"What kind of workshop?"

Lady St Clair shrugged. "I've no idea, he won't let anyone in. Even the servants are banned." She looked up then and Harriet was struck by the quality of her turquoise gaze, the same unusual colour her son had inherited. "Why don't you find out?"

Harriet quailed a little at barging into Jasper's private space. It was obvious he guarded it jealously, if he wouldn't even let the staff in. Naturally, she was now eaten alive with curiosity.

"The doctor told you a gentle stroll in the fresh air would be good for you, did he not?" Lady St Clair remarked, with a deal too much nonchalance.

"Very well," Harriet said, putting her book aside.

Ten minutes later and she was following Lady St Clair's little map past the stately stable buildings and farther along, past the vast kitchen garden that supplied the house with fresh produce, and past the hothouses where exotic fruits and blooms were lavished with tender care. On she went to the home farm, noting as she walked how neat, orderly, and well-kept everything was. Gardeners and farm workers doffed their hats and greeted her with cheerful smiles as she cast her eye over a large and well-run enterprise. There wasn't a roof in need of repair, or a pane of broken glass to be seen. Every yard and path was well swept. Memories rose in her mind of having played in and around these buildings as children, stealing soft fruit and petting the piglets and generally making a nuisance of themselves. It was such a long time since she'd been to this part of the property, and she smiled as she remembered a hundred adventures and squabbles, and a great deal of laughter. Harriet did not remember the place being in such excellent order back then, though. In fact, it had been a far more ramshackle collection of buildings, many of them in poor repair.

Had Jasper done all this?

Harriet looked at the map once more to get her bearings, concluding that the building she was searching for was on the very outer edge of the farm complex, before it gave way to fields. According to the map there was a cluster of buildings now, and they must all be new as she had no memory of there ever being anything but fields there. She walked on, skipping around puddles and enjoying the fresh air. The sun warmed her back and she breathed in lungfuls of sweet, clean air, grateful to breathe a deal easier than she had a few days ago.

The building, when she finally came upon it, was a solid red brick affair with high windows, far too high to allow Harriet a discreet peek before gathering her courage and knocking.

Well, she'd come this far, and it was only Jasper. Why on earth was she so nervous?

Harriet raised her gloved hand and rapped smartly on the door.

For a long moment there was no answer, and she'd just raised her hand to knock again when the door opened, and Jasper stuck his head out.

"Harriet!" he exclaimed, obviously surprised.

He came outside, closing the door behind him without allowing her the barest glimpse of what he was doing in there.

"What are you doing here?" he asked.

"Looking for you," she replied, studying his face. "I've not seen you since last night, when you left my room like I'd set light to your heels."

"I didn't." He stiffened at once, his expression guarded, and she was aware of tension vibrating through him.

"Yes, you did," she said, reaching out and taking his arm, which was stiff and unyielding under her hand.

"I had things to attend to. I told you I'd forgotten… *something*."

Harriet sighed and looked up at him, wondering why he was insisting on sticking to that hopeless excuse when it was patently untrue.

"Forgot what, Jasper?"

"Never you mind!" His voice was taut with irritation, and something else that she thought sounded remarkably like panic.

She remembered the panic she'd seen in his eyes yesterday, too.

"Everything was fine until I asked you to read to me," she mused, considering the possibilities until something obvious occurred to her. She sighed and looked up at his handsome face, trying to keep the smile from her lips. "Oh, Jasper, do… do you need spectacles? Is that why you made such a fuss?"

She started as he snatched his arm away from hers.

"No, I don't bloody need spectacles," he said, and Harriet gasped at the anger and hurt in his expression as he turned back to her. "Though I can hardly be surprised you'd think it. You believe me a brainless twit, don't you? You think I only care about how I look and what to wear. *Of course, Jasper's too bloody vain to wear spectacles to read, he'd prefer not to bother rather than ruin his pretty face*—that's it, isn't it, Harry? Christ, if that was all it took…."

He snapped his mouth shut and turned away from her, his arms folded tightly across his chest. She could feel misery and tension rolling off him in waves and did not know why, or how to help, though she longed to do so.

Harriet approached him cautiously, her heart thudding in her chest. His obvious hurt made her feel horrible, guilt weighing her down. It made her heart hurt to see him in such turmoil. Jasper had always been the one to laugh, the one with the quick smile and something witty to say, the one to cajole her out of the doldrums when her father had treated her like a silly little girl and refused to see she was more than that.

"Jasper," she said, close enough now to put a hand on his arm. She looked up at him, but he kept his face turned away from her. "Jasper, what is it? What's wrong?"

"Nothing."

She wanted to put her arms about him and hold him tightly, as that was clearly the biggest lie he'd ever spoken. That one word held a world of hurt and defiance, and she knew she must tread carefully. Whatever it was had injured his pride badly. Harriet had grown up among boys and knew what a fragile thing that pride was. A boy would sneer and laugh and say *I'm not scared*, when he was quaking in his boots, or, *that didn't hurt,* when he'd skinned his knees, even though the desire to be hugged and kissed shone in his eyes. She recognised that same fierce pride now, in every line of his body, and in the way he refused to meet her gaze.

"Why do you think I believe you're stupid, Jasper?" she asked, keeping her voice soft. "I don't, you know. I never have done."

He made a sound of disgust that suggested he didn't believe a word of it.

"I've been frustrated by your lack of interest in study, it's true," she said, deciding she'd best get him to talk about this, even if she had to make him angry to do it, for surely this was at the bottom of whatever problem he had. Had he been afraid to read to her in case she'd given him some scientific journal he couldn't follow? Surely not. "When you chose not to go to university I was annoyed and jealous, because I'd have given my right arm for such a chance and you just said no without a moment's thought. You didn't even consider it and—"

"Because I'm too bloody stupid to consider it!" he shouted, furious as he stalked away from her.

"No, you're not!" Harriet shouted in return, outraged that he should think such a thing when it was so clearly untrue. "I know you're not."

"You don't know a bloody thing about it, Harry!" He swung around and the pain in his expression devastated her, the glitter in his eyes making her chest tight. "You don't know...." he began again, the words raw but his voice cracked, and he turned away from her.

"Jasper!" she cried, running to him, throwing her arms about him. "Oh, my love.... Whatever it is, tell me, please. I can't bear to see you so unhappy. Why do you think such a thing? Who on earth has put such a thought in your head?"

"Who?" he said, the word incredulous, spoken with an edge of bitter laughter as he raked a hand through his hair. "Every tutor and school master I ever had, that's who!"

"But why? Because you skipped lessons and cheeked them?"

"No!" he cried, and it was such an anguished sound she could only hold him tighter.

He was breathing hard now, so obviously distraught that Harriet didn't know what to do or say, and so she did the only thing she could think of. She held him tightly as she looked up at him.

"I love you, Jasper. Whatever the problem is that won't change."

To her dismay, he shook his head and his throat worked.

"You'll leave me," he said, the words sounding so broken that she felt her heart shatter with them. "You'll despise me."

"I will not!" she exclaimed, wishing she had strength enough to shake him. "Good Lord, Jasper. I've been in love with you my whole life. My whole life! Do you think whatever dark secret you think you have can change that? Even when you sneered at me and made fun of me and made me feel like a dull little bookworm, I still loved you. I tried not to, believe me, I did, but I couldn't stop. I won't stop, Jasper. Please, my love," she said. "Won't you trust me?"

Harriet watched as he covered his face with his hands and she reached up, covering them with her own and drawing them away. She put them to her own face and kissed first one, then the other.

"Tell me," she urged, feeling her throat close with emotion as a tear slid down his cheek.

He was silent for a long moment and then he drew in a deep breath and she saw him steel himself for her response, her rejection.

"I c-can't read, Harry," he said, and it was an effort not to react, not to say *don't be silly, that's not possible...* because how on earth had he managed all this time if that were true?

She stared up into his beautiful face, recognising the fear in his eyes, knowing that he was waiting for her to laugh at him or reject him, or to recreate whatever it was he'd experienced in the past that had hurt him so deeply.

Harriet took a breath. "Why do you think that is?" she asked, her voice calm before adding, "and don't say because you're stupid, Jasper, because I won't have it. You're not stupid."

"You said I was," he countered, that brittle, defensive edge creeping into his voice.

"Perhaps that was because I didn't understand," she said. "Like I didn't understand why you were so cruel to me, and you didn't understand why I didn't love you anymore. I think we've made too many foolish mistakes over the past years, Jasper, and all of them could have been resolved so easily if we'd only explained ourselves."

He swallowed hard and then wiped his eyes with an irritated swipe of his hand. "I don't know why. I... I tried so hard, Harry," he said, and the anguish in his voice made her want to wail for the hurt he'd held inside all these years. "I m-mean I *can* read, only it's so difficult, and it takes forever and then when I try to write, it... it comes out all wrong. I get things back to front and it's... it's such a bloody mess."

"Jasper," she said, reaching up to touch his face, but he pushed away from her, out of her embrace.

"Don't pity me," he stormed, backing away from her and thrusting his hands into his hair like he'd tear it out by the roots. "Don't you dare! Not that."

"I don't pity you," she said, struggling to keep her voice even when she wanted to cry and hold him and rage at the world for having caused him such pain. "I'm in awe of you, Jasper. How hard you must have worked, how clever you must have been to conceal this from everybody all this time."

"Don't be so bloody patronising," he growled, pacing up and down now, like something wild that had been trapped in too small a space for too long.

"I'm not, I swear it. I can't imagine how you have run this vast estate all these years, let alone how you got through school. Good heavens, no wonder you didn't want to go to university." She paused, sucking in a breath as another thought occurred to her. "Oh, my God… and how I treated you, the things I said," she whispered, appalled by her cruelty, even though it had not been her intention to cause such hurt. If only she'd known!

"It doesn't matter," he said, kicking at a stone and sounding so weary that she longed to go to him and make it all better, but she didn't know how.

"Does anyone know?" she asked.

He shook his head, and she knew he'd been struggling with this alone his whole life, terrified someone would find him out.

"I think perhaps Merrick suspects," he said, still not looking at her.

"Your valet?"

Jasper nodded. "I have to ask people to read things for me. My secretary just thinks I'm too high in the instep to do it myself and that's fine. That's how I've got through most situations but… but it becomes tricky with more personal matters."

Harriet felt a lump rise to her throat. "That's why you didn't write," she said, blinking back tears now.

"I'm sorry," he said stiffly. "I wanted to, but—"

She couldn't hold back another minute, damn his pride. Harriet ran to him and wrapped herself about him as tightly as she could.

"I love you, Jasper. I love you, and you are the bravest person I've ever met, but you are not stupid, and you must never think it."

He was stiff and unyielding in her arms, the hurt he felt hidden behind a brittle wall that she needed to break down.

"Maybe not stupid," he allowed. "But I'm no great thinker, love. Not like—"

"If you say de Beauvoir, I will kill you," she snapped, before he had time to finish the sentence. "I tell you now, I admire many things about Inigo de Beauvoir, but I have concluded he is the stupidest genius I know."

Jasper gave her a blank look.

"His ideas on love are the most idiotic I've ever heard in my whole life," she said, shaking her head at him. "I tried to believe them for a long time, but I always knew he was wrong at heart. Honestly, how stupid do you need to be to think such a thing hasn't been proven over and again in infinite ways, since the beginning of the human race? What a great clod pole."

To her immense relief, his lips twitched.

"Well, I don't like to say I told you so," he said.

Harriet let out a little huff of laughter and stared up at him, touching her hand to his face.

"I'm so glad you told me, so relieved I understand, and we will work things out together, yes?"

He shrugged, his expression still wary and uncertain. "You can't fix me, Harry."

"I don't need or want to fix you," she shot back, irritated by the idea. "You're not broken, you...." She held his gaze as she thought about it. "Perhaps you just work differently from other people. Not badly, just... differently."

She watched him, hoping she'd said the right thing, relieved when he let out a long breath and leaned down, pressing his forehead to hers. "I love you so much, Harry. I couldn't bear for you to be ashamed of me, or—"

"*Never!*" she said, hearing her voice break on the word as she shook her head. She pulled him close and pressed a fierce kiss to his lips. "I could never, ever be ashamed of you."

"Thank you," he said, his smile a little surer now.

"Thank *you*," she replied. "For trusting me."

They stood together for a long while, holding each other tight and saying nothing at all, until Harriet looked up.

"Now. then," she said, her tone business-like. "Isn't it about time you showed me what you've got hidden in this secret workshop of yours? I'm dying of curiosity."

He laughed, and it was the carefree Jasper from her youth, the one she'd fallen in love with, without even noticing it was happening.

"All right," he said, looking almost shy. "As it happens, I just finished your wedding present."

Harriet stared at him. "You... You made me a wedding present?" she said, astonished that he'd taken such trouble for her. "Oh, Jasper, that's—"

"You haven't seen it yet," he reminded her, and she saw a flash of doubt in his eyes. "You might not like it."

She took his arm, wondering how she'd never noticed before how uncertain he was, how thin a veneer that confident, smiling countenance had been.

"You made it for me, Jasper. Whatever it is, I shall think it terribly romantic and love it more than anything else in the world."

He looked pleased by that and grabbed her hand. "Come along, then."

Chapter 18

Miss Butler,

I accept your apology. I regret to inform you, however, that I have no notion of how to deal with such inappropriate feelings. I strongly suggest that we endeavour to avoid each other at all costs.

I feel it is for the best.

Regards,

de Beauvoir.

— **Letter from Mr Inigo de Beauvoir to Miss Minerva Butler.**

8th September 1814. Holbrooke House, Sussex.

Harriet didn't know what she'd expected when she walked into the large workroom, but it wasn't what she saw.

The room was neatly swept and tidy, and it was clear there was a place for everything, and everything was in its place. Harriet looked around, enjoying the sweet, rather dusty scent of wood until her gaze landed on a shelf crammed with carved objects. With her heart in her mouth she reached for one, hardly daring to touch it, as it was so very delicate.

It was a carved horse, its proud neck arched, and its mane caught in the moment after it had tossed its head. He had captured every sinew and muscle in the fine grained wood, and with such precision.

"You... You did this, Jasper?"

She turned to him, feeling her throat ache with emotion.

He nodded, watching her intently.

"I... I don't know what to say." She looked along the shelves, at carvings of dogs and cats and cows, mice and birds. She set the horse down and reached for another, a tiny dormouse curled into a wooden nest. "You're an artist, Jasper," she said, smoothing a finger over the tiny creature, captured in perfect detail. Her voice was thick, and her eyes so full of tears he was blurred and out of focus when she looked back at him.

"Would you like to see what I made you?" he asked, and she nodded dumbly, too overwhelmed to speak as she set the little dormouse back on the shelf.

Jasper took her hand and led her to a sturdy workbench in the middle of the room. There was something large and oblong covered with a cloth on top of it, and as she drew closer Jasper reached for it and then hesitated.

"When I said it's your wedding present, I only mean it's one of your presents. I'll give you jewellery, too, of course, but... I made this for your trousseau," he said, and then tugged the cover away.

Harriet gasped, her hand moving to cover her mouth.

"Oh, my," she said, the words breathed more than spoken. "Oh, my."

She moved closer, unable to believe the detail, the care, the *time* that must have been lavished on this, for her.

"May I touch it?" she asked.

Jasper laughed and nodded. "Of course, it's yours."

Harriet ran her hand over the carving on the lid. A girl sat beneath an apple tree, reading a book. She blinked hard to clear the moisture in her eyes and a tear over spilled. All around the outside of the chest there were more books carved into the wood, life size, standing side by side or stacked in piles, or open with a few of the pages fanned open. She read some of the titles, Plato's *Republic* was there, Homer's *Iliad*, David Hume's *A Treatise of Human Nature*, and novels such as *Gulliver's Travels*. How hard it must have been for him to carve the writing. That he'd not only done this, against all the odds, but that he'd noticed what she was reading and gone to such trouble when his own difficulties made it so challenging for him to enjoy such things....

She could hardly take it in, emotion surging inside her like a rising tide.

"It's walnut," he said as Harriet struggled for breath. "Do you remember the big tree that got blown down in the storm? Down by the lake."

Harriet nodded. They'd loved that tree and had climbed in and picnicked beneath it. It had been like losing an old friend when she'd heard that a freak summer storm had torn it up by the roots. She could think of no finer use for the wood than this... with all the love and care that had been so lavished upon it. Her heart swelled until she thought it might burst. How could he have spent so long feeling as worthless as he clearly did when he was capable of such extraordinary things? She understood why he'd not shared his work publicly; it was not at all the thing for an earl to work with his hands, but that he'd not shared them with his family, his friends. It was only now that she truly understood him, that she realised how fragile his pride was, how much shame he'd endured, and how he'd believed he had only his looks to rely on.

"When... When did you do this, Jasper?"

She looked back at him, unable to hide the tears which were falling freely now.

He shrugged, smoothing his hand along the top of the marriage chest. "I began it when I came back from Russia," he admitted. "I've been working on it ever since. Not constantly," he added with a wry smile. "But during the times I dared hoped I might win you back. I never gave up hoping that I could change your mind about me."

Harriet made a sound, somewhere between a laugh and a sob and threw herself into his arms. "I love it, Jasper. I love it so much. More than anything else in the world, and I love you."

He kissed her then and Harriet sank into his embrace, knowing that she truly was loved. As strange and impossible as it was to believe that this beautiful, astonishing man loved her, she knew now that he did, and she'd not doubt him again.

***

10th September 1814, Holbrooke House, Sussex.

The picnic had been a wonderful idea. Matilda and Harriet, Ruth, Bonnie and Minerva had gone with Henry and Jasper and Jerome, down to the lake with baskets laden with goodies. Now, everyone was sleepy and replete, having stuffed themselves fit to bursting point.

Matilda sighed and put her parasol to one side, tipping her head back. Summer had decided it wasn't quite ready to hand over the mantle to autumn and was putting on one final show for them. The sun warmed her face, and she decided it was worth risking freckles to enjoy it. There couldn't be too many days like this left this year, and she wanted to revel in what remained of the summer.

The lazy afternoon was delicious and perfect; not so hot as to make everyone irritable, but warm enough to bask in the golden light burnishing every exposed inch of skin. There wasn't much skin exposed, naturally, but it was still a delight.

Jasper had taken Harriet out on the boat and Matilda smiled happily as she watched the two of them lean in and steal a kiss. There was a wistful sigh from beside her, and Matilda turned to see Bonnie gazing at the two lovebirds.

"Lucky things," she said, clutching her arms about herself.

Matilda nodded, unable to disagree. "Indeed."

"We're not all so lucky, are we?" Bonnie said, a bleak note entering her voice.

Matilda felt her heart ache, and not only for Bonnie.

"No," she said, for what was the point in pretending otherwise? "But you are young and pretty, Bonnie. There's time yet."

Bonnie shook her head. "No," she said, and Matilda heard the catch in her voice. "No, there's not. I told you, I'm already living on borrowed time."

Matilda reached out and took her hand, and Bonnie squeezed it in return. "You'll not be alone, Bonnie. Not forgotten or abandoned. Whatever happens. We won't allow that. Your friends will always be there for you. I'll come to Scotland and stay with you, I promise. No matter how far into the wilderness they try to bury you."

Bonnie made a choked sound and then laughed, and Matilda followed, blinking back tears.

"Lud, how maudlin we've become," she said, shaking her head. "This won't do at all."

"Aye, there's time enough for tears and wailing," Bonnie said, scrambling to her feet. "I won't waste a moment of what's left to me."

Matilda watched, rather daunted by what Bonnie meant as the girl took up her drinking cup and went to the water's edge, filling it to the brim.

"Oh dear," Matilda murmured as she saw Bonnie run unerringly towards Jerome, who was dozing on a blanket in the sun. Bonnie threw the water on him, laughing her head off as Jerome spluttered and cursed.

"Why, you little brat!" he shouted, pushing to his feet as Bonnie shrieked, dropping the cup and hitching up her skirts, running away as Jerome chased after her.

"I'm going to throw you in the lake, Bonnie Campbell," Jasper warned her as he set off in pursuit.

Bonnie crowed with laughter and turned back, sticking out her tongue at him.

"You've got to catch me first, clod pole," she taunted, before running off, into the trees.

"My, she's bold," Minerva said, shaking her head with admiration as she and Ruth came to sit beside Matilda.

"Yes," Matilda said, her voice faint with worry as she wondered how to get Bonnie back before there was another scandal to contend with.

"I wish I had half her nerve," Ruth admitted with a sigh. "Every time I think about my dare, I quake in my boots."

"To say something utterly outrageous to a handsome man?" Minerva said, grinning. "Oh, I'm sure you'll think of something. You must have a witness, though. We need proof."

Matilda looked back to Ruth, who looked rather sick.

"Does anyone know when Bonnie will do her dare?" she asked them. "I have a rather anxious feeling she will choose the engagement ball."

Both Ruth and Minerva shook their heads.

"No, she's been very quiet about it," Ruth admitted, which was the most worrisome thing she could have possibly said.

Bonnie was never quiet about *anything*. It meant she was up to something. Her dare, to wear a disguise in public, was the kind of thing Bonnie would delight in taking too far, and she'd likely ruin herself beyond saving.

"Oh, don't look so ill," Ruth said, smiling at Matilda. "I know she's rather wild, but she's not stupid. I think she's just gathering her rosebuds while she may, and it seems she cannot escape Gordon Anderson no matter what she does, or how badly she behaves. Morven is at his wits' end. He's threatening to send the brute down here to carry her back to Scotland. Even if she's ruined herself in the meantime she won't escape; he's told her as much. She'll be marrying Gordon Anderson, unless someone else marries her first, I suppose, but there's no sign of that. The earl has his heart set on it."

"Does anyone know anything of this Anderson fellow, apart from what Bonnie's said?" Matilda asked, wishing there were something they could do.

Ruth pulled a face and shook her head. "No, but every time she speaks of him the descriptions get more and more appalling. I admit I find it hard to believe any man is quite as vile as she paints him. I hope not, for her sake."

Matilda nodded, in complete agreement. Gordon Anderson had become the stuff of legend to the Peculiar Ladies, as Bonnie's descriptions of the man painted a vivid picture of an ignorant brute who ate small children for breakfast, smelled like a pig pen, and had as much personal appeal as a bout of typhoid. They were all torn between feeling desperately sorry for Bonnie at having to face such an unenviable fate, and dying to see the man in the flesh.

"At least she'll be a countess one day," Ruth said with a sigh. "It seems Morven's last direct heir died last month, and Anderson is his closest relation."

"Really?" Matilda said, astonished. "And the earl still wants him to marry Bonnie?"

Not that she meant it unkindly, but it seemed odd. From what she knew of Bonnie, she came from no great family, and—judging by the amount of trouble she'd caused Morven to date—one might have thought he'd just want rid of her, not to marry her to his heir.

"Apparently it was a deathbed promise or some such," Ruth said with a sigh. "Bonnie's father was loyal to Morven and a great friend. Morven swore to find Bonnie a good husband and see her settled before the man died. Despite being a thorn in his side, Morven is fond of her. I think he admires her spirit, and in some ways he even enjoys her defiance. She showed me one of her letters once, and it was very affectionate, in an insulting, rather coarse manner of speaking," Ruth added with a frown. "They don't hold back, I can tell you. Actually, it was rather refreshing."

"I can imagine," Matilda said with a sigh. "How freeing, to say whatever you want to a man who says exactly what he thinks."

"Quite," Ruth replied, nodding.

"Oh, I don't know." They turned to Minerva who had been quiet until now and was staring out at the lake, her expression troubled. "Too much honesty can be rather brutal."

Matilda wondered what she'd meant by that, but she didn't know Minerva well enough to pry. She frowned, deciding she must remedy that.

"What are you wearing to the ball, Minerva?" she asked, thinking that a safe topic to engage on with the girl.

"I've no idea. I've not really thought about it."

Ruth and Matilda exchanged a glance. When they'd first met Minerva, she'd seemed a shallow creature who only cared for appearances. They'd since learned there was a great deal more to her than that. Nonetheless, she was always beautifully dressed, and obviously took great care with her appearance.

"Well, why not come to my room later and you can help me choose? You always look so beautiful, Minerva. I should welcome your advice."

Minerva looked startled by the invitation, though pleased. "Really? Oh, I should enjoy that. Though I don't have the faintest idea why you'd want my help. Everyone looks to you, Matilda, surely you know that?"

Matilda chuckled, a little rueful. "Well, for an old spinster, I suppose I don't present too terrible a picture," she said with a quirk of her lips. "But nonetheless, a fresh pair of eyes is always a good thing."

"Well, you'd both best come and help me, then, or I'm bound to choose something diabolical. I don't know what possessed me to buy that hat with the cherries on. It was such a pretty bonnet, too, but when I put it on yesterday, I realised how dreadful it looked on me." Ruth gave a heavy sigh and shook her head. "I'm just not the right shape to wear such things."

"Nonsense," Matilda said, her voice firm. "You need simple cuts, Ruth, and beautiful tailoring, that's all. No frills and ruffles. What do you think, Minerva?"

Minerva nodded, her expert eye travelling over Ruth. "Yes, you're quite right. I say, why don't we go through Ruth's wardrobe too, find her something stunning?"

"Oh," Ruth said, looking delighted by the offer. "Oh, yes, please."

"That's settled, then," Matilda said, smiling with satisfaction until her eyes strayed to the tree line, and she realised… Bonnie and Jerome still had not appeared.

Chapter 19

I don't think I can ever forgive myself for the way I have treated Jasper, for how unhappy I made him. Whenever I think of it now, my heart hurts and I want to cry. If only he'd told me, confided in me, I would have gone to the ends of the earth to help him, to keep his secret. How could he ever believe I would think less of him when I idolised him so for so very long?

If only I had known. If only I had understood. How foolish it is to long to change the past and yet I do, but I have the future before me now, our future, and I won't ever let him down again. I won't ever allow anyone to make him feel inferior or anything less than the brilliant, wonderful man he is. I shall tell him every day how much I love and admire him, and it will be nothing less than the truth.

— Excerpt of an entry from Miss Harriet Stanhope to her diary.

18th September 1814. Holbrooke House, Sussex.

"Do you like it?" Jasper regarded the stunned expression on Harriet's face with amusement.

"*Like?*" Harriet breathed, staring down at the silk lined box that Jasper had just presented her with. "Oh, Jasper, how beautiful."

He grinned. "They're rubies, but I looked for the pinkest stones I could find. I know pink is your favourite colour."

She looked up at him, her lips curving into a delighted smile. "How did you know that?"

He shrugged. "You wear pink more often than any other colour."

Harriet shook her head, laughing softly. "I don't deserve you, Jasper. After all the dreadful things I thought and said."

Jasper chuckled and bent down, kissing the side of her neck, pleased as he felt the shiver run over her. "I think we're even on that score, love, but you can make it up to me if you insist."

"I do insist, and I'll spend the rest of my days doing just that, I swear it," she said.

Her tone such that his blood ran hot in his veins and he wished there wasn't a ball to attend, but there was, and it was in Harriet's honour and he wanted her to enjoy it.

"Put them on, then," he said, impatient now.

"I'm frightened to touch anything," she admitted. "You do it, please."

Jasper set the box down. Inside was a ruby and diamond parure set that would go beautifully with the deep pink gown she was wearing. He lifted the necklace out first and she turned so he could secure it about her throat. Next, he clasped the bracelet about her slender wrist, and handed her the earrings, one at a time, watching as she looked in the mirror to affix them.

"I've never worn anything so beautiful in my life," Harriet said, sounding rather breathless as she turned this way and that before the looking glass.

"Not as beautiful as you," Jasper said, still seeing the doubtful look in Harriet's eyes. "It's true," he insisted. "It shines from you, love, and it takes my breath away."

He pulled her against him, so her back was to his chest, and bent to press a kiss to her shoulder.

"I love you, Jasper," she said, and he looked up to see her eyes glittering with emotion. "I love you so much."

Jasper smiled, the truth of her words settling into his heart as he squeezed her a little tighter. "I love you too." He marvelled at how easy it was to say that now, at how simple it was now there were no misunderstandings and hurt feelings. "Now, then," he said, his words spoken against her skin as he kissed a path along her neck, watching the colour rise on her cheeks until it rivalled the rubies she wore. "I think we'd best greet our guests, or I will not let you leave this room at all."

***

"Thank you so much, Tilda. You and Minerva have worked wonders. I've had three people compliment me on my dress this evening already."

Matilda's eyes scanned the ballroom, searching, and it took a moment to realise that Ruth had been talking to her. "What? Oh! Oh, I beg your pardon, Ruth, I was wool gathering, and you are most welcome."

Ruth frowned, concern in her dark eyes. "Is something troubling you?" she asked, putting her hand to Matilda's arm. "You seem all on edge."

"No!" Matilda said, fixing a bright smile to her mouth and shaking her head, the little trill of laughter she gave sounded false and brittle however and Ruth was clearly unconvinced. "No, nothing is troubling me. I'm just so happy for Harriet and St Clair, and... and I am rather worried about Bonnie," she added, hoping to deflect attention from herself.

Besides, it was true enough.

Ruth followed her gaze to where Bonnie was dancing with Harriet's brother Henry. She was laughing, her head thrown back and every part of her bouncing with exuberance as she threw herself into the moment, as always. Henry looked amused and slightly stunned, which seemed to be the case for most of those watching too. Matilda's gaze travelled to Jerome who was also watching Bonnie dance, laughter glittering in his blue eyes.

"She's enjoying herself," Ruth said cautiously.

"Yes," Matilda replied with a sigh. "That she is."

"Has she still said nothing about her dare?"

Matilda shook her head. "Not to me."

"Oh, well." Ruth shrugged and gave Matilda a sympathetic smile. "We all rely on your good sense and guidance, Matilda, but you are not our mother and not responsible for our actions. We are grown women and our decisions are our own. You ought not spoil your own enjoyment with fretting for us all. Bonnie will do as she pleases, for good or for ill. You've warned her to have a care, now it's for her to heed your words or ignore them."

"I know." The words were quiet but heartfelt. Everyone made their own choices for their own reasons. Sometimes those choices seemed unfathomable to anyone looking on from the outside, but no one knew what went on in another's heart and mind. "Goodness, it's hot in here," she said, feeling the urgent desire to change the subject.

Matilda pressed the glass she held to her cheek, but the drink was tepid and offered no relief. Unbidden a memory stirred, of ice in a glass and the shock of cold against her skin, of a shady walkway, and a man she had no business thinking of. *Stop behaving like such a ninny,* she scolded herself. No wonder Ruth thought her all on edge, for she was, and had been ever since Lady St Clair had warned her that she'd invited Montagu. It was impossible not to, she'd said to Matilda, sympathy in her eyes, not when they knew he was still in the area.

Matilda stilled, aware of the sudden ripple of interest that thrummed though the entire ballroom. Between the dancers, between the flashes of colour as they flew past her, she gazed at the entrance, and the tall, flawless figure who stood there, staring at her across the vast space. She told herself she could not see the strange, wintry silver of his eyes, not from here, not over the length of a ballroom. Now the ice she'd sought to cool her skin shivered over her, followed by heat. Such an enigma he was, so cold, and yet he made her burn with nothing more than a look.

Matilda held his gaze for a long moment, her heart skittering in her chest like something trapped, and then she turned her back on him, and walked away.

***

Jerome helped himself to another drink. Though he shouldn't have another, he needed something to steady his nerves. He was in the very devil of a fix and he couldn't see how to get out of it. How Bonnie had talked him into such a madcap scheme he couldn't fathom. The trouble was, when he was with her, everything was a lark. She was funny and vivacious, and she made him laugh like no one else ever had. She was daring, too, and surprisingly clever. The truth was he'd never had so much fun in his life, but he knew things were getting out of hand. He also knew his brother had noticed, and he was edging inexorably closer to getting his head removed from his shoulders.

He'd already received a stern warning but, if Jasper got wind of this escapade, he'd be treated to a long walk off a short pier. Yet he'd found Bonnie impossible to refuse. These were her last days, she'd told him, her last chance to live and have some fun before Morven sent her husband-to-be to fetch her and bear her off to the wilds of Scotland.

Something uncomfortable tugged at Jerome's conscience and he quieted it. He wasn't the one condemning her to an unhappy marriage to a man she couldn't stand. It wasn't as if he'd given her the slightest reason to have hopes of him, either. He'd made it clear that they could never be more than friends, and Bonnie had laughed and told him he was an idiot. She no more expected an offer from Jerome than to sprout wings and fly. Yet he wasn't blind to the look in her eyes, and he'd been an utter bastard to take liberties with her, knowing that she had feelings for him. Not that it had been his idea. He'd tried to act the gentleman, but Bonnie hadn't wanted that. She knew her own mind and she wanted to fill these last days with memories that would warm her and make her smile once she was married and they had clipped her wings for good.

Anyone successfully clipping Bonnie's wings and subduing her restless spirit seemed unlikely at best, and Jerome could only wonder if Gordon Anderson had the slightest idea what he was doing. Taking an unwilling Bonnie to wife seemed like a recipe for disaster on an apocalyptic scale, but it was none of his affair. He was her friend, and he'd agreed to help her live as she wished until her time ran out, heaven help him. It was in his nature to help a damsel in distress, though he'd never met one with quite such odd notions of rescuing before. Jerome had not understood what he'd been agreeing to when she'd extracted that promise from him, and only now did he realise what an idiot he'd been. His promise bound him, however, so he could do nothing but his best to avoid a scandal. He groaned inwardly. Avoiding scandal was not something at which he excelled.

"There you are, old man. Been looking everywhere for you!"

Jerome jolted, torn from his thoughts by a hearty slap on the back. Irritated by the unfamiliar voice, he turned with a glower to face the young man who stood grinning at him.

"Who the devil are you?" he began, before the words died in his throat as he took in the unusual pale green eyes that were only too familiar.

"B-Bonnie?" he stammered, whilst his heart leapt to his throat.

"You didn't recognise me, did you?" she crowed, her face alight with triumph. "I told you I could do it."

Jerome swallowed and then looked her up and down. "Hell and the devil, you'll be the death of me, Bonnie Campbell. Oh, Lord, your hair! Bonnie, what have you done to your hair?"

She shrugged, apparently unconcerned, though there was a glint of something in those pale green depths that told him she was not quite as sanguine about it as she appeared.

"It's fashionable to wear it short," she said, defiance in her tone. "And I can hardly pass as a man with long hair, can I?"

Jerome took her by the arm and hauled her into a quiet corner. "This is madness," he said, resisting the urge to shake her. "We'll get caught and you'll be ruined, and my brother will have me locked up, if you don't get me consigned to Bedlam first."

Bonnie shook off his arm and glared at him. "It doesn't matter if I'm ruined, don't you see? It won't change anything. I'll still have to marry my cousin, no matter what I've done, so they may as well hang me for a sheep as a lamb. And don't you try to wriggle out of it. You gave me your word."

Jerome cursed and rubbed a hand over his face. She was right, damn it, and he was honour bound to do as he'd promised. "Fine," he said, angry with himself, with her, and with this whole ridiculous situation. "Fine, I'll take you, but don't come running to me when this goes to hell."

"I wouldn't dream of it, and it won't," Bonnie said soothingly. "You didn't recognise me, after all, and you knew what I was doing."

"For about five seconds," he retorted and then let out a breath, shaking his head. "I am so going to regret this."

"Ah, don't be like that," she coaxed, reaching for his hand and giving it a squeeze. "We'll have fun, I promise."

Jerome stared back at her, at her obvious excitement, at the curve of her lush lips and the mischievous glint in her eyes. "Oh, I don't doubt it, you little devil. I just wonder how long I'll be paying for it afterwards, that's all."

"It will be worth it," she said, her eyes fixed on his, something in her voice that made anticipation shiver down his spine. "I promise."

He nodded, believing her, because he always believed her. "I know," he said, before giving a short bark of laughter. "Well, then, if we're going to the devil, we may as well do it in style. What am I to call you, sir?"

Bonnie grinned at him, and in the fierce joy of that irrepressible smile all the terrible consequences fell away and there was nothing but this moment, this ridiculous adventure.

"Bartholomew Camden. A distant cousin on your mother's side, Jerry, old man."

Jerome snorted, disarmed by her enthusiasm, and a bubble of laughter rose inside of him. "Well, Coz, I'm very pleased to know you. Why don't we leave this place and find a bit of life?"

"I thought you'd never ask," Bonnie said, giving him a very tidy little bow. "Lead on, Macduff."

"It's actually 'lay on,'" Jerome began, correcting her, but Bonnie just huffed and rolled her eyes.

"Do shut up and come along," she scolded and dragged him out of the ballroom by his arm.

***

"A love match, it appears."

Matilda's heart leapt to her throat at the sound of the familiar voice so close behind her.

She forced herself not to turn, not to react. "It is certainly that, my lord."

She continued to watch Jasper and Harriet dancing together, their happiness so obvious it radiated from them across the ballroom. It was not them that held her attention now, though. Matilda could feel Montagu standing at her back, feel the heat of him standing just a little too close. If she closed her eyes, she might be able to detect the scent of him, too, that intriguing combination of bergamot and clean male skin, the faint trace of leather and horses... though perhaps it would be different tonight, as he would have arrived by carriage. The urge to lean in and sniff him was so outrageous that she almost smiled.

"How strange," he mused. "When everyone has believed she hated him, and he thought her a prim little bookworm."

"Appearances can be deceptive."

Her tone was wry, and she wondered if he smiled or felt the slightest bit guilty for all the slander attached to her name because of him. Though she wanted to turn around and study his face, Matilda continued to watch Harriet and Jasper, trying hard to appear indifferent to his proximity.

"So it appears, as they were caught in somewhat, er... delicate circumstances."

Matilda turned then, to look into the cool silver eyes that haunted so much of her time. A faint smile touched the corners of his mouth, softening the austere lines of his face not a whit. His hair shone like gilt beneath the candlelight, the harsh black and white of his formal evening attire only highlighting his extraordinary colouring.

"They have always loved each other. There was only misunderstanding and a lack of communication between them. If only they had talked together, if they had only been honest, things could have been resolved a long time ago."

He nodded at her words, surprising her. She'd assumed he'd make some cutting comment but he seemed to agree. "Honesty is to be prized above all things."

Matilda watched him closely for a moment. "You believe that."

"I do," he said, his gaze on her intent. "But sometimes it is a luxury one cannot afford to indulge."

Matilda gave a humourless snort. "That is not true," she said "As I remember the falsehoods you uttered to get me to Green Park with you. No, indeed, it sounds like the sort of thing a marquess would say to make himself feel better for lying through his teeth."

"I *never* lie," he said, his voice cold, clipped, and rather angry. "And that is a case in point. You knew my words were untrue as well as I did. I was simply managing the situation to my advantage and you knew it. I have always been honest with you."

"Too honest, my lord," she returned with a tight smile, wishing he'd leave her now.

Speaking with him was like dancing around a blade: sooner or later you'd misstep and find yourself cut to ribbons.

He moved closer, too close, his breath warm against her neck as his stark words shivered over her. "I want you very badly, Miss Hunt. I spend far too much time thinking of you, of how it would feel to take you in my arms. How is that for honesty?"

Matilda held herself still, refusing to show any reaction, though his words had set her blood alight, her nerve endings fizzing like tiny fireworks beneath her skin.

"I know," she replied, proud of herself for the coolness of her reply, for the fact her voice hadn't trembled when the rest of her was doing just that.

His fingers slid around her wrist, gentle yet firm, and her pulse thundered beneath his touch, his skin burning against hers as if he'd set a brand to her flesh.

"Have you accepted Mr Burton yet?"

The question caught her off-guard and she flushed before she had time to gather herself. His touch had scattered her wits and sent her heart thrashing in her chest like a wild thing.

"No."

"Why not?" he asked. "He's wealthy and handsome; he offers you everything you want, does he not?"

"Oh, and do you expect me to believe you remember what I want, let alone that you give a damn?" Matilda asked, wishing she had the strength to pull away from his grasp.

Instead, she turned away from his piercing gaze. Anger and frustration at the force of her reaction to him made her brittle. She stared around, wondering if anyone was watching their exchange, but all eyes were still on Harriet and Jasper.

"A home, children, and marriage to a man who loves and honours you."

Matilda felt her breath catch as he recited the words she'd spoken back to her with precision.

"You said it was of no matter if he was a lord or a common merchant, you said you would love him with all your heart and give him everything he could ever dream of."

Matilda could do nothing but turn back to him, staring into that startling silver gaze, as trapped in his presence as if his hand was a manacle, holding her in place, when it only encircled her wrist with the lightest touch. He'd remembered what she'd said, word for word.

"Why haven't you said yes, when he offers you everything you dream of?"

There was something hot and unsettling burning in his eyes, and his question echoed an identical one of her own, a question that had circled her brain incessantly and would not let her be. His thumb caressed the inside of her wrist, that slight touch connecting at once to somewhere far more intimate, making her body conspire against good sense as longing throbbed beneath her skin. Matilda fought to keep her breathing even, fought to find an answer when she had none. She considered telling him she meant to accept Mr Burton as soon as she returned to town, but she wasn't at all sure it was true and found she didn't wish to lie to him, foolish as that was.

"I...." she began and then let out a sigh. "I don't know," she admitted, sounding far too breathless. "He offers me so much of what I hoped for, only—"

"Only?"

Matilda stared at him in surprise. There had been a fierce edge to that question, a hint of something that perhaps he'd not meant to reveal. She met his gaze and, for no good reason she could think of, she told him the truth.

"Because I don't love him, because I fear he wishes to own me as he would a painting or a fine horse, and because... he frightens me a little."

"More than I do?"

His voice was soft now, shivering over her skin like a caress as his thumb slid up and down her wrist, and then settled over the place where her pulse thundered, frantic with fear and desire. Matilda swallowed and compelled herself to remember what it was he wanted from her.

"Oh, no," she said, the words hard and forceful and just as honest. "No, not nearly as much as you do, my Lord Montagu. So... if you'll excuse me, I believe I promised this dance to St Clair."

Matilda turned, tugged her wrist from his grasp, and hurried away from him.

Chapter 20

I know I ought not have done it, but I love him, and it was wonderful, so perfect. I love him so much it hurts. What option did I have?

Oh Lord, I'm so unhappy.

— Excerpt of an entry from one of the Peculiar Ladies to her diary.

19th September 1814. Holbrooke House, Sussex.

It was a warm afternoon, though the scent of autumn lingered in the air, the sunshine gilding the colours about them to deeper shades of red and gold as the summer gave way at last. Everyone was languid today, sleepy and content after a lazy morning recovering from last night's excesses.

"I'm so tired," Minerva said, smothering a yawn. "And my feet hurt. I don't think I've ever danced so much."

"It was a splendid party, wasn't it?" Ruth said, setting down her teacup.

Matilda nodded, regarding the remaining Peculiar Ladies who sat on the terrace with her, enjoying the afternoon.

"Splendid," she agreed, looking over at Harriet.

As ever, the young woman sat with a book in her hands, but she was not engrossed in it as she usually was. Instead her eyes were fixed on a figure walking the gardens, her expression so full of adoration that Matilda felt her throat tighten.

Ruth followed her gaze to where Lord St Clair was walking, deep in conversation with his brother. Matilda suspected Jerome was receiving a scolding. They watched as Harriet set down her book and got up, walking across the grass towards him. St Clair turned before she was anywhere near him, as if he'd known she was there the moment she'd got to her feet. He held out his hand and Harriet ran the last few steps, reaching up for a kiss as Jerome turned his back on the happy pair and pretended not to notice.

"Do you think there's the slightest hope of finding something like that, or does it only come from knowing someone since childhood?" Ruth asked with a wistful sigh. "Like for Kitty and Luke."

"My brother fell for Alice the first time they met," Matilda said, smiling a little. "I think love is different for everyone, but if you find it, you must hold on to it very tightly indeed, for you may not be as lucky as Harriet was and get a second chance."

"I agree," Minerva said. "I think you must be brave and pursue it, even if it seems hopeless."

"I don't think I'll ever know it," Ruth said, though there was no despair in the words, just acceptance. "I think it would be foolish of me to hope for it."

"What do you hope for?" Matilda asked, wondering if Ruth was correct. In her own case she feared it was all too true and that she should heed her words.

Ruth smiled her no-nonsense smile and placed her hands in her lap, considering the question for a moment. "I hope to please my father and make him proud by marrying a titled man to elevate the family, as he dreams I will. I hope that man and I can be friends and allies and that we can make each other comfortable, and perhaps even content. I hope to have children to love, a household to run, and a position of respect and security. That is what I hope for. What about you?"

"I hope I can be satisfied with everything you just said," Matilda replied, meaning it. "For I know it is also everything I should wish for, and it ought to be more than enough, more than I have a right to expect in my circumstances."

"It isn't what you want at heart, though, is it?" Ruth's tone was sympathetic, and far too understanding.

"Of course it isn't!"

Ruth and Matilda looked up in surprise at Bonnie's terse words. Matilda had thought her asleep as she'd been sitting between them with her eyes closed this past half hour, but apparently she had been attending the conversation.

"How can either of you hope to merely be comfortable or content?" she demanded, startling them by the force of her outburst. She sounded angry, and her eyes glittered with the threat of tears. "Perhaps that is the best reality will give us, but surely to goodness you *hope* for more than that? Don't you hope and dream and wish for love and happiness and a life that's full of all of those things, a life worth living, a life that touches others and leaves them changed by it?"

Matilda reached out and took Bonnie's hand, squeezing it tight. "Yes," she said, holding on tight. "Yes, I do. Of course I do."

"Me too," Ruth admitted, reaching out and taking Bonnie's other hand. "Though I am well aware it's a forlorn hope, I do still dream of it."

"And me," Minerva getting to her feet and putting her arms about Bonnie, kissing her cheek. "I dream of impossible things all the time, every day, and I shan't stop, though no doubt that makes me a fool."

"Not a fool," Bonnie said fiercely. "It makes you alive, and I refuse to live as though I've one foot in the grave. Not yet, at least. I'll not give in yet."

Matilda reached out and ruffled Bonnie's short curls. Though Matilda had to admit the daring hairstyle suited her, they'd all been shocked by her appearance this morning, though more so when they considered how she'd excused herself early last night and retired to her room with a headache… and a full head of hair. As yet, Matilda hadn't dared ask her what she'd been up to.

"Has Morven written to you again?" Matilda asked, wishing there was something she could do as the bleak look entered Bonnie's eyes and she shook her head.

"He'll not write again," she said, her gaze fixed on St Clair's brother as the two men strolled with Harriet, down to the lake. "He's said all he has to say."

"Well, you can't leave before the wedding, that's for certain," Minerva said, sitting back down again. "Lady St Clair has been so generous, offering to let us stay until the big day. So, we have two full weeks at least, and with that dashing new haircut you're bound to turn heads, Bonnie. Perhaps some man will fall in love with you at first sight."

Bonnie snorted. "Turning heads is easy enough. I've been doing that my whole life, if not for the right reasons. It's getting them to see you, to see past all the things they thought they wanted, to the things that are important, the things they really need." She sighed and closed her eyes again. "Ach, I'm a fool and dreaming of impossible things, just as Minerva said, but I'll do it to the last all the same, for there's nothing else I can do."

"As will we all," Matilda said as Ruth and Minerva nodded and added their confirmation to her words.

Bonnie's eyes opened again and she looked from Matilda to Ruth and Minerva. "I'm so very grateful for your friendship, all of you," she said, a real smile at her lips. "For all the trouble I cause and all the advice I don't heed, don't ever forget that. I know I've been blessed with my friends, and that's more than many people ever have. Thank you for putting up with me," she added, humour in her eyes.

"It's a great pleasure, Bonnie, and I think we would all say the same. How blessed we are to have such friends. To the Peculiar Ladies," Matilda said, raising her teacup in a toast as the other ladies followed suit. "And to all our futures, whatever they might bring us."

***

2nd October 1814. Holbrooke House, Sussex.

The wedding was an informal affair, held in the private chapel at Holbrooke House. Harriet's brother gave her away as the letter informing her parents of her nuptials probably would not even have reached them yet. Lady St Clair assured Harriet that her mother had always hoped that she would marry Jasper, and there was no reason to delay. They dare not, in any case. Harriet needed the protection of Jasper's name and he was too eager to give it to countenance the slightest delay.

Harriet was glad of that, and proud to have her brother walk her down the aisle. After his initial shock, Henry seemed pleased as punch that his best friend was marrying his sister, even though he still seemed a little bemused by the idea.

Many of the Peculiar Ladies were in attendance, too. Kitty had come running back with her new husband in tow, heedless of Harriet's protests at having interrupted her and Luke's honeymoon, and nearly knocking Harriet flat in her exuberant delight at seeing her friend again, and in such happy circumstances. Prue and her husband, the Duke of Bedwin, arrived with Bedwin's sister, Lady Helena, all of them flushed with the success of Prue's latest book, which was taking the country by storm. Matilda's brother Nate and a blooming Alice also accompanied them. Now the first three months of her pregnancy had passed without incident, Alice seemed in fine fettle, her eyes sparkling and a smile always at her lips, though there was no question as to why, as her husband fussed over her comfort and she looked upon him with adoration. Harriet had started at the burst of longing that had surged through her when she saw Alice smooth a protective hand over the slight swell of her belly, and wondered whether she might be with child too. She waited for panic to set in at the idea but found nothing but a smile curving her lips. How wonderful and extraordinary to think it. How happy Jasper would be, and how she wanted to make him happy.

Harriet turned to him now, trying to attend to the words of the service but utterly spellbound by the sight of the man beside her. He was unspeakably handsome, and she was so very proud of him, for so much more than just his beautiful face. She would spend her married life making up for any hurt she had caused him over the past years. She would protect him from anything that could hurt or embarrass him, for she realised now that Jasper needed protecting, not that he'd ever say so. Not because he wasn't clever enough, how could she think that when he had hidden his difficulties from the world for so long? Not because anyone need pity him either, for he was quite clearly a brilliant artist, and Harriet was in awe of anyone who could create such beauty when she couldn't so much a draw a straight line. No, he needed protecting only from the things that made him uncomfortable and unhappy, and made him feel less than he was, and Jasper must never feel that way ever again.

Perhaps he felt the weight of her gaze, for he turned to her then, those incredible turquoise eyes fixing on her, and the depth of emotion she saw there turned her heart inside out. He smiled and squeezed the hand he held, and Harriet squeezed back, wanting to kiss him so badly that she very nearly missed the next words....

"Jasper Augustus Louis Cadogan, wilt thou have this woman to be thy wedded wife, to live together after God's ordinance in the holy estate of matrimony? Wilt thou love her, comfort her, honour, and keep her in sickness and in health; and, forsaking all others, keep thee only unto her, so long as ye both shall live?"

Harriet held her breath as Jasper smiled at her, a smile that knocked the air from her lungs and filled her heart with every dream she'd ever dared dream since she was a little girl.

"I will," he said.

***

"Where are you taking me?"

Harriet looked over her shoulder at her husband and grinned. "It's a surprise," she said, laughing at his delighted expression.

They'd slipped away from their guests at Harriet's insistence, not that Jasper had taken much persuading. She led him across the gardens, her slippers growing damp in the grass as the warmth of the day departed with the sinking sun. It glowed now, streaking the sky with gaudy blazes of pink and orange, setting the lake aflame as it reflected the startling colours back at them.

Harriet admired the scene. "How beautiful," she said, smiling as Jasper slipped his arm about her waist.

"Is this your surprise?"

She laughed and shook her head. "Sadly, my talents don't run to organising such a show for you, though I would if I could. You deserve such magnificence."

Jasper snorted and pulled her closer. "Stop," he said, cupping her face in his hands. "I shall become impossible if you keep saying such things. I shall long for one of your set downs if you keep on."

Harriet's smile fell, and she buried her face in his waistcoat, clutching her arms about him.

"Don't," she said, her voice muffled. "I can't bear to remember all the stupid, hateful things I said."

"Ah, love," Jasper said, kissing the top of her head. "I goaded you to it more often than not, and we both know it. We've both been foolish. I ought to have trusted you enough to know you'd never judge me in the way I feared. You always knew I wasn't as clever as you, and you always took time to explain things without making me feel a fool. I underestimated you because of my own pride and that's my fault, not yours."

"But you are clever, Jasper," she said, clutching at his lapels and wanting to shake him for thinking otherwise. "That's the point. I always knew you were, and that's why I was so angry with you. I thought you were just wasting your talent through laziness and now... now when I know how hard you must have worked...."

Her voice quavered and Jasper bent and kissed her, stealing whatever words she may have found with a kiss that softened her bones and stole her ability to think, let alone speak.

He let her go at last and smiled down at her in satisfaction. "Your spectacles are crooked," he said, the smug devil.

"I'm surprised they haven't melted," Harriet replied, straightening them with a dignified little sniff. "There ought to be a law against you, Jasper Cadogan. You're a dangerous man. I can't think when you kiss me like that."

"Well fair's fair. A fellow has to have some advantages, love," he said, taking her hand again. "Now, weren't you taking me somewhere to have your wicked way with me?"

"Is that what I was doing?" Harriet replied, trying to sound tart, which was difficult when her mouth refused to do anything but grin stupidly at him.

"I believe so."

Harriet gave up and laughed, tugging at his hand. "Come along, then."

She pulled him on farther until he realised where they were going. "The summerhouse?"

"Of course, the summerhouse," she said, blushing a little all the same. "Our first kiss was here and so I thought...." Harriet felt her blush increase but he looked so pleased she carried on regardless. "I thought it would be the perfect place for our first night."

"It's hardly that." Jasper smirked, no doubt remembering just as she was that they'd hardly been parted during the endless wait for their wedding day.

Harriet huffed at him, knowing he was teasing. "Our first night as a married couple," she clarified.

"Well, that sounds very romantic, love," he admitted, though he sounded a little dubious. "But I think my bedroom might be more comfortable."

"Ah, that's what you think," Harriet said, pleased with herself as she led him to the door.

Jasper gave her a curious look before setting his hand on the knob and pushing the door open. She heard his gasp of surprise and clutched her arms about herself, bursting with delight as he saw everything she'd done. It looked rather magnificent. Swathes of red silk hung from the centre of the ceiling and down the walls, and the floor was thick with rugs and huge cushions in dozens of jewel bright colours. There were gilt platters, heaped with grapes, strawberries, exotic fruits, and tiny pastries, every item a perfect little mouthful. A fire blazed in the hearth and lamps glowed, making the space intimate, warm, and desperately romantic.

"*A Thousand and One Arabian Nights*," Jasper said, his voice little more than a whisper.

"It was always your favourite," Harriet said, closing the door behind her and taking his hand.

Jasper turned to look at her, his eyes sparkling. "You must have read it to me a dozen times, and you never complained when I asked for it again."

Harriet shrugged. "I loved reading it to you, it was the only time I had your undivided attention, even if it was the book that captured you, and not me."

"It's been you for a very long time, Harry," he said softly. "And it will only ever be you."

Harriet's heart did a mad little dance in her chest, happiness bubbling up inside her and she flung her arms about his neck, pulling his head down for a kiss.

"I love you," she said breathlessly when she finally let him go. "And I have a present for you."

She laughed, thrilled by the pleasure in his eyes as she went to retrieve the carefully wrapped parcel.

"Actually," she said, feeling a little mischievous. "If I'm honest, it's a present for me, not you."

Jasper returned a curious look and reached for the parcel, tugging at the ribbon holding it closed. He let the paper fall to the ground and shook out the garment folded inside. The fabric was a stunning gold, intricately embroidered and fit for a king.

He looked up at Harriet in surprise. "A banyan?"

Harriet nodded, blushing a little now. "When… When I read the stories to you, I…." Her mouth grew dry, and she felt a little foolish admitting to her fantasies, but she owed Jasper a great deal and she wanted him to know this, to know everything she had dreamed. "I used to imagine that you were Prince Shahryar and I—"

"You were Scheherazade," he finished for her. "Spinning her tales and leaving each one on a cliff hanger, hoping to live another night."

Harriet nodded, her shyness evaporating as she saw the way his eyes had darkened.

"I imagined you as the prince," she said, breathless now. "Dressed in silks and laying back against colourful cushions as I told you my stories."

"Well, then," he said, stroking a finger over the heavy silk of the dressing gown. "I would not want to disappoint you." Harriet's mouth grew dry as he shrugged out of his coat, throwing it in a careless heap on the floor. He paused then, his lips quirking as he noted the rapt look on her face and made a circling motion with his fingers. "Turn away, please. I would like to give you the full effect."

Harriet huffed, not wanting to miss out on the tantalising sight of her gorgeous husband disrobing, but did as she was told. The rustle of fabric was a torment that made her long to turn around and steal a glimpse, but she did not, and finally she heard him speak.

"Well, Scheherazade, do I meet with your approval?"

Harriet turned, and the air left her lungs in a rush as she took in the scene before her. Jasper lay back on a tumble of cushions, and every part of him glinted gold in the firelight. He looked every inch the image of the Persian prince she'd imagined, or perhaps an indulged pasha awaiting one of his wives to peel him a grape, or even a pagan god lounging in expectation of his supplicant's devotions. The banyan fell carelessly from his shoulders, gaping to show an expanse of smooth skin and a line of golden hair that disappeared in a provocative trail beneath the loose tie about his hips.

"Oh, yes," Harriet murmured, wondering how Scheherazade had kept her wits about her for so long if her prince had looked anything like Jasper. The threat of losing your head must focus the mind rather, she supposed.

Harriet moved closer and knelt before him. She could do nothing but stare, too enraptured by the beauty of him, clothed in silk and firelight and surrounded by the decadent sprawl of brightly coloured rugs and cushions.

"What, no clever story to spin for me, love?" Jasper teased her, his beautiful eyes dark with anticipation.

Harriet shook her head. "No," she breathed. "Not a one. I must try to please you another way, I suppose."

Jasper's lips quirked, and he put one hand behind his head, making an expansive gesture that encompassed the rest of him with the other. "I am at your disposal, wife."

She leaned in, sliding her hand beneath the warm silk and laying it flat against his chest. His body burned beneath her palm and her breath caught.

"You are always so much hotter than me," she said, curious as ever, though too impatient to consider why that might be.

She slid her hand down, over his taut belly, until the robe's belt impeded her path. Harriet gave it an impatient tug and pushed the lush fabric aside, exposing him to her view.

His eyes were upon her, she knew it, but she didn't care if he saw the adoration in her gaze, the depth of her desire. She could do nothing but drink him in, admiring the sheer masculine beauty before her.

"Mine," she whispered, daring to meet his eyes.

He stared back at her, his expression serious. "All yours."

Harriet let out a little sigh of pleasure and then took off her spectacles and set them carefully aside.

"Hmmm, Scheherazade has removed her spectacles. Should I be worried?"

"Certainly," Harriet said, feeling quite indecent and very pleased with herself as she leant down and pressed her mouth to his cock. It leapt at her touch and Jasper groaned as she kissed him again, and again and then gave him a cautious lick. This earned her a gasp and his hips canted towards her, demanding more, so she did it again. She knew he liked this, and loved the urgent sounds he made, but she knew too that she was dreadfully inexperienced and wanted to know more, wanted to be good at this for him.

"Teach me," she said, staring up at him as her own skin burned with desire. The dark look in his eyes made her feel hot, achy, and impatient, but she wanted to learn this, wanted to give him as much pleasure as he'd given her.

"I think you're doing admirably," he said, the words breathless as he curled his fingers into her hair.

Harriet shook her head. "Teach me, I want to learn."

She saw his throat working, held her breath as he found the words to instruct her. "Take it in your mouth," he said.

She did as he asked, closing her eyes and sliding her mouth down over him and back. The sound he made sent the blood fizzing through her veins with a surge of triumph and she did it again, her confidence soaring as he gasped and moaned, his hips bucking beneath her as she increased the speed. Feeling extremely pleased with herself, it was a shock then when he pulled away from her and moments later she found herself flat on her back.

Jasper flung the golden banyan aside and tugged at the skirts of Harriet's wedding dress, bunching them up and moving between them with frantic, almost desperate movements.

"Oh, God, Harry," he said, settling between her thighs and sliding his arousal against her. Harriet leapt at the contact, his silky skin so hot and perfect that pleasure spiked through her. "Let me in," he begged, and Harriet could say nothing in reply, too focused on wanting the same thing, on the need to feel him inside her.

"Yes, yes," she said helplessly, tilting her hips as he sought and found and slid inside her in one, hot surge. A startled cry was wrung from her lips and she clung to him, clutching at his shoulders as he rose up over her. Harriet arched as he pulled back and sank into her again and she laughed with the sheer joy of it.

"Do you like that, Harry?" he asked, staring down at her, his eyes lit with pleasure.

"I like all of it, all of you," she said, gasping again as he tilted her hips just so and stole her breath.

"Tell me," he said urgently. "Tell me how much you like it."

"I love it," she said, fighting to get the words out as her mind fogged with desire and her body melted beneath his touch, at his pleasure. "And I love you."

"Say it again," he demanded, wrapping his arms about her and holding her tight.

"I love you," she said, and then he claimed her mouth but the words were still between them, in the caress of her hands over his skin, in the touch of her lips against his, and she vowed it would be obvious to him from now on, in everything she said and did.

"Harry," he said, her name torn from his lips as his body convulsed and his climax surged through him, taking her with him as the two of them clung together, bound together at last, with no foolish misunderstandings to ever keep them apart again.

***

"The Chronicles of the Sasanians, the ancient kings of Persia who extended their empire to the Indies, over all the dependant islands, to a considerable distance beyond the Ganges, and as far as China, acquaint us that there was formerly a king of that potent family, the most excellent prince of his time...."

Jasper lay back against a tumble of silken cushions, the golden material of the banyan swathed over them both as Harriet sat in the cradle of his arms and read to him from the stories of The Arabian Nights. He'd teased her for having brought it to their wedding night, making her blush by demanding if she'd thought she'd be bored, but in truth he was beyond touched that she'd remembered, that she'd thought of it. Memories of other nights, a lifetime ago now, flooded back to him... memories of being enraptured by Harriet's quiet telling of Scheherazade's stories, and the way he would look up and catch her eye and she would stumble over the sentence she was reading and blush, before finding her place and carrying on again. He'd spent his entire youth knowing that she loved him, that she adored him and thought him without fault. She'd put up with being dragged through mud and half-drowned and kidnapped and rescued and never had that worshipful gaze faltered.

When he'd returned from Russia to find his world so changed, he'd been bereft and confused, and he'd realised how badly he'd taken her love for granted. It wasn't until he'd lost her than he'd realised what he'd had. Now he knew. Now they both knew. They both knew how close they'd come to losing what mattered most and they'd not risk such folly again.

Harriet's voice wrapped around him as she spun the first of Scheherazade's tales and he tightened his arms around her, holding her to him. She paused and turned her head, looking up at him with a smile.

"I'll not be able to breathe, let alone read, if you hold me any tighter," she murmured, though it was clear enough that she was not complaining.

Jasper gazed down at her, utterly charmed by the picture she made, her hair tumbled about her in disarray, her body naked and barely covered by the golden fabric of his gift, her spectacles perched on the end of her sweet little nose and, as ever, a book in her hand. He bent his head and stole a kiss.

"Are you happy?"

Harriet laughed, her expression rather incredulous. "You know I am. If I were any happier, I'd burst."

"Good," he said, settling back against the pillows. "I wish everyone we care for could find the same happiness too."

"What a romantic you are," she said, turning in his arms to regard him.

He shrugged but did not deny it. "I wish Jerome would fall in love with someone suitable," he added with a sigh. "I despair of him."

"Oh, there's time yet, surely?"

Jasper frowned, troubled. "I don't know. I fear he's getting himself into a tangle."

Harriet sat up, anxiety in her eyes. "You mean Bonnie," she said, and he heard the edge to her voice. "Jasper, I won't hear anything against her. She's a lovely girl, and she's my friend, and if your brother has taken advantage of her—"

Jasper reached out and pressed a finger to her lips. "Then he shall take the consequences," he said firmly. "But I cannot pretend I think it is a good match."

"Why not?"

There was a defiant note to the question that made Jasper smile. He knew that Harriet had always had difficulty making friends. She was too shy, too unsure of herself in company to be at ease, but she had found friends within the odd collection of women that comprised The Peculiar Ladies. He was glad of it, and unsurprised by her loyalty. So, he spoke carefully.

"Bonnie seems like a lovely young woman, and I can see Jerome is fond of her, but I fear he views her as he views his friends, not as… not as a lady he wishes to wed. Jerome has always felt the need to rescue fair maidens. He wants someone to protect and cosset, someone who needs him, and Bonnie—"

"Bonnie is utterly fearless and would face the world head on and spit in its eye."

Jasper laughed a little and nodded at her description. "Precisely that."

"You really think it's doomed, Jasper?" Harriet asked, and his heart sank as he realised his fears had been well founded.

"Why?" he asked, though he knew the answer before she said it.

"Because I'm very much afraid she's fallen hopelessly in love with him, and I can't bear to see her hurt."

Jasper sighed, wishing he'd not seen this coming, wishing he'd been more successful in steering his idiot brother out of trouble. "She's promised to Morven's heir," he said, shrugging. "Even if Jerome announced his undying love for her, which I really can't see happening, she's all but engaged."

Harriet shook her head. "You'd best not let Bonnie hear you say so. I suppose your mother wouldn't be best pleased, either?"

"She would not," he admitted. "Though hopefully today has gone a long way to softening any disappointment Jerome may bring her."

Harriet smiled as he kissed her forehead. "She had hopes of Lady Helena, I think?"

Jasper nodded. "Yes, I think so, but Jerome didn't even notice her. Not that she seemed to care a whit either, mind."

"Well, we shall do what we can," Harriet said thoughtfully.

"Harry?" Jasper said, feeling anxious himself now. "Whatever do you mean?"

"Oh, nothing really. Only… it's like you said. All our friends should be as happy as we are, and our brothers too, and if there's anything we can do to help…."

"Oh, no." Jasper shook his head. "No matchmaking. I forbid it."

"You *what* it?" Harriet repeated, eyes wide behind her spectacles.

Jasper hesitated and tried again. "I believe I meant to say…. We'll see what we can do."

Harriet snickered and Jasper poked her in the ribs until she squealed.

"Bully," he murmured against her ear, before giving it a little nip.

"Who, me?" Harriet replied, all innocence. "I'm Scheherazade. You're the one threatening to cut off my head."

Jasper chuckled and settled her more comfortably in his arms. "Well then, wife, you'd best carry on with your story, and make sure it has a happy ending."

Harriet looked up and planted a kiss on his cheek. "Always, Jasper. I'll make sure of it."

Girls who dare– *Inside every wallflower is the beating heart of a lioness, a passionate individual willing to risk all for their dream, if only they can find the courage to begin. When these overlooked girls make a pact to change their lives, anything can happen.*

Ten girls – Ten dares in a hat. Who will dare to risk it all?

Next in the series

To Dance with a Devil
Girls Who Dare, Book 6

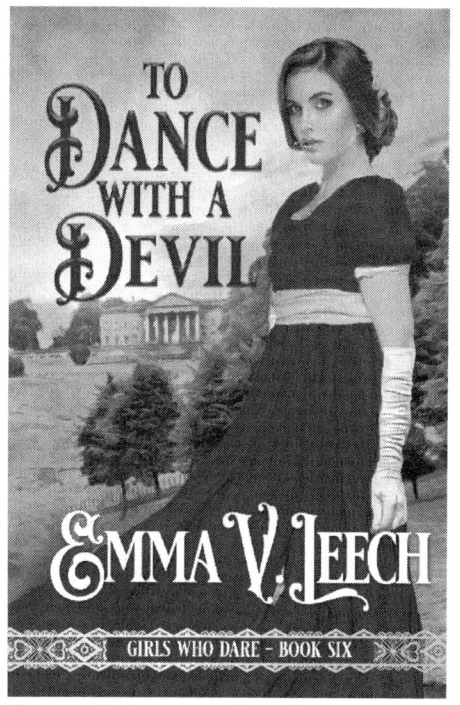

A young woman desperate to escape her fate.

Bonnie Campbell's time is almost up. In the light of no better offers, her guardian, the Earl of Morven, is forcing her to marry her cousin, Gordon Anderson. Vivacious Bonnie will have no option but to comply, condemning her to spend the rest of her life in the wilds of the Scottish

Highlands, far from her friends and any possible chance of fun. During her final weeks of freedom however, she will live as though these were her last days on earth and find the courage to show the man she truly loves, just how she feels.

A young man determined to prove his older brother wrong.

Jerome Cadogan, younger brother to the Earl of St Clair, is a good-natured scoundrel. His blond, blue-eyed looks are not the least marred by his broken nose, his reputation for trouble, nor his predilection of falling in love with unsuitable women. Reeling from a stinging lecture delivered by his brother the earl, Jerome faces having his allowance cut off if he can't mend his ways. Determined to prove that he can be every bit as mature and sensible as St Clair, Jerome swears off drinking, carousing and getting into trouble.

A scandal looking for a place to happen.

Sadly, his dearest friend Bonnie has other ideas. Lurching from one disaster to the next in her wake, Jerome is tearing his hair out and knows he must end their friendship before his brother ends him.
Yet when a hulking Highlander turns up to claim Bonnie for his own, Jerome ought to breathe a sigh of relief, but it appears his heart has done something unforgivable and fallen in love with the most unsuitable woman of all.

Keep reading for a sneak peek!

Chapter 1

I feel like I'm running pell-mell towards a cliff's edge, and though I know there's a sheer drop to face, I can't seem to stop myself. I never considered myself a stupid girl, but surely this is madness. Yet the alternative is to give in and do as I'm told and marry a man I don't want and live in a place I have no wish to be.

The cliff's edge it is then.

—**Excerpt of an entry from Miss Bonnie Campbell to her diary.**

10th September 1814, Holbrooke House, Sussex.

Bonnie contemplated the inside of her eyelids, shining red as the sun warmed her face. Sleep tugged at her mind, drowsy from the lazy afternoon and the delicious picnic she'd eaten with her friends. It would be easy to drift off, to forget all the worries that crowded her mind of late, like spectators to another's misfortune, gathering to gawk and gossip and thank the heavens it wasn't them run down by the mail coach, or fallen on their face in the dirt.

Bonnie was used to spectators, used to people casting her disapproving glances and tutting and whispering. It was jealousy, she told herself, they were simply jealous that she had the guts to do the things they wanted to do but hadn't the nerve. What did she care if they thought her a hoyden?

She opened her eyes, dazzled by the midday sun, and blinked up at a sky of azure blue, as blue as Jerome Cadogan's eyes. Lord but she was a cliché, a foolish little nobody in love with a devilishly handsome man far beyond her reach. He was a wicked charmer with a roguish laugh and twinkling blue eyes, and no more mind to put a ring on her finger that he had to become the next Archbishop of Canterbury. She might be a ward of the Earl of Morven, but her family were not illustrious. Respectable enough certainly, but Jerome Cadogan, brother of the Earl of St Clair could do a great deal better.

Her only hope had been to get him to fall as madly in love with her as she had with him. Bonnie let out a soft huff of laughter as she considered just how well that plan had worked. Jerome loved her all right, just like he loved the rest of his motley band of friends. He thought her a *jolly good sort* and *merry as a grig,* and treated her just as he might one of his boisterous roaring boys, not like a gently bred young lady. Not that Bonnie *was* frail and gently bred. There was nothing the least bit fragile about her. Her figure was voluptuous, verging on plump, she considered herself nigh on unshockable, and she had a knack for saying the first thing that came into her head, usually loudly enough to be heard several streets away.

No, she knew the type of lady Jerome fancied well enough by now and it wasn't her. Not even nearly. He had a reputation for falling in love at the drop of a hat, and always with women who were far from suitable, much to his older brother's despair. Apart from their unsuitability these women had other things in common. They were blond and blue-eyed, daintily pretty and in obvious need of rescue. Bonnie might be the epitome of unsuitability but there the comparison ended. She had dark hair, vaguely green eyes, a robust figure and was more than capable of knocking a man out cold with a well-aimed blow to the nose if the need arose. She sighed, aware of her own idiocy and worse, aware that her friends all knew of her infatuation and pitied her for it.

They'd done their best to warn her off, to tell her that Jerome just didn't see her that way, would never see her that way, and it wasn't that she didn't believe them, she did. She knew they were right. Even Jerome, bless his soul, had warned her he wasn't the marrying kind when he'd caught her eyeing him with something more than friendly affection and the penny had finally dropped. He'd been sweet about it too, making sure she knew how much he valued her friendship and assuring her that it was his loss, for he'd make the most appalling husband if ever he was forced to take a wife. He'd caught at an imaginary rope and pretended to hang himself with it at this point, and Bonnie had laughed at his antics even though her heart was breaking. Ah well, better to have loved and lost ... pfft. What drivel. If she could fall out of love with Jerome Cadogan as easily as she'd tumbled into it, she'd do so in a heartbeat, but her heart beat for him alone, and she didn't know how to make it stop.

Why couldn't she have just pleased everyone and fallen for Gordon bloody Anderson? The idea of it made her shudder. The glowering, bad tempered fellow and his glowering, unwelcoming castle, Wildsyde, had nothing to recommend them in Bonnie's view. He wouldn't know fun if it fell on its head with a label attached pronouncing FUN in capital letters. Well she was damned if she'd marry a man who thought her frivolous because she liked to laugh and longed to dance and enjoy life, no matter what plans Anderson had for her dowry or what Moven had promised her father before he'd died. That had been his promise, not hers. She'd not let them lock her up in some ghastly castle in the Highlands, away from all her friends and with no other occupation than to give her husband as many brats as she could manage before the activity killed her like it had killed her mother. No thank you.

The trouble was, she couldn't avoid it indefinitely. She was living on borrowed time. Anderson would come for her soon, she knew, and as she lived on Morven's money, there was no escaping her fate, not really. She could, and would, put it off for as long as possible, however. Perhaps if she behaved badly enough Anderson would refuse to marry her. He only wanted her for her dowry in any case, and if she was damaged goods...

Perhaps that would be enough to make him refuse her?

The idea persisted though she knew it was dangerous. Yet it meant she could have what she wanted, for a brief time at least. She could give herself to the man she loved and be honest with Anderson about what she'd done. Either it would change her fate, or it wouldn't. Perhaps Morven would disown her, but she didn't think so. No doubt he'd pack her off somewhere she'd cause him no further embarrassment, but that had to be better than mouldering in some Godforsaken castle in the backend of nowhere, surely.

Well, it would likely come to naught anyway, she thought gloomily. Jerome simply didn't see her in that light, so he'd probably not want to ruin her, even if she handed herself to him on a platter, though, it had to be worth a try.

Bonnie stared at the lake in front of her as she considered the idea, her gaze falling upon St Clair and Harriet. They'd finally sorted themselves out and were very clearly in love. Lucky Harriet, she thought with a sigh.

Matilda, who was sitting beside her, glanced over at the sound.

"Lucky things," Bonnie said, smiling wistfully as Matilda nodded her agreement.

"Indeed."

"We're not all so lucky, are we?"

"No," Matilda said, and there was a bleak note in that one word that Bonnie heard and recognised. "But you are young and pretty, Bonnie. There's time yet."

Bonnie shook her head. "No," she said, wishing her voice hadn't quavered, there was no point in bleating about it. "No, there's not. I told you, I'm already living on borrowed time."

Matilda reached out and took her hand and Bonnie squeezed it in return, grateful for the woman's unerring support and understanding. Matilda understood because her time was running out too. "You'll not be alone, Bonnie. Not forgotten or abandoned. Whatever happens. We won't allow that. Your friends will always be there for you. I'll come to Scotland and stay with you, I promise. No matter how far into the wilderness they try to bury you."

Bonnie made a choked sound as her emotions swelled, and then laughed, and Matilda followed, blinking back tears.

"Lud, how maudlin we've become," Matilda said, shaking her head. "This won't do at all."

Bonnie nodded. She couldn't agree more. You were a long time dead and the living could join them in the blink of an eye as she well knew.

"Aye, there's time enough for tears and wailing," Bonnie said, scrambling to her feet, determination swelling in her heart. "I won't waste a moment of what's left to me."

Taking a deep breath, Bonnie snatched up her drinking cup and headed for the lake.

***

Jerome sighed, content, and stretched in the sun like a lazy cat. He considered himself a simple fellow with simple tastes and it took little to please him. A sunny day, convivial company and good food and he wouldn't have swapped places with a duke or a king. He certainly didn't envy his brother the responsibilities of the earldom. No, no, the life of a younger son was by far preferable. No accounts legers and tenants bleating about this problem and that roof and the price of barley, no expectations to marry well and provide an heir and a spare, though it seemed Jasper had that well in hand, the sly devil. Harry Stanhope, who would have thought it?

Why hadn't he seen it earlier, he wondered, for now it was as clear as the besotted grin on his brother's face. The two of them adored each other. They been at each other's throats for years and all the time... well, it just went to show, no one knew for sure what went on in another fellow's head. Probably for the best that too, he thought, suppressing a grin as he turned his own thoughts to a comely new barmaid he'd spotted down at The Swan in the village. She was blonde and pretty, slender as a reed but with curves in all the right places, and she'd given him a smile that might have stopped short of *come hither*, but only just.

He'd just settled himself down to indulge in an agreeable daydream of how to get an invitation to come hither, when a shock of icy water hit him in the face, and he sat up with a yelp. For a moment he sat, dripping, too stunned to react further, and then he saw her.

"Why you little brat!" he thundered, as his outraged glare fell upon the culprit.

Who else?

"I'm going to throw you in the lake, Bonnie Campbell," he warned her, pushing to his feet as she hitched up her skirts and gave a shriek. Jasper cursed and set off in pursuit. Bonnie glanced over her shoulder to see him belting after her and crowed with laughter, turning back and sticking out her tongue at him.

"You've got to catch me first, clod pole," she taunted, before running off, into the trees.

Despite his annoyance Jerome laughed, charging after her into the cool shade of the woods. Bonnie squealed as he lunged for her and twisted away, just out of his grasp as she ran on again. She was faster than she looked though her face was flushed now, her eyes sparkling with devilry.

"Wretch!" he yelled, before snagging his toe on a root and falling heavily to his knees. "Curse it," he muttered, hauling himself up to discover Bonnie had vanished. He could still hear her though, so he ran on, following the sound of crunching leaves and snapping twigs. What felt like a lifetime later, he paused to lean against a tree gasping. Good Lord but his lifestyle was beginning to take a toll on his stamina. He really did have to make more of an effort before he ran to fat like his friend Cholly, who was looking increasingly portly. Forcing himself onwards, he broke from the tree line where it gave out onto the edge of the lake.

There was a small inlet here, out of sight and secluded, which was just as well as he took in the sight in front of him and froze with shock.

"Bonnie Campbell, you'll be the death of me yet," he murmured as his gaze snagged and held on the woman before him, wearing nothing but her shift. She turned to grin at him, standing on a large rock that jutted out into deeper water.

"Bonnie, no!" he called, but too late. With quite remarkable grace, considering what a hoyden she was, she dived into the water.

Jerome ran to the lake's edge, his heart in his mouth as he stared down into the dark water beneath him. It was deep here, so deep neither he nor Jasper had ever swam to the bottom. Not so much as a ripple disturbed the surface and panic gripped him. No. Oh, no, no, no.

He stripped off, never taking his eyes from the water and then dived in, swimming down and down until his lungs were bursting and he was forced to surface, coughing and spluttering. About to take a breath and dive once more he almost screamed as hand gripped his shoulders and dunked him under.

It was only for a second, but when he came up he found Bonnie shrieking with laughter and he had to fight the urge to throttle her.

"Plague take you!" he shouted, wiping water from his eyes. "That's not funny you diabolical creature. I thought you'd drowned, curse you."

"In this little puddle?" she said, pulling a face and obviously unimpressed. "I hardly think so. I've been swimming in lochs since

I was a bairn, far deeper and darker and colder than this. This is like taking a bath."

"Perhaps I'll drown you myself then," he muttered, and swam after her.

She gasped and tried to evade him, but was too slow this time and he grabbed her about the waist.

"Let go," she protested, wriggling in his grasp, but Jerome was too incensed to do as she bid him. Though she had likened the temperature to bath water, in truth it was icy and in normal circumstances quite enough to cool any man's ardour. Having a generous armful of barely clad female in his arms however was enough for Jerome's body to sit up and take note of the situation.

Behave, he told himself sternly. Bonnie was out of bounds. He knew it. If he hadn't known it, his brother had hit him over the head with the fact so repeatedly there was really no escaping it. Jasper had warned him his last little *mésalliance* was the last one he'd bail Jerome out of. To be fair, it *had* cost a pretty penny and *hadn't* been his finest hour and Jerome had been trying to behave himself. Besides, Bonnie wasn't his type at all, except when she turned in his arms and the fine fabric of her shift did absolutely nothing to make a barrier between her nearly naked form and his own, his cock didn't seem to be of a mind to make a distinction.

Though the water was too bloody cold, her breasts were still warm and plump and pushed against his chest, the hard little nubs of her nipples a more insistent pressure upon his skin that made his blood heat despite the frigid lake. She gasped with surprise as his erection pressed into the softness of her belly and Jerome held his breath, waiting for her to shriek in horror and slap him. Except this was Bonnie, bold, wicked Bonnie, and he ought to have known better. She wrapped her legs about his waist, and pleasure jolted through him as his cock nestled between her thighs, and her mouth pressed against his. The pleasure was so intense and so unexpected, that he forgot to swim, and they plunged under the water again.

They came up a moment later, coughing and splashing and laughing. Jerome threw back his head and roared with the insanity of it and Bonnie watched him with delight ablaze in her eyes. He saw the devil in her then, recognised it as it called out to the devil in him, a terrible siren song which would lure them both into deep water and destroy them on the rocks if they weren't very careful. It was why they ought to stay far, far away from each other, and why it was so very hard to keep her at bay. They were alike, two wicked peas in a pod, and all too ready to go to hell together.

With regret, Jerome turned away from her and swam back to the shore, stumbling across the rock to the grass and sitting down in a heap, gasping for air and willing his arousal to perdition. He looked up then and knew that was never going to happen as Bonnie emerged from the water. Her long dark hair was plastered to her, dripping in thick coils about her shoulders, framing the mouth-watering abundance of her breasts. Jerome's tastes had never run to excess, a tidy handful was quite enough for any man in his opinion, yet he wondered now if he'd not been a bit hasty as his gaze took in Bonnie's lush curves. His breath hitched as the shift was all but transparent, clinging to her body and leaving nothing to the imagination. Her nipples were clearly defined, as was the dark triangle of her sex as his gaze travelled over her.

Heat exploded under his skin and his body throbbed, all the hotter and more insistent for knowing she'd welcome his advances, she'd made that plain enough. Yet she was an innocent, a young lady, not a willing petticoat or a Cyprian. There were rules. If one did not expect to offer marriage, one had no business in dallying with virgins.

As Bonnie knelt beside him, however, her pale green eyes darker than he'd ever seen them, this was almost impossible to remember. She pressed her lips to his again and he groaned, pushing her down onto the grass and filling his hands with her. She arched beneath his touch and sighed with pleasure as he gave a her full breast a gentle squeeze and then took her nipple in his mouth, suckling.

Oh God, he was doomed.

He licked and teased and grazed her with his teeth, desire a wild thing in his blood now, thrashing inside him and demanding release, and then he looked up. For just a moment he was caught in her gaze, in the emotion he saw there, the love. For just a moment longer his heart squeezed in his chest, and then panic won out and he pushed away from her, getting to his feet. He strode away, his heart thudding unevenly in his chest.

"Jerry," she said, the disappointment in the sound of his name all too clear. She should get used to that, he supposed. He'd always be a disappointment to her if she looked at him like he'd hung the moon.

"No," he said, trying to keep the word soft, as gentle as he could make it when frustration and desire were simmering beneath his skin like he was boiling in a cauldron, the witch's brew that Bonnie seemed to stir in his blood fighting to control him. "We can't, Bonnie. No."

"We could," she persisted, and he wanted to curse her for putting temptation in his way. "I wouldn't..."

"No!" He almost shouted the word, his fists clenched against the desire to fling himself to the ground beside her and take everything she was offering him.

"No," she repeated, and he hated the sound of it, the way it sounded so defeated, as though she'd known it would be the answer.

Of course she'd known, he raged to himself. He'd told her so, hadn't he, told her there was no future for her with him. He had no intention of marrying, not for a long, long, time at any rate. Why on earth would he tie himself down with a wife and children when his life was so agreeable? He need only stay out of trouble and Jasper wouldn't nag him to settle down, not for a good few years at least.

He dried himself off as best he could, discarding his wet drawers for now. He'd have to retrieve them another time before they scandalised some visitor or another, or his mother, heaven forbid. By the time he turned around Bonnie was dressed too. He caught her eye and let out a breath, smiling at her. If he wasn't so dashed fond of her this wouldn't be so hard, but he was. He did love her, but not in the way she wanted him too. He'd been too much the wide-eyed innocent in his youth, giving his heart away at the drop of a hat and making a blasted fool of himself. Never again. He'd sworn to his brother and himself, never again, and he'd meant it.

"We're friends, Bonnie," he said, his voice soft. "Don't spoil it."

She nodded and flashed him a grin which he didn't believe because it didn't reach her eyes and that unpleasant ache took up residence in his chest again.

"Come along, you nuisance of a female," he said, holding out a hand to her. "We'd best find a way to smuggle you into the house, *again,*" he added, tsking at her. "You look like a half-drowned cat."

"Such a way with words you have, Jerome," she said, pressing her free hand to her heart and pretending to swoon. "I'll faint if you keep saying such romantic things."

He snorted and tugged her hand into the crook of his arm. "If you faint, I'll leave you here and you can find your own way home. I'm famished and I've not energy enough to haul your lifeless corpse all the way to the house I can tell you."

This time Bonnie slapped the back of her hand to her head. "Oh, my," she said, as her knees buckled, and she slid elegantly to the floor. A moment later she peered up through her fingers at him and grinned. Laughing and shaking his head, he reached down and grasped her hands.

"Addlepate," he said, with too much affection in his voice but unable to stop it.

"I know," she said with a sigh, before hauling herself to her feet with rather less elegance than she'd fallen with.

Relieved that she'd recovered her good humour, Jerome tucked her hand back in the crook of his arm and escorted her back to the house.

Chapter 2

Dear Alice,

I'm so sorry you're missing out on all the fun. We've all been so lucky to be asked to stay on for St Clair and Harriet's wedding. You'd think Lady St Clair would have had enough of us by now – me anyway – but she's always so gracious. I wish I had an ounce of her sophistication, I'm sure she thinks me an unruly hoyden and will be glad to see the back of me.

—Excerpt of a letter to Mrs Alice Hunt from Miss Bonnie Campbell.

18th September 1814, Harriet and Jasper's engagement ball. Holbrooke House, Sussex.

Bonnie laughed, delighted as Harriet's brother Henry spun her around. He looked a little unnerved by her unabashed enthusiasm, as well he might. Well behaved young ladies did not laugh their heads off and bounce about the floor like Bonnie did. Well behaved young ladies gave shy smiles and glided about like they floated just above the parquet on a little fluffy cloud made of innocence and rainbows and pink ribbons or something equally nauseating.

If such a thing had existed Bonnie would have stomped her little cloud into the dirt and gladly a long time ago. She didn't want to simper and be a good girl and do as she was told. She'd had done, once, a long time ago, so long ago that she could only just remember it, only just remember the cold stone beneath her bony knees as she prayed to a God who'd refused to listen to her pleas, her promises to be a good girl. Being good hadn't gotten her what she'd wanted then, and it never would, so she was done trying. She'd get what she wanted through her own efforts or she'd fail but it would be her doing and no one else's, certainly not some capricious deity who'd ignored a desperate child.

She didn't dare look at Jerome, too certain he'd be glowering at her. He'd promised to help her with her dare before troubling himself to discover what she had in mind, poor fool, and now he was stuck. He'd tried everything he could think of to change her mind but once Bonnie had focused her brain on something that was an end to it. She'd made her plans and he had promised, it was a *fait accompli* and so she'd told him.

She waited until almost eleven o'clock before she slipped away. For what she had in mind that would hardly be considered late in the evening and yet it was long enough. She hadn't wanted to miss Harriet and Jasper's engagement ball, but it was likely her last chance for such a scheme. This way she could plead fatigue after having danced herself into exhaustion without anyone thinking it suspicious. Smiling to herself and with anticipation simmering in her veins she hurried up the stairs to her room.

***

"There you are, old man, been looking everywhere for you!"

Bonnie had to stamp on the urge to crow with laughter as Jerome jolted in response to her hearty slap on the back. He glowered at her, affronted by the temerity of the young man who'd taken such a liberty when they'd not been introduced.

"Who the devil are you?" he began and then stopped, his handsome face leaching of colour as his gaze travelled over her to her feet and back again. "B-Bonnie?" he stammered, quite obviously horrified.

"You didn't recognise me, did you!" Bonnie barely restrained herself from doing a little dance of triumph. She couldn't afford to draw attention to them.

"Hell and the devil, you'll be the death of me, Bonnie Campbell," he cursed, before his mouth fell open. She'd thought he'd seemed quite horrified enough before but now he looked like he might swoon. "Oh, Lord." His voice was rough, almost breathless. "Your hair! Bonnie what have you done to your hair?"

Bonnie felt a tremor of regret as she lifted a hand to her shorn locks. She'd almost changed her mind when her maid had burst into tears, begging her not to make her cut off her thick dark tresses. The sight of it piled on her bedroom floor had almost made Bonnie weep too, but what was the point. Jerome didn't think it her crowning glory, he didn't think of her at all, not in such a way. She was just one of his chums, not a woman whose appearance he admired, so what difference did it make if she cut it off or not. Except now, looking at his appalled expression she wanted to cry. *Stop it,* she scolded herself. *You couldn't seduce him when you were all but naked and flat on your back, cutting off your hair won't make him want you any less, you ninny.*

"It's fashionable to wear it short," she said, defiantly. "And I can hardly pass as a man with long hair, can I?"

Jerome took her by the arm and hauled her into a quiet corner where he proceeded to scold her and do his best to wriggle out of his promise. Bonnie held firm and refused to budge. He'd promised her and she was holding him too it. She didn't care if she was ruined. It wouldn't change anything. Morven had told her she'd marry Anderson no matter what she did to try and get out of it. She believed him. All she could hope was that good old Gordy would be so disgusted with her he'd refuse, dowry be damned.

Jerome muttered and cursed some more as Bonnie reminded him he'd not recognised her. This did not seem to appease him one little bit.

"Ah, don't be like that," she coaxed, reaching for his hand and giving it a squeeze. "We'll have fun, I promise."

Jerome stared back at her. "Oh, I don't doubt it, you little devil. I just wonder how long I'll be paying for it afterwards, that's all."

"It will be worth it, I promise."

Something in his eyes softened a little and she knew she had him. "I know," he said, before giving a short bark of laughter. "Well, then, if we're going to the devil, we may as well do it in style. What am I to call you, sir?"

"Bartholomew Camden, a distant cousin on your mother's side, Jerry, old man."

Jerome snorted. "Well, Coz, I'm very pleased to know you. Why don't we leave this place and find a bit of life?"

Bonnie grinned at him, wanting to hug him for forgetting his concerns and getting into the spirit of it. "I thought you'd never ask," she said.

***

Jerome's heart had been lodged firmly in his throat for the past hour or more but as he looked around the card table at the disreputable faces of some of his friends, it cautiously returned to the vicinity of his chest. Bonnie grinned at him, a cheroot clamped between her teeth, and Jerome had to stamp on the urge to snicker.

Cholly or more correctly, Lord Chalfont, Mr Gideon Newman and The Honourable Algernon Fortescue—known affectionately as Algae to his intimates, had all accepted Bonnie as his cousin Bart without so much as a blink. Admittedly by the time he'd tracked them down through a variety of dubious drinking places they were all drunk as wheelbarrows but nonetheless—were the brainless idiots blind? How could they possibly not see she was a woman?

Her skin was too soft, too perfect and her heart shaped face far too pretty. There were pretty lads about, he knew, but surely not with the lavish curves of the dreadful girl across the table. Bonnie had bound her breasts, and so severely her shape had morphed into something that gave her the silhouette of a plump pigeon. It made him want to laugh every time he looked her. It also made his hands itch with desire to unwind her like a spinning top, unravelling whatever it was restraining her charms as his palm burned with the memory of having those generous mounds in his grasp. He rubbed a hand over his face, increasingly heated and agitated now. Hell and the devil, he didn't even want Bonnie, not like that. He'd not given her a second glance when she'd turned up with her friends and would have continued to not glance her way if not for her outrageous sense of humour and devilish tongue. Here he was though, lusting over her breasts. He wanted to kiss and lick and soothe that tortured bounty once he'd freed them from the ridiculous cage she'd trapped them in and then he'd...

Jerome cleared his throat and returned his attention to his cards. *Behave, Cadogan.* Grimacing at the inadequate hand he held the threw it down to the table in disgust.

"I'm out," he said with a sigh.

"Bad luck, Jerry," Bonnie murmured as he glowered at the tidy stack of counters before her. Why he should be surprised she was wiping the floor with them he had no idea. She was utterly diabolical. He watched as she took a draw on the cheroot and blew a perfect smoke ring across the table to him with a wink. He glowered back and snatched the brandy decanter from her grasp before she could reach for it. She'd already had a generous measure and he dared not think what might happen if he allowed her to get foxed. There were limits to his depravity. Allowing a virginal young woman to cut off her hair, dress as a man and gamble in a low dive like the one they were inhabiting at present would put quite enough paving slabs on his personal road to hell for one night, thank you very much.

Bonnie returned an impatient glare but said nothing, instead going on to relieve his friends of what remained of their coin. Algae groaned and put his head in his hands.

"Someone will have to pay my shot," he said, shaking his head mournfully. "I'm cleaned out."

"I say, Jerry," Cholly said, throwing down his cards with a grimace. "If you've any more cousins do us a favour and leave 'em where ye find 'em."

"You need have no fear on that score," Jerome muttered. "Come on Bart, my lad. That's enough excitement for one night. I'd best get you back or we'll both be in the basket."

"Oh, but, Jerry…"

Jerome ignored Bonnie's complaints, knowing well enough what the rest of the evening would likely hold as Gideon crooked his finger at a comely serving wench. He watched, amused despite himself while Bonnie's eyes grew wide and the young woman sashayed over, settling herself in Gideon's lap.

"Now, Bart," he said, smirking a little.

Bonnie got to her feet and followed him out the door.

It was gone three in the morning by the time they got back to Holbrooke House. By some miracle he managed to put the curricle away and bed down the horse without waking any of the stable lads.

"Well, then, you dreadful girl, I hope you're satisfied?" he said, sliding the bolt across on the stall door and turning to her.

"Oh, yes, Jerome, thank you so much. It was fun, wasn't it?"

He laughed despite himself, shaking his head. "I suppose so, once I'd convinced myself that my friends really are blind and even more thick headed than I'd supposed. I thought I was going to have a heart attack in the first half an hour, I can tell you."

"You worry too much," she said, shaking her head at him.

"You don't worry enough," he muttered.

She rolled her eyes and then winced, her mouth tightening.

"What is it?" he asked, frowning at her obvious discomfort.

"It's the binding," she said, her voice tight. "It's really hurting now, and Mary will be a bed. I'll have to sleep in the blasted thing for I can't risk going to wake her. Not that I'll sleep, I can barely breath."

"You fool girl," he said, impatient now. "You'll do yourself an injury."

"Oh, Jerry, please help me get it off," she pleaded, shrugging out of her coat and letting it fall to the floor.

Jerome stared at her, his mouth growing dry as the visions he'd been lingering on earlier bloomed behind his eyes. No. No. No, no, no. Behave Cadogan.

"I don't think..." he began, his voice creaking like a rusty gate, but her slender hands had already undone the buttons on her waistcoat.

"Oh, don't be so missish about it," she said, huffing with impatience as the waistcoat joined the coat in a heap on the floor. "It's not like you've not seen everything before, and you've made it plain enough you're not interested."

Not interested?

He blinked but said nothing, not that he could have. How the devil had she gotten the idea he wasn't interested? He was a man and she was suggesting he unwrap her breasts like the best Christmas present a fellow had ever received. Also he wasn't dead. Not interested? She was unhinged if she thought that likely.

Before he could find any way of stopping her, which with Bonnie would be as futile as trying to put out a fire with a decanter of brandy, she'd tugged the shirt off over her head.

Jerome stared.

She was bound, mummy like, from her waist to beneath her armpits, so tightly he could see her skin was red and abraded where the edge of the wrappings had rubbed against her delicate flesh. He swallowed, heat climbing up his neck as she turned her back.

"The fastenings are in the back there somewhere. I can't do it by myself, so you'll have to undo them for me."

Just undo the bindings and walk away, he counselled himself as his heart began to thud in double time. *You can do that. It's not difficult.*

Jerome licked his lips and reached out to where the bindings had been tightly knotted, the ends tucked back under and out of sight. His hands trembled a little as he tugged the ends free and fumbled with the knot.

"Oh, do hurry," she pleaded.

"I'm going as fast as I can, curse you," he muttered. "And it's your own dashed fault so don't go chastising me."

"I wasn't chastising," she retorted. "I was only asking you to hurry."

"Well don't. I'll do it in my own good time." Except at that moment the knot came apart in his hands and he wasn't ready, hadn't steeled himself to say, *there you go, you're free. I'll leave you to it now.* He couldn't leave her half dressed and alone in the stables in any case, he reasoned. Anyone might come across her and think her fair game for a tumble. No. No, he'd have to stay. Just to … be on the safe side.

He tugged, just as he'd imagined earlier, and just as he'd imagined she turned round and round before him as he unravelled her bindings along with his own sanity. His breathing grew ragged as she turned and turned, and the tight wrappings tumbled to the ground as his pulse beat in his ears and his body grew taut with interest.

She was faced away from him as the last length of fabric fell and she let out a heartfelt sigh that he felt somewhere in the pit of his belly.

"Oh, thank heavens," she murmured. "That's better."

As though he was watching someone in a dream—some poor fool bent on destruction no doubt—he reached out and traced one of the red lines across her back where the bindings had left imprints in her soft skin.

"Look what you've done to yourself," he whispered, hearing the breathless quality of his own words. His finger trailed to her waist and he put his hand on her at the point where the curve of her hips began.

She stilled beneath his touch and then looked back, over her shoulder at him. Her eyes were wide and dark and she licked her lips.

"It's worse this side," she said, her voice low. "I wish you'd kiss it better."

Oh God, he was doomed.

Bonnie reached down and took his hand, guiding it to her breast.

"Bonnie," he said, shaking his head even as his body throbbed with desire. His heart was a drumbeat in his ears, his swelling cock pulsing in time with it, with need. Oh, good Lord he was in deep trouble. "Bonnie, no," he said, though it was a pitiful effort to act the gentlemen as his hand curved about her breast and squeezed as he spoke.

"Your hands are so warm," she said, the words spoken on a sigh. "So big and warm." She leaned back against his chest and he took it for the invitation it was, filling both his hands with her soft flesh, gently kneading and stroking and then pinching her nipples, rolling them back and forth between finger and thumb.

She gasped and tilted her head back, exposing the pale line of her throat.

Jerome stared down at it, willing himself to find the strength to move away from her, to stop, when the desire to kiss a path down that slender neck was so fierce he could taste it. She turned her head and looked up at him.

"It's all right, Jerome," she said, and her eyes were clear, focused entirely on him. "I know we're not going to marry, I'm not trying to trap you. I want this. I want you."

"It's wrong…" he said, forcing the words out. "I ought not…"

"Nonsense," she said, smiling at him. "I want you. I want this night for myself before my life is no longer my own. That's not so much to ask is it? Unless… unless you don't want to."

He watched uncertainty flicker in her eyes, saw the glimpse of vulnerability before she turned away from him, and hated it.

"Seriously?" he asked, pulling her closer so that her bottom cradled his arousal. She let out a breath as he pressed against her. "Don't be so bird witted."

"Jerome," she whispered, and turned in his arm, tugging at his neck, pulling him down and down into a kiss that drowned out good sense and any notions of gentlemanly behaviour. After all, she wanted him, wanted this, her last chance to make her own decision about anything before she was married to a man she didn't even like. How could he refuse her?

Somehow he guided her back, into an empty stall, thickly bedded with clean straw, praise be to God. Not that he liked straw, it always ended up sticking you in the arse, blasted prickly stuff, but beggars couldn't be choosers.

The tumbled into it, the sweet scent of summer past rising around them as Jerome found the buttons on the fall of her trousers and flicked them undone, sliding his hand beneath. His hand moved over the gentle swell of her stomach, over skin like satin until he found the feather curls he sought and trailed his fingers through them.

Bonnie's breath caught and her hips arched, seeking more of the tentative touch his fingers teased her with. Jerome smiled at her impatience.

"Wicked girl," he crooned, nipping at her earlobe. "Always in such a hurry."

"I'm afraid you'll change your mind and leave me alone," she admitted, before tugging his shirt free and sliding her hands beneath. Jerome closed his eyes as her hands moved over him, the caress making him want to purr like a cat to announce his approval.

"I'm not that noble," he said, bending to swipe his tongue over her nipple and grazing the tender bud with his teeth, enjoying her soft cries and exclamations as his fingers slid through the curls between her thighs and caressed her intimate flesh. He groaned as his fingers moved deeper and found her hot and wet, wanting and needing him.

"Please," she begged him, clinging to his neck. "Please."

How could he refuse such a plea? It was the work of moments to shed his clothes and tug her legs free of the trousers she wore, easier still to take his place between her thighs, sliding his aching flesh against her until she cried out and he thought he'd go mad if he didn't have her. Yet she was a virgin and though Jerome had never deflowered one before he knew he must prepare the way to make it easier for her.

So he continued the glide of his flesh over hers, until she was writhing beneath him, her pale skin flushed and rosy as she clutched at him, grasping at his shoulders and holding tight. He moved back then, returning his hand to that tender spot and sliding a finger inside as his thumb circled and caressed.

"Is this what you want?" he asked, as his finger moved slowly back and forth.

"Yes," she gasped, and then. "No, I… I don't know."

"Yes, you do," he said, smiling down at her. "Tell me."

"It's… It's… lovely," she managed, staring up at him from heavy lidded eyes. "But…"

"But?"

"But it's not enough."

Jerome chuckled and moved over her, kissing her neck and then her mouth. "Greedy girl," he murmured against her lips. "Are you sure?" And then he crooked his fingers inside her, finding the tender spot that made her cry out again and again until she shattered beneath him and he swallowed her cries with his mouth. He didn't wait until the pleasure had ebbed, thrusting inside her as it still pulsed within her and she cried out again, pleasure and pain and she let him inside her.

"Bonnie," he whispered as the pleasure took over, sweeping him up with it. "Bonnie you feel like heaven."

Available December 20, 2019

Pre-Order your copy here: To Dance with a Devil

Want more Emma?

If you enjoyed this book, please support this indie author and take a moment to leave a few words in a review. *Thank you!*

To be kept informed of special offers and free deals (which I do regularly) follow me on *https://www.bookbub.com/authors/emma-v-leech*

To find out more and to get news and sneak peeks of the first chapter of upcoming works, go to my website and sign up for the newsletter.
http://www.emmavleech.com/

Come and join the fans in my Facebook group for news, info and exciting discussion...

Emmas Book Club

Or Follow me here......

http://viewauthor.at/EmmaVLeechAmazon
Emma's Twitter page

About Me!

I started this incredible journey way back in 2010 with The Key to Erebus but didn't summon the courage to hit publish until October 2012. For anyone who's done it, you'll know publishing your first title is a terribly scary thing! I still get butterflies on the morning a new title releases but the terror has subsided at least. Now I just live in dread of the day my daughters are old enough to read them.

The horror! (On both sides I suspect.)

2017 marked the year that I made my first foray into Historical Romance and the world of the Regency Romance, and my word what a year! I was delighted by the response to this series and can't wait to add more titles. Paranormal Romance readers need not despair however as there is much more to come there too. Writing has become an addiction and as soon as one book is over I'm hugely excited to start the next so you can expect plenty more in the future.

As many of my works reflect I am greatly influenced by the beautiful French countryside in which I live. I've been here in the South West for the past twenty years though I was born and raised in England. My three gorgeous girls are all bilingual and the youngest who is only six, is showing signs of following in my footsteps after producing *The Lonely Princess* all by herself.

I'm told book two is coming soon ...

She's keeping me on my toes, so I'd better get cracking!

KEEP READING TO DISCOVER MY OTHER BOOKS!

Other Works by Emma V. Leech

(For those of you who have read The French Fae Legend series, please remember that chronologically The Heart of Arima precedes The Dark Prince)

Girls Who Dare

To Dare a Duke

To Steal A Kiss

To Break the Rules

To Follow her Heart

To Wager with Love (November 15, 2019)

To Dance with a Devil (December 20, 2019)

Rogues & Gentlemen

The Rogue

The Earl's Temptation

Scandal's Daughter

The Devil May Care

Nearly Ruining Mr. Russell

One Wicked Winter

To Tame a Savage Heart

Persuading Patience

The Last Man in London

Flaming June

Charity and the Devil

A Slight Indiscretion

The Corinthian Duke

The Blackest of Hearts

Duke and Duplicity

The Scent of Scandal

The Rogue and The Earl's Temptation Box set

Melting Miss Wynter

The Regency Romance Mysteries

Dying for a Duke

A Dog in a Doublet

The Rum and the Fox

The French Vampire Legend

The Key to Erebus
The Heart of Arima
The Fires of Tartarus
The Boxset (The Key to Erebus, The Heart of Arima)
The Son of Darkness (October 31, 2020)

The French Fae Legend

The Dark Prince
The Dark Heart
The Dark Deceit
The Darkest Night
Short Stories: A Dark Collection.

Stand Alone

The Book Lover (a paranormal novella)

Audio Books!

Don't have time to read but still need your romance fix? The wait is over...

By popular demand, get your favourite Emma V Leech Regency Romance books on audio at Audible as performed by the incomparable Philip Battley and Gerard Marzilli. Several titles available and more added each month!

Click the links to choose your favourite and start listening now.

Rogues & Gentlemen

The Rogue

The Earl's Tempation

Scandal's Daughter

The Devil May Care

Nearly Ruining Mr Russell

One Wicked Winter

To Tame a Savage Heart

Persuading Patience

The Last Man in London

Flaming June

The Winter Bride, a novella (coming soon)

Girls Who Dare

To Dare a Duke

To Steal A Kiss

To Break the Rules (coming soon)

The Regency Romance Mysteries

Dying for a Duke

A Dog in a Doublet (coming soon)

Also check out Emma's regency romance series, Rogues & Gentlemen. Available now!

The Rogue
Rogues & Gentlemen Book 1

1815

Along the wild and untamed coast of Cornwall, smuggling is not only a way of life, but a means of survival.

Henrietta Morton knows well to look the other way when the free trading 'gentlemen' are at work. Yet when a notorious pirate, known as The Rogue, bursts in on her in the village shop, she takes things one step further.

Bewitched by a pair of wicked blue eyes, in a moment of insanity she hides the handsome fugitive from the local Militia. Her reward is a kiss that she just cannot forget. But in his haste to escape with his life, her pirate drops a letter, inadvertently giving

Henri incriminating information about the man she just helped free.

When her father gives her hand in marriage to a wealthy and villainous nobleman in return for the payment of his debts, Henri becomes desperate.

Blackmailing a pirate may be her only hope for freedom.

Read for free on Kindle Unlimited

The Rogue

Interested in a Regency Romance with a twist?

Dying for a Duke
The Regency Romance Mysteries Book 1

Straight-laced, imperious and morally rigid, Benedict Rutland - the darkly handsome Earl of Rothay - gained his title too young. Responsible for a large family of younger siblings that his frivolous parents have brought to bankruptcy, his youth was spent clawing back the family fortunes.

Now a man in his prime and financially secure he is betrothed to a strict, sensible and cool-headed woman who will never upset the balance of his life or disturb his emotions ...

But then Miss Skeffington-Fox arrives.

Brought up solely by her rake of a step-father, Benedict is scandalised by everything about the dashing Miss.

But as family members in line for the dukedom begin to die at an alarming rate, all fingers point at Benedict, and Miss Skeffington-Fox may be the only one who can save him.

FREE to read on Amazon Kindle Unlimited.. [Dying for a Duke](#)

Lose yourself in Emma's paranormal world with The French Vampire Legend series…..

The Key to Erebus
The French Vampire Legend Book 1

The truth can kill you.

Taken away as a small child, from a life where vampires, the Fae, and other mythical creatures are real and treacherous, the beautiful young witch, Jéhenne Corbeaux is totally unprepared when she returns to rural France to live with her eccentric Grandmother.

Thrown headlong into a world she knows nothing about she seeks to learn the truth about herself, uncovering secrets more shocking than anything she could ever have imagined and finding that she is by no means powerless to protect the ones she loves.

Despite her Gran's dire warnings, she is inexorably drawn to the dark and terrifying figure of Corvus, an ancient vampire and master of the vast Albinus family.

Jéhenne is about to find her answers and discover that, not only is Corvus far more dangerous than she could ever imagine, but that he holds much more than the key to her heart …

FREE to read on Kindle Unlimited The Key to Erebus

Check out Emma's exciting fantasy series with hailed by Kirkus Reviews as "An enchanting fantasy with a likable heroine, romantic intrigue, and clever narrative flourishes."

The Dark Prince
The French Fae Legend Book 1

*Two Fae Princes
One Human Woman
And a world ready to tear them all apart*

Laen Braed is Prince of the Dark fae, with a temper and reputation to match his black eyes, and a heart that despises the human race. When he is sent back through the forbidden gates between realms to retrieve an ancient fae artifact, he returns home with far more than he bargained for.

Corin Albrecht, the most powerful Elven Prince ever born. His golden eyes are rumoured to be a gift from the gods, and destiny is calling him. With a love for the human world that runs deep, his friendship with Laen is being torn apart by his prejudices.

Océane DeBeauvoir is an artist and bookbinder who has always relied on her lively imagination to get her through an unhappy and uneventful life. A jewelled dagger put on display at a nearby museum hits the headlines with speculation of another race, the Fae. But the discovery also inspires Océane to create an extraordinary piece of art that cannot be confined to the pages of a book.

With two powerful men vying for her attention and their friendship stretched to the breaking point, the only question that remains...who is truly The Dark Prince.

The man of your dreams is coming...or is it your nightmares he visits? Find out in Book One of The French Fae Legend.

Available now to read for FREE on Kindle Unlimited.

The Dark Prince

Acknowledgements

Thanks, of course, to my wonderful editor Kezia Cole.

To Victoria Cooper for all your hard work, amazing artwork and above all your unending patience!!! Thank you so much. You are amazing!

To my BFF, PA, personal cheerleader and bringer of chocolate, Varsi Appel, for moral support, confidence boosting and for reading my work more times than I have. I love you loads!

A huge thank you to all of Emma's Book Club members! You guys are the best!

I'm always so happy to hear from you so do email or message me :)

emmavleech@orange.fr

To my husband Pat and my family ... For always being proud of me.

Printed in Great Britain
by Amazon